SIDEWINDERS:
MANKILLER,
COLORADO

WLC/#4
7ns

SIDEWINDERS: MANKILLER, COLORADO

William W. Johnstone
with J. A. Johnstone

PINNACLE BOOKS
Kensington Publishing Corp.
www.kensingtonbooks.com

PINNACLE BOOKS are published by

Kensington Publishing Corp.
119 West 40th Street
New York, NY 10018

Copyright © 2010 William W. Johnstone

PUBLISHER'S NOTE

Following the death of William W. Johnstone, the Johnstone family is working with a carefully selected writer to organize and complete Mr. Johnstone's outlines and many unfinished manuscripts to create additional novels in all of his series like The Last Gunfighter, Mountain Man, and Eagles, among others. The novel was inspired by Mr. Johnstone's superb storytelling.

If you purchased this book without a cover, you should be aware that this book is stolen property. It was reported as "unsold and destroyed" to the publisher, and neither the author nor the publisher has received any payment for this "stripped book."

All Kensington titles, imprints, and distributed lines are available at special quantity discounts for bulk purchases for sales promotions, premiums, fund-raising, educational, or institutional use. Special book excerpts or customized printings can also be created to fit specific needs. For details, write or phone the office of the Kensington special sales manager: Kensington Publishing Corp., 119 West 40th Street, New York, NY 10018, attn: Special Sales Department; Phone: 1-800-221-2647.

PINNACLE BOOKS and the Pinnacle logo are Reg. U.S. Pat. & TM Off.
The WWJ steer head logo is a trademark of Kensington Publishing Corp.

ISBN-13: 978-0-7860-2123-9
ISBN-10: 0-7860-2123-3

First Printing: June 2010

10 9 8 7

Printed in the United States of America

Give them great meals of beef
and iron and steel,
they will eat like wolves
and fight like devils.

—William Shakespeare, *King Henry V*

I reckon we've always liked a ruckus
just a mite too much.

—Scratch Morton

CHAPTER 1

"We're gettin' too old for this," Scratch Morton said.

"Amen," Bo Creel agreed. "But we signed on to do it. We don't have any choice but to get it done."

He lifted the posthole digger and brought it down hard against the rocky ground. The blades didn't penetrate very far into the stubborn dirt. With a sigh, Bo lifted the digger and then slammed it down again. He pulled the handles apart, lifted them, turned to empty a pathetic amount of dirt onto a pile that seemed to be growing with infinite slowness.

Then he threw the digger and said with uncharacteristic anger, "Damn it, I hate digging postholes!"

Scratch stepped forward. "Lemme work on it for a while. You can unload the next roll of wire from the wagon."

The New Mexico sun beat down mercilessly on the two old friends. They were stripped to the waist, revealing fish-belly-white torsos that had started to thicken with age but were still muscular and powerful.

Despite not having any shirts on, both men still

wore their hats. Scratch's headgear, in keeping with his personality as something of a dandy, was a big, cream-colored Stetson that was beginning to show some wear but retained vestiges of its fanciness . . . much like the man who wore it.

Bo's hat was plain, flat-crowned, black. He didn't put on any airs. He just wanted something to keep the sun off his head.

They were working in a semi-arid valley bordered by low hills on the south and a string of rugged mesas on the north. The range on which they had parked the ranch wagon was part of Big John Peeler's Circle JP ranch, but the cattleman's land ended here and Bo and Scratch had been given the job of stringing barbed wire from the hills to the mesas to mark that boundary.

Bo sat down for a second on the wagon's lowered tailgate and pulled off his work gloves so he could wipe sweat off his face, which was tanned to a permanent shade matching that of saddle leather. "I don't see why somebody had to go and invent that blasted devil wire in the first place," he complained bitterly.

Scratch dug the posthole digger into the ground. The blades grated in the gravelly soil. He grinned over at Bo.

"You're the one who always talks about what a good thing progress is. I thought you liked civilization."

"Not when I have to dig holes for posts to string it on."

"I know what you mean." Scratch drove the digger into the ground again. "I sort of miss the open range days, too. But once everybody gets wire strung up, I reckon there won't be near as many range wars."

Bo shook his head. "Folks'll just find something else to fight over."

"Well, ain't you a gloomy cuss today. Look at it this way . . . You're out in the fresh air, ain't you? You ain't wearin' an apron, stuck behind some store counter somewhere, clerkin' or sweepin' up in a saloon. That's all most folks think fellas our age are good for anymore."

Bo took off his hat and scrubbed a hand over his face. "Yeah, I guess you've got a point."

The digger's blades *chunked* into the ground again. "Sure I do. Nobody's shootin' at us, either, and that's a welcome change, ain't it?"

Bo gazed off into the distance and said quietly, "I'm not so sure."

He wasn't seeing the sweeping vistas of the landscape outside of Socorro, New Mexico Territory. Instead, in his mind's eye he saw the decades that had rolled by since he and Scratch had left Texas.

It had been an adventurous life. Bo had needed plenty of adventure to help him forget the pain of losing his wife and children to sickness, and his old friend Scratch had been more than willing to help provide it. As boys, they had fought side by side against Santa Anna's thousands at the Battle of San Jacinto where Texas had won its independence. That had given Scratch an appetite for excitement he had never gotten over.

As grown men they had drifted, from south of the Rio Grande to north of the Canadian border. They had seen the stately flow of the Mississippi past grand homes in Memphis and Vicksburg, and they had stood on cliffs and looked out over the vast Pacific Ocean as its waves crashed powerfully on the rocks below them. They had ridden through deserts, climbed high mountain passes, seen giant redwoods reaching for the heavens. They had known the solitude of far, lonely places, as well as the smoky camaraderie of saloons and gambling dens and bunkhouses.

There had been some trouble along the way, of course, because Bo and Scratch, being Texans born-bred-and-forever, naturally couldn't stand aside and do nothing when they saw someone being threatened or taken advantage of. They had a deep and abiding dislike of outlaws, bullies, cheap gunmen, tinhorn gamblers, whoremongers, horse thieves, con artists, and all other sorts of miscreants. Scratch liked to say that they were peaceable men who never went looking for a ruckus to get into. The truth of that statement was debatable.

But by and large, it had been a good life, and Bo was damned if he understood how he and Scratch had wound up here in this hellhole, doing the most menial labor available to cowpunchers, for a jack-ass like Big John Peeler. They'd had quite a bit of money in their poke when they came up out of Mexico, following a little dustup down there.

"Red Cloud," Bo said softly.

Scratch paused in his digging. "The old Indian chief?"

Bo frowned at him. "You know good and well what I'm talking about."

Scratch leaned on the posthole digger and shook his head. "I told you, Bo, that was a good tip. That fella in Las Cruces swore the horse hadn't lost a race yet."

"If that was true, you wouldn't have been able to get such good odds, now would you?"

Scratch grimaced. "Well, yeah, I reckon you're right about that. I guess I wasn't thinkin' too straight—"

"Because you'd had nearly a whole jug of hooch in that parlor house."

Scratch shook his head stubbornly. "You know whiskey don't muddle me none, and neither do the señoritas. Sometimes my ambition gets a mite ahead of my thinkin', though."

Bo had to laugh. "Well, if I didn't know that after all these years, I don't reckon I'd have been paying much attention, now would I? Anyway, it's like a tumbleweed. It's blown away, and there's no point in worrying about it anymore."

"Now, that's a right smart way to look at it." Scratch resumed digging, adding over his shoulder, "Anyway, this ain't so bad. We'll work for Big John for a while until our poke's fattened up again, and then we can light a shuck outta here."

"Sounds good to me." Bo pulled his gloves on again and slid off the tailgate. He went along the side of the wagon until he could reach over and grab hold of one of the rolls of barbed wire he and Scratch had loaded into the vehicle before leaving Circle JP headquarters that morning.

Scratch was right. Jobs weren't easy to come by at this time of year. All the roundups were already over. A fella with empty pockets had to take what he could get, and by the time he and Scratch had reached Socorro, about halfway between Las Cruces and Albuquerque, they had barely had two coins to clink together. Usually when their funds ran low, Bo could find a poker game in some saloon and replenish them, but this time they didn't even have the wherewithal to buy into a game. It was ranch work or nothing, and Peeler was the only cattleman hiring.

Bo glanced off to the west as he dropped the roll of wire on the ground next to the line of posts. His eyes narrowed as he straightened.

"Somebody coming," he told Scratch.

Scratch paused in his digging and looked in the same direction Bo was looking. A plume of dust curled upward in the distance.

"Three or four riders, I'd say."

"Yeah," Bo agreed. "Coming from the Snake Track."

Peeler's neighbor to the west was Case Ridley, who called his ranch the Snake Track because his brand was just a squiggly line. The name fit, because from what Bo and Scratch had seen of Ridley, he was snake-mean, all right. There was bad blood between Peeler and Ridley, but also an uneasy truce. The Texans knew that Peeler hoped putting up this fence would settle some of the disputes between them.

Scratch carried the posthole digger over to the wagon and leaned it against the tailgate. "I don't know about you," he said to Bo, "but I reckon I'll feel a mite better if I'm packin' iron."

He reached into the wagon and took out a coiled

gun belt with two holsters attached to it. He strapped it around his hips and then grasped the ivory handles of the two long-barreled Remington revolvers in the holsters. Scratch slid the guns up and down a little, making sure they were riding easy in the leather.

Bo followed suit, taking a gun belt with a single holster from the wagon. The gun in the holster was a Colt with plain walnut grips. He buckled on the belt, then stood beside the wagon with Scratch, waiting for the riders who were coming toward them.

The black dots at the base of the dust plume resolved themselves into four men on horseback. As the riders came closer, Bo recognized one of them as Case Ridley, whom he had seen in Socorro. Ridley was a tall, whip-thin man with a hawk nose and a narrow black mustache. His face was all hard planes and angles. Bo didn't like him a bit.

The other three men were some of Ridley's crew, hard-bitten, beard-stubbled men who'd been hired as much for their skill with their guns as for what they could do with a horse and a rope.

The riders came to a stop on the other side of the fence line. Ridley edged his horse forward a couple of steps and demanded, "Who the hell are you men, and what are you doing here?"

Bo answered the second question first. "We're stringing fence for the Circle JP. We work for Big John Peeler. His name's Morton. I'm Creel."

"Peeler told you to do this?"

"That's right."

"That son of a bitch!" Ridley flung out a hand to gesture at the posts. "That fence is on my range!"

Scratch drawled, "I reckon you must be mistaken, Mr. Ridley."

The rancher sneered at him. "You know who I am, eh?"

Scratch nodded. "Seen you around in town."

"If you know who I am, you must know I don't take kindly to being called a liar."

"Scratch didn't call you a liar," Bo pointed out. "He said you were mistaken."

"It's the same damn thing! Now pull those posts up, and be damned glad you hadn't strung any wire I'd have to go to the trouble of tearing down!" Ridley pointed. "Peeler's range ends a thousand yards east of here."

"I don't think so," Scratch said. "The boss gave us pretty good directions. He told us right where all the landmarks are. We're in the right place."

"Now you *are* calling me a liar!"

"This is where Mr. Peeler told us to build the fence," Bo said. "I reckon this is where we'll build it."

"You'll play hell doing it!" Ridley gestured to his men. "Boys, get down and teach these old bastards a lesson."

Bo and Scratch were both tough, but Ridley's men were tough, too, and a lot younger. The Texans knew they probably couldn't win a fistfight, which meant that Ridley's men would give them a thrashing.

They weren't going to stand for that. Their hands edged toward their guns.

"You fellas best stay on your horses," Bo said in a quiet, dangerous voice.

Ridley's angular face darkened with fury. "You

old codgers are going to shoot it out with us?" he demanded as if he couldn't believe it.

"If we have to," Bo said.

The dust that had been kicked up by the riders had blown away. Now the air was filled with the tense expectation of gunplay and sudden death instead.

CHAPTER 2

Before anybody could slap leather, one of Ridley's men spoke up, saying, "Somebody comin' over yonder, boss."

He was looking back to the east, behind Bo and Scratch, and for a second Bo thought it was just a trick to get the two of them to turn around so Ridley's gun hawks could get the drop on them.

But then Bo heard the distant pounding of hoofbeats.

"Hold it," Ridley snapped to his men. "Don't start anything. Not until we find out who that is."

Bo had a hunch who the newcomers were. They were coming from the direction of Circle JP headquarters, so in all likelihood they were some of Big John Peeler's men.

That turned out to be the case. After a couple of tense minutes, eight riders led by Joe Archibald swept up. Big John ramrodded his own crew, but Archibald was his *segundo* and gave all the orders that Peeler didn't.

"What the hell's going on here?" he demanded of

Bo and Scratch, unwittingly echoing what Ridley had said a few minutes earlier.

Scratch nodded toward the rival rancher. "Mr. Ridley here's got a problem with this fence Big John told us to put up, Joe."

"Of course I've got a problem," Ridley said. "The damn fence is on my range!"

Archibald looked toward the hills, then turned his head to gaze toward the line of mesas. Then he faced Ridley again and said, "Looks like it's in the right place to me."

"It's half a mile too far west!"

"A minute ago you said a thousand yards," Scratch said, drawing a murderous glower from Ridley.

Archibald leaned forward slightly in his saddle and said, "This fence is stayin' right here, Ridley . . . unless you think four against eight is good odds for an argument."

Ridley's face turned an even darker, mottled shade of red, but before he could say anything, Bo spoke up.

"Wait a minute, Archibald. This is between Ridley and his men, and Scratch and me. We're the ones he came up to and started bellowing at and ordering around."

Under his breath, Scratch said, "Bo, what're you doin'?"

Bo ignored his old friend's question. "If anybody settles this, it ought to be Scratch and me."

Archibald grunted. "Is that so? Have you gone loco, Creel? They outnumber you two to one."

"We've faced long odds before, haven't we, Scratch?"

"Yeah, but not when we didn't have to. Dang it, Bo, what's got into you?"

"I just think we ought to fight our own fights—"

Archibald sent his horse forward, and the men with him followed suit. They bulled past Bo and Scratch to face Ridley and his men across the fence line.

"You two saddle tramps just stay out of this," Archibald snapped. "This is between Ridley's bunch and ours, and anyway, you're too old to be gettin' mixed up in ruckuses like this. Just stay out of the way."

Bo's jaw clamped tight. His breath hissed between his teeth. Scratch watched him with a worried frown.

Ridley shook a finger at Archibald. "This isn't over!" he blustered. "There'll be another day, Archibald. And tell Peeler that this damned fence won't stand, either!"

"Tell him your own damned self if you want to come callin'," Archibald said.

Ridley spun his horse around and jabbed his spurs cruelly into its flanks. He galloped away, back toward his ranch headquarters, with his men following him.

Archibald watched them go for a moment, then turned to the men with him. "All right," he said. "I want this fence finished today, so you're all gonna work on it."

"Mr. Peeler gave that job to us," Bo protested.

"Well, you ain't gonna get it done quick enough.

You and Morton can still help, but we'll finish it. Then we can have men ridin' patrol on it all the time to make sure Ridley doesn't try anything."

Scratch touched his old friend's arm. "Come on, Bo. Look at it like this—at least we don't have to work out here in the hot sun all day by ourselves."

"Yeah," Bo said with bitter cynicism in his voice. "Aren't we lucky?"

No cowboy enjoyed stringing wire, so there was plenty of complaining going on as the men set to work, but nobody was going to contradict Archibald's orders. And, Bo had to admit, with ten men working instead of two, the fence went up a lot quicker. It would have taken him and Scratch days to string the wire across the valley by themselves. With the other men pitching in, the job could be done in a day, as Archibald had commanded.

As the day went on, a sneaking suspicion began to lurk in the back of Bo's mind. It seemed to him like Archibald and the other men had shown up awfully conveniently. Maybe Peeler had sent him and Scratch out by themselves as bait of a sort, to find out if Ridley was keeping an eye on the valley. Archibald could have followed them, with orders to step in if Ridley showed up at the fence line. Forcing Ridley to back down was just the sort of slap in the face that Big John would enjoy dealing out to his rival.

By late afternoon, the fence was finished. Archibald told a couple of the men to stay there and patrol the length of it until he got back to headquarters and sent some relief out to them. Then he said, "Creel, you and Morton load up the wire that's left and take the wagon back."

Bo looked up at the *segundo*, who was mounted again, and said, "Listen, Joe, did the boss set this up just to get Ridley's goat?"

Archibald frowned at him. "What are you talkin' about?"

"I thought Big John and Ridley had agreed about putting up a fence and where it was supposed to be."

"It's supposed to be right here where it is. If you got a problem with that, Creel, maybe you better draw your time and ride on."

"Now, hold on," Scratch said. "We don't want to go jumpin' to no conclusions such as that. I reckon Bo was just a mite curious, that's all."

"It don't pay to be curious when you ain't in charge of anything." Archibald wheeled his horse. "Get that wagon back to the ranch before dark!"

He and the others rode away, including the two men who would ride along the fence line to guard it, leaving Bo and Scratch to finish loading the wagon.

"Who put a burr under your saddle?" Scratch asked as he shrugged into his shirt and started to button it. "I'm usually the hotheaded one who goes off half-cocked and gets us into trouble."

"I don't know," Bo replied with a shake of his head. "I've just got a feeling that something's not right here. Like maybe Big John's just using us."

"Well, of course he's usin' us. He's payin' our wages, ain't he?"

"That's not what I mean."

"When you figure out what you *do* mean, be sure and let me know. In the meantime, try actin' more like the Bo Creel I been ridin' with for all these many years, and not like me."

Bo managed a grin. "Yeah, we wouldn't want that."

They threw a partially used roll of wire into the back of the wagon, along with a small stack of fence posts they'd wound up not needing. Then they climbed onto the seat and Bo took up the reins, slapping them against the backs of the two horses hitched to the wagon. The team started toward Circle JP headquarters in a plodding walk.

The sun was almost down when the wagon rolled up to the largest of the three barns scattered around the ranch. An elderly cowhand who was too stove up to ride the range anymore came out and took charge of the team. Bo and Scratch climbed down from the seat, and Scratch started toward the bunkhouse, going several yards before he realized that Bo wasn't with him.

Frowning, Scratch turned and saw that Bo was striding resolutely toward the sprawling, two-story, whitewashed house where Big John Peeler lived. Scratch hurried after him and caught up.

"Bo, what are you thinkin' about doin', now?"

"I want to ask the boss a question, that's all."

"About that blasted fence? Let it go, Bo. It ain't like you to stir up a hornets' nest."

"If I'm going to risk getting killed, I want to know what for."

"Nobody got killed," Scratch pointed out. "Wasn't even any gunshots."

"What about the next time some Circle JP riders

wind up facing Snake Track men across that barbed wire? What do you think is going to happen then?"

"I don't know," Scratch replied honestly. "Could be trouble."

"That's right."

They had reached the steps leading up to the wide verandah that ran along the front of the house. Peeler must have seen them coming from inside, because the door opened and he stepped out to meet them.

"Howdy, Creel. Morton. Joe tells me you got that fence put up, with a little help."

Big John Peeler lived up to his name. He stood a couple of inches over six feet, and with his barrel chest and his thick gut, weighed well over two hundred pounds. He was about fifty years old and had been in this part of the country for almost thirty years. His squarish head and rugged face looked like they had been chiseled out of a chunk of granite.

"Did Joe tell you we almost got in a shootout with Case Ridley and three of his men?" Bo asked.

Peeler nodded. "He mentioned it." A grin spread across his face. "I sure would've liked to have been there when Ridley had to take water and run." Big John slapped a hamlike hand against his thigh in amusement. "Mighty funny, and the joke's all on him!"

"Because that fence really is in the wrong place, isn't it?"

Peeler sobered and frowned at Bo. "What do you mean by that?"

"You're trying to put one over on Ridley by taking more range than you agreed to. You figure once the fence is there and you have men patrolling it, there won't be anything Ridley can do about it."

"That's not any of your business, Creel. You just do what you're told and don't worry about anything else." Peeler snorted in disgust. "Hell, you're lucky that I gave a couple of broken-down old saddle tramps like you and your friend any kind of job at all. If you don't like what you've been doing, you can help old Jonas muck out the stables, by God! See if you like shoveling horse shit better."

"Now wait a minute, boss——" Scratch began.

"Wait a minute, hell! I'm not used to anybody questioning what I do, and I'm sure not gonna take it from some crazy old codger."

"I'm not that much older than you," Bo said, tight-lipped.

"Well, maybe it's not the years so much as it is the miles," Peeler waved a hand. "You two get out of my sight. You can spend the next few days working in the barns with Jonas. It's probably all you're good for, anyway."

Scratch had had just about enough of being talked to like that. He put a foot on the bottom step and said, "Now look here——"

Bo stopped him by taking hold of his arm. "Let it go, Scratch."

Scratch looked over at him in surprise. "What, all of a sudden you're the voice of reason again? I swear, Bo, you've got as changeable as the wind."

"I'm just too tired to argue about this anymore. Let's go to the bunkhouse."

Scratch hesitated, then reluctantly nodded. "All right. I reckon it ain't worth fightin' over."

Behind them, Big John Peeler laughed. "That's right. Just like Ridley will wise up and decide that extra ground isn't worth a range war."

Bo stopped in his tracks. He looked back. "You're admitting that the fence isn't in the right place? That you're grabbing that range just to spite Ridley?"

"Well, what of it?" Peeler shot back at him. "I knew when he saw where you fellas were building the fence, he'd come out there and start blustering around. That's why I had Joe and some of the boys ready for him."

"Then I was right," Bo said quietly. "Scratch and I were just bait that you dangled in front of Ridley."

"What of it? What else are a couple of old fools like you good for, anyway?"

Scratch made a grab for Bo's arm but missed. With speed that belied his age and weariness, Bo bounded up the steps to the verandah and charged Big John Peeler. He slammed into the surprised rancher and drove him backward so that Peeler fell and both men crashed through the doorway, disappearing into the house.

CHAPTER 3

For a few stunned seconds, all Scratch could do was stand there and stare. Then he regained his wits and hurried up the steps. He saw Bo and Peeler rolling around on the floor just inside the door, wrestling and slugging at each other.

Some of the cowboys gathered around the bunkhouse in the fading light, smoking and talking while they waited for the supper bell to ring, must have seen the way Bo had charged Big John. They let out indignant yells and ran across the ranch yard toward the house.

"Bo! Damn it, Bo!" Scratch jerked the door open more. It had torn loose from its top hinge and flopped around, getting in his way. He gave it a vicious yank that tore the other hinge free and shoved the door aside. "Bo!"

Bo didn't pay any attention. He hammered his fists into Peeler's body. Even though the rancher was bigger and younger, Bo's actions had taken him by surprise, and Bo clearly had the upper hand in the fight.

Scratch bent down, hooked his hands under his friend's arms, and hauled Bo off Peeler, lifting him and dragging him back toward the door. At that moment, the group of cowboys pounded into the house.

Joe Archibald was one of them, and when he saw his boss lying on the floor, bloody and battered, and Scratch holding Bo back, he jumped to the correct conclusion. The *segundo* yanked his gun from its holster and leaped toward Bo, yelling, "You son of a bitch! I'll beat you within an inch of your life!"

Scratch twisted around, still holding Bo with his left arm. His right hand flashed toward his hip, and the ivory-handled Remington on that side seemed to leap out of its holster as if by magic and appear in Scratch's hand. Archibald came to a sudden, startled stop as he found himself staring down the long barrel of the .44.

"Nobody's beatin' anybody," Scratch said in a flinty voice. "This has gone on long enough."

Archibald lowered his gun and used his other hand to point past Bo and Scratch at Peeler, who lay there groggy from the punches Bo had landed. "Your pard jumped the boss! You reckon we're gonna let him get away with that?"

"Big John . . . had it coming," Bo panted. "He knew he told us to put that fence . . . in the wrong place. He was just . . . trying to get the best of Ridley."

"I don't care what he did. He's the boss. We do what he says," Archibald made a curt gesture to his companions. "Some of you help Mr. Peeler up, damn it."

Three of the men went around Bo and Scratch, all of them warily eyeing the gun in the hand of the silver-haired Texan. They took hold of Big John and lifted his considerable bulk to his feet, then stood there bracing him as he shook his big, square head like an old bull.

"I told you earlier that if you don't like the job, you can draw your time and ride on," Archibald continued. "Well, you're not gonna do that. You don't get any wages for attacking the boss. Just gather your gear and get off this spread . . . *now*."

"You can't do that," Scratch argued. "Lord knows Peeler wasn't payin' us much. Slave wages is more like it. But what we earned, we got comin'."

"You're lucky you don't get a rope and a necktie party! Or I can send somebody into Socorro to fetch the sheriff, and you can spend the next six months locked up in jail for attackin' one of the county's leading citizens. Would you like that better, Morton?"

Bo said, "Let go of me, Scratch."

"You ain't gonna go loco again if I do?"

"No, I reckon that's over and done with."

Scratch released his grip on Bo, who looked around and then bent over to pick up his hat, which had fallen off when he tackled Peeler. He brushed off the hat and straightened a dent in it, then put it on and said, "We'll go."

"Wait a minute," Scratch objected. "Peeler owes us money."

"I don't want his money. I just want to be away from here."

Archibald sneered. "We want you away from

here, too, Creel. You've got the place stinkin' of old man."

Scratch gave the *segundo* a hard look. "This old man got the drop on you, mister, when you already had your gun out."

Archibald didn't like being reminded of that. He glared at Scratch.

"Step aside," Scratch said.

"Don't push it," Archibald warned.

"You wanted us gone, we're leavin'. Come on, Bo." Archibald motioned for the other men to step aside. The Texans moved past them through the ruined doorway, crossed the porch, and went down the steps.

Quietly, Bo said, "Sorry I lost this job for us, partner. I just couldn't keep the rein tight enough on my temper."

"Shoot, don't worry about it, Bo. Peeler's a jackass, and Archibald ain't any better. They don't appreciate us here. We'll be better off somewheres else."

"Yeah, but at least here we could eat."

"Well, that could be a problem, seein' as we're broke. But we'll think of something."

When they trudged into the barn to get their horses, the skinny old hostler called Jonas met them. "What was all the commotion over to the big house?" he asked. "I heard a lot of yellin'."

Scratch grinned and jerked a thumb at his old friend. "Bo here got in a tussle with Big John."

Jonas's eyes widened. "You tangled with the boss? Good Lord, Bo, even if he wasn't the boss,

I've seen Big John bust fellas plumb in half with his bare hands. He could'a killed you!"

"Yeah, well, Bo was gettin' the best of the fight when I pulled him off," Scratch said.

"What'd Big John do?"

"Nothin'. He was still too groggy from Bo handin' him his needin's. But Archibald threw us off the place. Said we weren't even gonna get the wages we got comin'."

Jonas shook his head. "Now ain't that a damned shame. Don't tell him I said it, but Joe Archibald is a plumb mean-spirited hombre. He's all the time sayin' things about me being old and broke-down and worthless, and he don't ever seem to notice that I work like a sumbitch takin' care of all the saddle stock around here."

Bo put a hand on the hostler's shoulder. "You do a good job, Jonas. I've noticed how you care for our horses, and I appreciate it."

"So do I," Scratch added. "Guess you better bring 'em out now, come to think of it. Bo and me got our marchin' orders."

"Where will you go?" asked Jonas.

"Socorro's not far," Bo said. "I guess we'll ride in there and start looking for work again."

It didn't take long to get Bo's rangy lineback dun and Scratch's big bay saddled and ready to ride.

He didn't mention how they had had trouble finding work in Socorro before. That was how they'd wound up on the Circle JP. But maybe the situation had improved since then and something better would turn up.

"You got any money at all?"

Scratch shrugged. "Not to speak of. Big John hadn't gotten around to payin' us."

Jonas hesitated. "Listen here. I don't like to see any man tryin' to make his way in the world when he's flat-broke busted." He delved in a pocket of his overalls and brought out a coin. "Here, take this. It's only five dollars, but it'll buy you some grub and a place to sleep, maybe."

Bo shook his head. "We can't take that, Jonas. Five dollars is a lot of money."

"Yeah, but I got plenty. I don't do nothin' with my wages but save 'em, anyway. I'm too old for women, and I never developed a taste for whiskey."

Scratch reached out and took the coin from the hostler's fingers. "We're much obliged, Jonas. This is mighty kind of you."

"Consider it a loan," Bo said. "When we get on our feet again, we'll send it back to you."

"You do that," Jonas said with a nod. "I'll be here, I reckon. Ain't nowheres else for me to go."

Bo and Scratch shook hands with the old-timer, then swung up into their saddles. As they rode out of the barn, they saw Archibald and some of the other Circle JP hands arrayed in front of the house, watching them with hostile glares. Other cowboys were in front of the bunkhouse, looking equally unfriendly.

"Looks like a gauntlet," Bo said under his breath.

"Yeah," Scratch agreed. "I hope we don't have to shoot our way outta here."

None of the men reached for a gun as the Texans rode between them. Bo and Scratch kept their pace deliberate. They might be leaving, but they weren't going to run. That wasn't in their nature. They didn't nudge their horses into a trot until they cleared the ranch yard.

"You know," Scratch mused as they rode off into the gathering dusk, "maybe we ought to mosey over to the Snake Track. We could tell Ridley that Big John knows good and well he's claimin' land that don't belong to him."

Bo shook his head. "I don't like Ridley any more than I do Peeler. He can look out for his own interests. I don't want to be in the middle of those two anymore."

"Yeah, I understand that. Tell you the truth, Bo, I'd just as soon head for some other part of the country as soon as we can put a stake together. Got that damn ugly *Jornada del Muerto* off to the east and nothin' but mountains and hardscrabble range to the west. We can find some place better to spend our time."

Bo nodded and said, "Yeah. All it'll take is money."

"We got five dollars," Scratch pointed out. "That'll buy your way into a poker game."

Bo rubbed his jaw. "Yeah. With that and a little luck . . ."

Biting back a groan of despair, Bo stumbled toward the outhouse behind the livery stable in Socorro early the next morning. His muscles were stiff because he and Scratch had slept in the stable's hayloft. The owner had agreed to that in return for them mucking out the stalls. Even though they had left the Circle JP, they'd wound up having to shovel horse shit after all.

The five-dollar stake had lasted less than half an hour in the game at Socorro's Desert Queen Saloon before Bo was cleaned out. When a man's luck turned, it turned hard, he supposed. The bartender had taken pity on them and let them scrounge some hard-boiled eggs from the jar on the bar, and that was all they'd had to eat. Then they had made the deal with the liveryman so they wouldn't have to sleep on the ground.

"I'll buy both those horses from you," the man had offered. "They look like fine animals."

"Our horses ain't for sale," Scratch had responded indignantly.

"Well, I just thought that from the looks of you, you'll be selling your saddles any day now, anyway, so you might as well sell the horses, too."

Scratch would have gotten mad at that comment—no self-respecting Texan would ever sell his saddle—but Bo had intervened. His bout of melancholia and resentment had gone away—unfortunately not in time to save their jobs on the Circle JP—and he was once again the voice of reason in the duo.

Now, stiff muscles protesting, Bo headed for the outhouse on this frosty morning. Around here, the nights were chilly, even during the summer. He had left Scratch curled up in the hay, snoring, and headed out into the dawn to tend to his personal needs.

He tried not to think about what the rest of the day might bring. He and Scratch were just about at the ends of their ropes.

The privy wasn't occupied. Bo tried to tell himself

that *that* was a bit of good luck. Maybe their fortunes were turning. He pulled the door with its half-moon cutout closed behind him. The outhouse was just a one-holer. He lowered his trousers and long underwear, then sat down and sighed, trying not to shiver from the cold.

Before leaving the stable to come out here, he had grabbed a few sheets of newspaper from a stack of them, folded them, and tucked them under his arm to warm them a little. He took them out now and unfolded them, idly scanning the stories in the dim light that came in through the half-moon.

Suddenly, Bo felt his heart start to pound faster. He checked the date on the piece of newspaper he was holding. It had been published in Albuquerque three weeks earlier, so the news in it was fairly recent. His eyes fastened on one particular headline, and even though he wasn't a superstitious man by nature, he had to wonder at that moment if there really was such a thing as an omen.

The headline read BIG GOLD STRIKE! TOWN BOOMS! BONANZA FOUND NEAR MANKILLER, COLORADO!

CHAPTER 4

Bo thrust the ragged piece of newspaper in front of Scratch's face. He had torn out the story about the gold strike in Colorado and used the rest of the newspaper for the purpose for which God had intended it.

"Wake up, Scratch," he said as he shook his old friend's shoulder. "Take a look at this."

Scratch cracked one eye open a little. "Bo? What the hell are you doin' up in the middle of the night?"

"It's not the middle of the night. It's morning. And I have an idea what we need to do."

Scratch closed his eye, groaned, and snuggled deeper in the hay. "I was havin' me the nicest dream. I was surrounded by a bunch of pretty little señoritas . . ."

"The only things surrounding you in that hay are bugs and rats," Bo said. "Come on, wake up."

"You're gonna keep on pesterin' me until I do, ain't you?"

"More than likely."

Scratch heaved a sigh. He forced both eyes open,

rolled onto his side, and pushed himself up into a sitting position. "All right, all right. What'n blazes are you goin' on about? It ain't like you to be that worked up about anything, Bo."

Bo shoved the newspaper story in front of Scratch's face again. "Read that."

Scratch grimaced. "My eyes are a mite blurry this mornin'. Why don't you just tell me what it says?"

"It says there's a big gold strike up in Colorado, at a town called Mankiller."

"Never heard of it," Scratch muttered as he rubbed his hands wearily over his face.

"It's not far from Durango, according to this story."

"Well, I still never— Wait a minute." Scratch looked up with a frown. "Did you say gold strike?"

"That's right. A real bonanza, the paper says. Mankiller's gone from being a sleepy little wide place in the road to a boomtown almost overnight."

Bo shrugged. "Of course, this paper was published three weeks ago, so it's not exactly overnight anymore . . ."

"So we don't know for sure if the boom's still goin' on, or if the the gold petered out in a hurry."

"No, but I think it's worth checking out, don't you?"

"Gold," Scratch mused. "Seems like we just got tangled up with a gold mine down yonder in Mexico not that long ago. We could have stayed down there if we wanted to be gold miners."

"Maybe we made the wrong decision. Things haven't worked out that well for us since we left Mexico, have they?"

"Well . . . no, I reckon not."

Bo tapped a finger against the newspaper story. "Maybe this is telling us that we have another chance. We should go to this Mankiller, Colorado, and see if we can get in on the strike."

Scratch frowned again. "I never knew you to go chasin' after gold before, Bo, or any other sort of wealth, for that matter. You've gotten downright jumpy these days. You're supposed to be the calm, steady one."

Bo looked out the window in the hayloft. It faced east, which meant the view overlooked the Rio Grande and the vast, arid ugliness of the *Jornada del Muerto.*

"Time's running out," Bo said.

"What?"

"You ever think about how many years we've drifted, Scratch? And how little we've got to show for it? We're both still in pretty good health now—"

Scratch thumped his chest with a fist. "Speak for yourself. I'm healthy as a horse!"

"Yeah, but what about ten or fifteen years from now? What if we get sick? Who's going to take care of us?"

Scratch stared at his old friend for a long moment, then exploded. "What the hell is wrong with you? The odds are that neither of us will live to be old and feeble, the way we keep runnin' into trouble! Blast it, Bo, ever since we left Texas, we've worried about *today,* not tomorrow. We live for right now."

Bo looked around at the hayloft. Rats scrabbled around here and there.

"Right now doesn't look like much at the moment."

"Our lack of dinero is just a temporary setback. We'll get on our feet again, get us a stake built up——"

"How? We can't even afford to buy a cup of coffee for breakfast."

"That's right," Scratch said. "So how in hell do you think we're gonna be able to go all the way to Colorado to look for gold?"

Bo shrugged. "That's a problem, all right. But I still think we should have a goal——"

"I got a goal." Scratch heaved himself to his feet and groaned again as he straightened his back and legs and joints creaked and popped into place. "My goal's to make it to the outhouse. After I've managed that, I'll figure out what to do next."

Scratch went to the ladder and climbed down, grumbling and muttering as he went. Bo tucked the torn-out newspaper story in his pocket and sighed. He followed Scratch down the ladder. The silver-haired Texan had already disappeared out the rear door of the livery barn.

The elderly proprietor of the stable came out of his office running knobby fingers through a thatch of snowy white hair. "Mornin'," he said to Bo with a nod. "How'd you fellas sleep?"

"All right, I guess."

"If you fellas'd like to stay on for a spell, I got some other chores that could use doin'. Roof needs patched, and there are some rotten boards in the walls that ought to be replaced. Things like that. If you boys want to take care of those jobs for me, you can keep on sleepin' in the loft."

"How about wages?" Bo asked.

The old man shook his head. "Oh, no, I can't afford to pay you no wages. This place don't make that much money."

"You'd feed us?"

The man's eyes widened. "Do I look like a rich man? No, a place to sleep in return for the work, that's all I can offer you."

"Even slaves got fed," Bo snapped.

"Don't get testy with me now. I'm just tryin' to help you fellas out."

If that was the old-timer's idea of helping out, Bo hated to think what he would do to someone he was trying to take advantage of. "No deal," he said as he headed for the front entrance.

"Hold on just a minute."

Bo looked back, thinking that the proprietor was going to be more reasonable.

Instead, the man said in an irritated voice, "Your horses ate some of my grain and drank my water. You got to pay me for that. I'll take a day of roof patchin' for what you owe."

"What we owe?" Bo felt anger welling up inside him. He told himself to get a grip on his temper. Losing control with Big John Peeler had cost him and Scratch that job. It hadn't been a good one, but it was better than nothing, which was what they had now. "We worked until almost midnight cleaning those stalls. That ought to be enough to care of any debt."

"This is my livery stable, mister. I'll be the judge of what's enough and what ain't. And if you don't like it, I'll fetch the marshal and see what he thinks about it. If you ain't careful, you and your pard are gonna wind up behind bars as vagrants."

If that happened, it wouldn't be the first time he and Scratch had been in jail, Bo reflected. In fact, the accommodations would probably be better, and the local law would have to feed them.

The only problem was that being locked up was hell on both of the Texans because of the wanderlust that always gripped them. They might not have anywhere to go, but their nature cried out for them to be free to ride on any time they chose.

"Don't get a burr under your saddle," Bo told the liveryman. "I'll talk to my partner as soon as he gets back from the outhouse, and we'll figure out what we're going to do."

"That's another thing. You fellas used my outhouse. That ought to be worth somethin'."

Bo bit back the angry retort that sprang to his lips. The money-grubbing old-timer was damned annoying, but Bo was determined not to let his temper get the best of him.

He unlatched the big double doors at the front of the barn and swung them open. The hour was still early, but people were moving around and folks could show up at the stable to pick up their horses at any time. Bo stood there, watching the rosy glow in the sky grow brighter as the sun climbed above the horizon.

Idly, he looked down the street and spotted a couple of men walking toward a large, redbrick building a couple of blocks away. One of the men wore a town suit and a hat, while the other was dressed in range clothes, including a battered old

Stetson, a cowhide vest, and a pair of chaps strapped over denim trousers. The two men made an unlikely pair, and something about the sight caused Bo to frown.

"Say, is that the bank two blocks down?" he asked over his shoulder. "Big building made of red bricks?"

"Sure is. Why do you want to know?" The oldster cackled. "You ain't got no money to put in it."

"Is the fella who runs it in the habit of showing up early?"

"Yeah. Frank Mosely's the president. He usually gets there about this time of mornin'. Says he likes to get an early start on the day. You ask me, I think he goes in there while nobody's around and throws money on the floor of the vault and rolls around in it, the danged old miser. I never knew anybody to love money as much as that old skinflint does."

The old saying about the pot and the kettle occurred to Bo, but he shoved the thought aside.

"Mosely's a portly fella about sixty?"

"That's him."

As Bo watched, the two men reached the door of the bank. The one in the suit took a key from his pocket and started to unlock the door. He fumbled with it, missing the hole on the lock several times before he was able to insert the key and turn it.

"Is there any reason for some cowpoke to be going into the bank with Mosely?" Bo asked.

The stableman came up beside him. "What the deuce are you talkin' about? I told you, Frank goes in there alone so's he can play with other people's money. He wouldn't be takin' anybody in with him. Bank don't open to the public for a couple hours yet."

Bo nodded. "That's what I thought." Both men had disappeared into the bank building now, and the door was shut forcefully enough that he could hear it a couple of blocks away. Bo turned and walked toward the tack room where he and Scratch had stowed their saddles and gear.

"Hey!" the old man called after him. "What are you doin'? You ain't fixin' to run out on me, are you?"

Bo ignored the questions. He went into the tack room and picked up his Winchester, working the rifle's lever to throw a cartridge into the firing chamber. As he walked down the center aisle of the barn, holding the repeater at a slant across his chest, the liveryman looked at him, gulped, and stepped hurriedly out of the way.

Bo left the barn and started down the street toward the bank, which appeared quiet and deserted. Anyone would think so, if they hadn't seen Frank Mosely and his mysterious companion go inside a couple of minutes earlier. Bo knew they were in there, though, so he wasn't surprised when the door opened again and the man in range clothes reappeared, toting a canvas bag in his left hand. The man's right hand rested on the butt of his holstered revolver.

Bo's gaze flicked along the street. A couple of storekeepers were sweeping off the boardwalks in front of their establishments. A man came out of a café and paused to pick his teeth. Another man walked along the street, his head down as he packed tobacco into a pipe. A wagon pulled by a couple of mules and driven by a stocky man in a tall straw sombrero was at the far end of the street, rolling slowly toward the center of town.

It took Bo only a split second to assess the situation. It could have been better, as far as bystanders were concerned, but it could have been a lot worse, too. He walked a little faster as the man who had just come out of the bank turned toward a horse tied at a nearby hitch rail.

Before the man could reach the horse, Bo stopped and leveled the Winchester at him, calling in a loud, clear voice, "Hold it right there, mister!"

At that same moment, Frank Mosely, the president of the bank, staggered out of that establishment's front door, holding a hand to his bloody head as he yelled, "Stop him! Stop that man! He just robbed the bank!"

The bank robber cursed and yanked his pistol from its holster.

CHAPTER 5

Moving swiftly, Bo snapped the Winchester to his shoulder. He fired, getting off the first shot while the robber was still clearing leather.

Fate took its usual capricious hand, though. As the outlaw clawed his gun out, he swung the canvas bag up with his other hand. Bo didn't know what the hombre intended to do with it, but as luck would have it, the bullet he fired struck the bag and drove it back against the robber's chest. The man staggered under the impact and let go of the bag. When it fell to the ground at his feet, Bo saw there was no blood on the robber's shirt. Something in the bag had stopped the bullet.

The robber jerked his gun up and fired. Bo was already moving, so the slug whipped past his ear rather than blowing his brains out. As he darted to the side, he levered the Winchester and fired a second shot, this time from the hip.

The bullet kicked up dust at the robber's feet and made him jump, but that was all the damage it did.

The man whirled around and leaped back up onto the boardwalk.

Mosely was still squalling for help, but he stopped short as he realized that the robber was lunging at him. The man grabbed Mosely and jerked him in front of him, looping his free arm around the terrified banker's neck to hold him there.

As the robber dragged Mosely back toward the door, he thrust his gun past the hostage and fired two more shots at Bo, who threw himself to the ground and rolled behind a water trough as he felt the wind-rip of the slugs pass his head. He raised up and coolly took aim with the Winchester, knowing that if the robber succeeded in getting back in the bank with Mosely, it would be hard to get him out of there without the banker being killed.

For a split second, Bo had a clear shot at the robber's left thigh. He took it, stroking the trigger. The rifle cracked, and blood flew from the outlaw's leg as the bullet ripped through it. The man howled in pain and stumbled.

Mosely seized the opportunity to twist around and put his hands against the robber's chest. He shoved hard, breaking the man's grip on him. As soon as he was free, Mosely dove to the boardwalk to get out of the line of fire.

Bo's rifle slammed out another shot. This one caught the robber in the body and drove him back. The man managed to trigger his gun again. The bullet thudded into the water trough. Bo levered the Winchester and fired again, then again. Both slugs punched into the robber's chest. They flung him backward against the front window of the bank. The collision shattered the glass. Splinters and shards of it flew in the air as the wounded man fell through the window into the bank.

Bo leaped to his feet and bounded onto the boardwalk. He kept the rifle pointed at the window as he cautiously approached it. Glass crunched under his boots. The robber's knees had caught on the windowsill. His legs from there down hung motionless outside the window.

When Bo reached the point where he could look through the broken window, he saw that the robber would never be a threat to anyone again. The man's shirt was sodden with blood from the bullet holes. He lay on his back, arms flung out at his sides, and his eyes stared sightlessly at the ceiling of the bank.

"Is . . . is he dead?"

The question came from Frank Mosely. The banker was on hands and knees a few yards away, his hair in disarray and hanging in front of his face, blood from the gash on his forehead dripping on the boardwalk.

"He's dead," Bo confirmed. "I reckon he must have walloped you with his gun?"

Mosely gave a shaky nod in reply. "Yes, he . . . he said I was taking too long getting the vault open, so he hit me. Then after he got the money, he told me to stay inside until he was gone, or he'd kill me. But I couldn't let him get away with all that money. It would have ruined too many people here in town to lose it."

The banker didn't sound like the sort of hombre who would dump other people's money on the floor and roll around in it. Bo figured the liveryman just thought everybody was as venal and greedy as he was. Lowering the rifle, Bo went over to Mosely to help him to his feet.

Running footsteps made him look around. A man wearing trousers and long underwear, with his suspenders still loose, hurried toward them carrying a shotgun.

"Is that the marshal?" Bo asked Mosely.

The banker nodded. "Yes, that's Ralph Peterson."

"I'd appreciate it if you'd tell him *I'm* not the robber. I hate to see any man holding a shotgun get nervous."

Mosely held up a hand, palm out, and called, "Take it easy, Ralph, it's all over! A man tried to rob the bank, but he's dead."

The lawman came to a stop in the street next to the boardwalk and squinted suspiciously at Bo. "Who's this old varmint?"

"I don't know, but he saved my life and the bank's money as well." Mosely looked over at Bo. "What's your name, friend?"

"Bo Creel!"

"Well, Mr. Creel, I think you've just earned yourself a reward."

Bo drew in a deep breath. He hadn't even thought about the possibility of a reward when he decided to get his rifle and see what was going on. He was just curious, more than anything else, and he had suspected that a bank robbery was under way.

"Bo! Bo, you all right?"

That worried shout came from Scratch, who came running down the street from the livery stable with both Remingtons in his hands. Bo motioned for him to slow down. "Friend of mine, Marshal," he told Peterson. "Nothing to get alarmed about."

"Well, tell him to put those fancy hoglegs up," Peterson snapped. "I don't like people waving guns around in my town."

"Pouch those irons, Scratch," Bo said as his friend came to a stop in front of the bank. "The trouble's all over."

Scratch hesitated, then slid the long-barreled revolvers back into leather. "What in blazes happened?" he asked. "I go off to commune with nature for a spell, and when I come out, the fella at the livery stable tells me you're down here fightin' the Battle of San Jacinto all over again."

"Somebody tried to rob the bank," Bo explained.

Scratch looked at the legs hanging out the broken window. "I reckon he saw the error of his ways?"

"You could say that."

Mosely took hold of Bo's arm. "Come inside, Mr. Creel," he invited. "Come inside. I know it's awfully early in the morning, but I have a bottle of brandy in my desk, and I think this occasion warrants breaking into it." He looked at Peterson. "Ralph, you'll see about getting the undertaker down here to, ah, clean up this mess?"

The marshal nodded. "Looks like you need to have the sawbones take a look at your head, too, Frank. I'll send for Doc Holmes. You'll need the carpenter to board up that window, too, until you can replace it."

"If you'll tend to all that, I'd appreciate it."

"Sure thing," the lawman agreed. The town banker was one of the most important men in any settlement, and most folks liked to stay on his good side, even the local star packer.

"Come along," Mosely said to Bo. "Your friend, too."

"To tell you the truth, Mr. Mosely," Bo said, "I think we'd rather have some coffee and something to eat instead of that brandy."

Scratch grinned. "Now, Bo, don't go offendin' the man by turnin' down his offer of a drink."

"Once we've settled the matter of that reward, you'll have plenty of money for coffee and breakfast," Mosely said.

Scratch licked his lips and repeated, "Reward?"

Bo said, "Grab that money bag and bring it in, Scratch. I want to find out what stopped the first shot of mine."

As it turned out, there was a smaller pouch inside the bag, packed tightly with double eagles. The .44-40 slug from Bo's Winchester had struck the coins as such an angle that it penetrated several of them before its force was finally spent. The rest of the bag was full of greenbacks.

"He didn't actually clean out the vault," Mosely said as he sat at his desk, looking at the spot on the floor just inside the window where the dead robber's body had sprawled until the undertaker arrived to remove it. There was a dark stain on the highly polished wood. "But he got enough that it would have been a severely damaging blow to the bank to lose it."

The doctor had shown up as well and cleaned and bandaged the gash on Mosely's forehead. The local handyman had swept up the broken glass and was now measuring the window so he could see about nailing up some boards to cover it.

A short, squat glass with a little brandy in it sat on the desk in front of Mosely. Scratch held a similar glass and sipped the amber liquid in it. Bo had turned down the drink.

Mosely picked up some bills from the pile he had dumped onto the desk from the bag. "I want you to have this," he told Bo as he extended the cash across the desk. "You deserve it for saving the bank's money . . . and my life."

"He probably wouldn't have killed you," Bo said. "But with all that lead flying around, you might've gotten hit by a stray bullet, especially if he'd made it back into the bank with you as his hostage."

Scratch reached out and took the bills. "What Bo means to say, Mr. Mosely, is thanks. We're much obliged to you for your kindliness and your generosity—" He stopped and let out a low whistle as he riffled through the money. "There's five hundred bucks here!"

"A small price to pay for a man's life," the banker said solemnly.

"That's not depositors' money, is it?" Bo asked.

Mosely shook his head. "I'll replace it from the bank's operating fund. Don't worry, Mr. Creel. None of the depositors will lose a penny today . . . thanks to you."

"In that case . . ." Bo nodded. "Thank you."

Marshal Peterson came into the bank carrying a piece of paper. As he walked over to Mosely's desk, opening the gate in the railing along the way,

Bo recognized the paper as a wanted poster. The marshal placed the paper on the desk and asked, "Recognize this gent?"

Bo looked at the harsh, beard-stubbled face drawn on the reward dodger and knew good and well where he'd seen it recently. "That's the fella who tried to rob the bank."

"Yep. Bill Page, sometimes called Indiana Bill. Wanted in three states and four territories for bank robbery and murder. There's a five-hundred-dollar reward for him, dead or alive. I thought I'd seen the jasper before."

"Five hundred dollars?" Scratch said with a frown. "That's all he's worth, charged with all them robberies and killin's?"

The marshal shrugged. "I guess they were small banks and he didn't kill anybody all that important. Anyway, five hundred dollars is nothin' to sneeze at."

"Especially when you combine it with the reward I'm paying," Mosely put in. "You have a nice cool thousand dollars coming to you, Mr. Creel. What are you going to do with it?"

Bo rubbed his chin. "Well, we still haven't gotten that coffee and breakfast, and there's a little debt to settle up with the fella who owns the livery stable . . . ."

"Johnny Burford?" the marshal asked. "Watch yourself around him. He'd steal pennies out of a blind man's cup."

"What about the *other* nine hundred and ninety-five dollars?" Mosely asked.

"Scratch and I were thinking about taking a little trip up north," Bo said.

CHAPTER 6

"So that's it," Scratch said as he and Bo reined their horses to a halt atop a ridge a couple of weeks later and looked down at the settlement below them. "Mankiller, Colorado."

Durango lay a day's ride behind them. Off to the left, the Animas River snaked its sparkling course through a narrow valley. Farther to the northeast towered snowcapped Mount Wilson and Lizard Head Pass. A number of other rugged peaks in the San Juan range loomed all around them. It was pretty country, no doubt about it, but Bo and Scratch were more interested in what lay below the surface.

Gold.

They had heard in Durango that the boom was still going on in Mankiller, and even if they hadn't, they would have been able to tell that much from what was happening in the streets of the settlement. Wagons, men on horseback, and more men on foot clogged those streets. The boardwalks were equally crowded, although without the wagon and horse traffic.

Bo wouldn't have been surprised to see some drunken miner ride a horse right up onto the boardwalk, or even into one of the numerous saloons that lined the street. In Durango, the Texans had also heard about how Mankiller was wide open and lawless. Saloon shoot-outs, rampant prostitution, lynchings, and murders were the order of the day. In this boomtown, getting killed was as easy as plucking a dandelion.

Mankiller sprawled over a hillside, surrounded by pine trees. Other trees had been cleared to expand the town; stumps were still visible here and there in the streets. The three main streets ran upward for several blocks, starting at the base of the slope. Side streets were laid out across the slope.

Most of the buildings were frame structures, made from rough boards probably whipsawed out of the trees that had been felled to make room for them. There were still some tents and tar paper shacks, though, and they were probably some of the original dwellings in town. At the other end of the spectrum were several solid-looking brick structures that appeared to be built to last. Someone, at least, believed that Mankiller would have a life beyond this gold-fueled boom.

Bo and Scratch hadn't wasted any time getting up here after leaving Socorro, but it was a long ride up the valley of the Rio Grande and then over across the Colorado Plateau, past the majestic and mysterious cliff dwellings at Mesa Verde, and on through Durango and up the Animas River.

They had bought a packhorse and supplies in Socorro, using the reward money. They'd had to overpay for the horse, since they bought it from Johnny Burford, but it was a good animal. They had more than half of the thousand dollars left, which gave them a good stake. They would be able to outfit themselves, find a good claim, and start prospecting right away.

That was the plan, anyway.

"We're here," Scratch went on. "Feel any better now?"

"We'll see," Bo said. "I guess it depends on what we find down there."

He lifted his reins and hitched the dun into motion again.

The Texans rode down the hill and started across the river on a wooden bridge. The hooves of their horses thudded on the planks, providing counterpoint to the bubbling music of the swift-flowing stream.

A couple of men came out of a tar paper shack not far from the western end of the span. Bo's eyes narrowed in instinctive dislike as he watched them walk toward the bridge.

Both men wore patched denim trousers held up by suspenders. One was shirtless. The other wore only long, faded red underwear above the waist. Their hats were old and floppy-brimmed. The shirtless one had a long red beard that came down over the top of his bare chest. The other was clean-shaven, revealing a lantern jaw so extreme that his face looked almost like a figure eight. There was some resemblance between the two, probably not enough for them to be brothers, but maybe cousins.

Each man carried a shotgun as well.

"I don't much like the looks of this," Scratch said under his breath.

"Neither do I," agreed Bo. "But we'll wait and see how it plays out."

The two men planted themselves in the middle of the road where it began on the other side of the bridge. The shirtless, bearded one tucked his scattergun under an arm and held up his hand.

"Howdy, fellers," he said as Bo and Scratch reined in. "Come to Mankiller to look for gold?"

"That's the idea," Bo said.

Shirtless grinned. "Well, good! Let me be the first one to wish you all the luck in the world. And Thad here'll be the second. Ain't that right, Thad?"

Lantern-Jaw nodded. "That's right, Luke. Good luck to you fellers. Hope you find a lot of gold."

"We appreciate that," Scratch told Luke and Thad. "And it's mighty nice of you boys to give us a warm welcome like this. Now, if you'll move aside so we can get on into town . . ."

Luke shook his head. "Oh, we can't do that."

"You can't?" Bo said.

"Nope. Not until you pay the toll for crossin' the bridge. We're the official toll collectors today."

Bo wasn't surprised by the demand. He had expected something like that as soon as he saw the two men blocking the road. He said, "I didn't see any sign about a toll at the other end of the bridge."

"Has that ol' sign fallen down again?" Luke laughed and shook his head. "Well, it don't really matter whether the sign's up or not. Rules is rules, and it's a rule around here that you got to pay to use the bridge to get into Mankiller."

"What about to get out of Mankiller?" Scratch asked.

"Oh, there ain't no charge for that. But you got to pay to come in again."

"How much is the toll?" Bo asked.

Luke held up a couple of grimy fingers. "Two dollars."

"For each horse," Thad added.

"Yeah, so you'd owe us six dollars, seein' as how you got a packhorse, too."

Scratch said, "Kind of steep, ain't it?"

"Well, there's an old sayin' about what the traffic will bear. Folks been payin' two dollars, so I reckon that's a good price."

"Does the money go to the town?" Bo asked. He figured he knew the answer.

The question brought laughter from both men. Thad dug an elbow into Luke's side and repeated, "Does the money go to the town? That's a good'un, ain't it, Luke?"

"It sure is." Luke looked up at Bo and Scratch and shook his head. "The money goes where it's supposed to, don't you worry none 'bout that, mister. Now, do you fellers want to pay the toll, or are you gonna turn around and go back where you come from?"

"Maybe we'll find some other place to cross," Scratch suggested.

Luke shook his head. "Ain't no other place to cross for miles up and down stream, and I wouldn't recommend tryin' to swim them horses across, neither. This river's mighty cold and fast. You might get swept away, and nobody'd ever see you again. Not alive, anyway."

Bo was fast running out of patience. "I don't believe this is actually a toll bridge," he said. "I think the two of you are just trying to extort money out of us. But I'll check with the sheriff to be sure, and if I'm wrong, we'll come back and pay you what we owe. Fair enough?"

The false affability that Luke and Thad had been displaying vanished. Thad's lips twisted in a snarl.

Luke said sharply, "No, it ain't fair enough. We've told you how it is, you danged old codger. Now pay us the twelve bucks, or you ain't gettin' into Mankiller."

"I thought it was six," Scratch said.

"Price has gone up to four dollars per horse while you been wastin' our time with all that jawin'."

"This is ridiculous," Bo said. "We're not paying you. Now get out of our way if you don't want us to ride you down."

Thad cursed and started to swing his shotgun up.

"Why, you damned old—"

Bo's Colt came out of its holster and leveled before Thad could raise the Greener enough to fire it. Thad stopped short and gulped as he found himself staring down the revolver's barrel.

At the same time and with equal swiftness, Scratch drew his right-hand Remington and pointed it at Luke, who in his arrogance still had his shotgun tucked under his arm. "I wouldn't be gettin' any ideas if I was you," advised the silver-haired Texan.

Luke glared at them but didn't try to move his gun. "Take it easy, Thad," he said. "I ain't quite sure how they did it, but these old mossbacks got the drop on us."

"That's right, we do," Bo said. "Now toss those shotguns over there in the brush."

"The hell we will!" Thad burst out.

"It's either that or toss them in the river," Scratch said. "Choice is up to you. But if you think we're gonna ride past you boys while you're still armed, you're loco."

"Not as loco as you are for buckin' us, old man," Luke said through tight lips. He jerked his head at Thad. "Throw your gun in the brush, like they said."

"But Luke——"

"Do it." As an example, Luke tossed his shotgun into the thick brush on the left side of the road.

"Don't worry, Thad. This ain't over."

"No, it's not," Bo agreed as Thad grudgingly followed suit and threw his Greener into the brush.

"Like I told you, if I find out we were wrong about you boys, we'll come back and pay what we honestly owe."

"You were wrong, all right." Luke sneered. "Dead wrong."

"Man could take that as a threat," Scratch said.

"Take it any way you want,"

Bo motioned with his Colt. "Step aside now."

Luke and Thad rode past to the side of the road. Bo and Scratch rode past after Bo holstered his gun so he could lead the packhorse. Scratch kept his Remington in his hand and hipped around in the saddle so he could watch the two men. They didn't make any move to retrieve their weapons.

"Looks like they're gonna let it go," Scratch commented.

"For now." Bo didn't look around. "I'll bet Luke meant what he said about it not being over, though."

"You believe they really had a right to charge us that toll?"

Bo shook his head. "Not for a second. But if it turns out we're wrong, we'll settle up."

A humorless laugh came from Scratch. "I don't think payin' the toll's gonna be enough. Not after we made 'em back down like that. We better keep an eye out for trouble."

"Just like always, you mean?"

Scratch grinned. "Yeah. Just like always."

They started up the sloping main street. At the far end of it, sitting square in the middle of where the road would have run if it had continued past the town, was a large, ramshackle old house that looked older than any other building in Mankiller. It had a broad verandah along the front with a roof supported by thick, square beams.

As Bo and Scratch rode along the street, Bo looked for the sheriff's office. They passed a number of businesses, including a couple of hotels, a bank, a newspaper office, an assayer's office, a pair of decent-looking restaurants, a hole-in-the-wall hash house, and more than a dozen saloons. In fact, there were so many saloons that each of the more respectable businesses seemed to be completely surrounded by them, as if they were little islands in a sea of debauchery.

Tinny music came from each of the saloons, the competing tunes blending together to create a discordant racket. Men laughed and cursed. Women shrieked and cursed. A fat man in a derby and a gaudy checked suit stood outside the door of a gambling hall and bellowed, "Honest games! Honest games of chance!"

Scratch leaned over in the saddle and asked Bo, "What do you reckon the odds are he's tellin' the truth?"

Bo shook his head and said, "I wouldn't bet a hat on it."

They passed a two-story frame building with a number of windows on the second floor where women in low-cut gowns leaned out and called obscene invitations to the men in the street. One of the soiled doves looked at Scratch and yelled, "Hey, handsome! You there in the buckskin jacket!"

Scratch looked up at her and ticked a finger against the brim of his Stetson as he nodded. "Ma'am."

"Come on up here!" She squeezed her ample breasts together so that they seemed to be on the brink of spilling completely from her thin wrapper. "These'll make you feel young again!"

Bo and Scratch rode on, although Scratch sighed a little.

"You'd be taking your life in your hands if you went in that place," Bo told him.

"Maybe so, but I'd be takin' somethin' else in my hands, too."

Bo laughed, pointed, and said, "There's the sheriff's office."

It was a blocky building made of the same sort of whipsawed planks that had been used in many of the other buildings in Mankiller. A sign nailed above the door read SHERIFF'S OFFICE AND JAIL. The sign was pocked with holes.

"Those are bullet holes all over that sign, ain't they?"

"That's what they look like," Bo agreed.

"Well, that don't bode well. Seems like a lawman wouldn't take it kindly if folks did that."

"Let's go in and see if he's there."

The Texans dismounted and tied their horses and pack animal at a hitch rail in front of the sheriff's office. It was just about the only hitch rail in town that wasn't already full up, Bo noted. In a boom-town like this, he was a little leery of leaving their supplies outside, so he said, "I'll watch the horses. You can go inside and talk to the sheriff."

Scratch shook his head. "Let's swap those chores around. You're better at talkin' to lawdogs than I am. I always feel like they're suspicious of me, even when I ain't done nothin'."

"That's because you know you've gotten away with enough in your life that you always feel a little guilty," Bo said with a smile.

"Hey, if nobody saw me, they can't prove I done it! And if I did, I had me a good reason."

Bo laughed and went to the door of the sheriff's office. He opened it and stepped inside. The room was gloomy, choked with thick shadows. No lamp was burning, and the windows were so grimy they didn't admit much light. Bo's eyes adjusted quickly, though, and he stiffened as he spotted the figure sitting at the desk.

The man was sprawled forward, his head twisted to the side and lying on a scattering of papers. Those papers were stained by the dark pool that spread slowly around the man's head, as if his throat had been cut and his life was still seeping out.

CHAPTER 7

Bo backed away until he was standing in the doorway. His hand moved toward his gun, just in case any threat still lurked in here. The office was quiet and apparently deserted, though, except for the man sprawled on the desk.

"Scratch!" Bo called over his shoulder. "Get in here."

Scratch was there instantly, alert for trouble. "What is it?"

Bo nodded toward the desk.

"Son of a bitch," Scratch said. "You reckon he's still alive?"

"I don't see how, with that much blood on the desk. But we'd better make sure."

They started forward warily, splitting up so that Bo went to the right of the desk and Scratch to the left. Bo glanced through an open door that led to a small cell block. He could see into two of the cells. They were empty, and when he called, "Anybody back there?" no answer came from the cell block.

"Who could've cut the sheriff's throat in his own office?" Scratch asked in a low voice.

"That's assuming he's the sheriff," Bo pointed out. "We don't know that."

"No, I reckon we don't. But if he is, I wonder if he's got any deputies. We'll have to report this to somebody."

Bo nodded. "And hope that we don't get blamed for it."

"Yeah, that's just the way our luck runs sometimes, ain't it?"

They were at the desk now, and as both Texans leaned toward the body, Scratch suddenly sniffed and said, "Bo, somethin's wrong here. Up close like this, that don't really look like blood. It don't smell like it, neither. In fact, it smells like——" Scratch reached out, dipped a finger in the dark pool, and lifted it to his nose. He sniffed again, then licked his fingertip. "Yep. Rum."

Bo sighed in mingled relief and disgust. "Yeah, I can see part of a flask lying there under him now. I guess——"

The man chose that moment to give out with a loud, gasping snore that filled the office. He jerked, then lifted his head from the desk, having woke himself up.

Seeing the two Texans standing there so close to him must have startled him, because he shoved his chair back so hard and abruptly that it started to tip over backward with him still in it. He waved his arms in the air frantically and yelled, "Whoa, Nelly!"

Scratch grabbed hold of the man's right arm while Bo caught the chair and kept it from tipping over. He righted it, causing the chair's front legs to thump heavily on the floor. That threw the man sitting in it forward again, and only Scratch's strong hand on his arm kept him for falling face-first on the desk again.

The man's bleary eyes opened wide at the sight of the dark, liquid pool on the desk. "Godfrey Daniel!" he cried. "What a catastrophic turn of events!"

He wrenched free of Scratch's grip with unexpected strength and leaned forward, plunging his face toward the desk so that he could start lapping up the rum like a dog.

"Good Lord, man," Bo said, completely disgusted now. "Don't you have any self-respect?"

The man glanced up at him and said, "There are some circumstances, sir, when shelf-respect is . . . is painfully inshufficient for a man's needs."

Scratch went behind the chair and reached down to take hold of the man under each arm. He straightened, hauling the man up and out of the chair.

"What you need is to have your head ducked in a water trough a few times, mister. You scared us outta some time we can't afford to lose at our age!"

"Take it easy, Scratch," Bo advised as he caught sight of the tin star pinned to the man's vest. "You'll get arrested if you start manhandling the law."

"You mean this pathetic drunk really *is* the sheriff in these parts?"

Bo leaned closer to peer at the badge in the bad light. "That's what the tin star says, anyway."

"Un . . . unhand me, sir!" the drunken lawman demanded. "Or I'll be forced to . . . to throw you in the calaboose!"

Scratch lowered the man back into the chair. "Sorry, Sheriff," he said. "I figured you must just be some drunk who wandered in from the street to sleep off a bender. I thought maybe we'd be doin' you a favor by gettin' you out of here before the real sheriff found you."

The man let out a huge belch, then grabbed hold of the desk's edge with both hands as if the room had started spinning around him. "I . . . I am . . . the real sher'f. Sher'f O'Brien at your . . . your shervice. What can I . . . do for you two . . . fine gennelmen?"

Sheriff O'Brien was a thickset man who wore a dirty flannel shirt that was missing a button so that some of his ample belly showed where it bulged against the garment. He had a close-cropped salt-and-pepper beard and a thatch of graying hair that stuck up in wild spikes as if O'Brien had run his fingers through it several times before passing out. The butt of a handgun stuck up from a holster attached to a gun belt strapped around his hips.

Lawman or not, Bo wasn't sure it was a good idea for somebody like this to be carrying a gun. O'Brien might shoot himself or somebody else without even knowing what he was doing.

Bo looked around and spotted a battered old coffeepot sitting on a cast-iron stove in the corner. "You want a cup of coffee, Sheriff?"

O'Brien shuddered. "Can't stand coffee. Keeps me awake at night. Man with . . . an important job like mine . . . needs his sleep at night." He peered at Bo and Scratch, looking back and forth between them. "Who . . . who are you? I don't remember . . .

don't remember seeing you around our fine community before."

"That's because we just rode in. He's Scratch Morton. My name's Bo Creel. We're from Texas."

"Well, you're welcome in Mankiller anyway."

O'Brien hiccupped. "Ever'body's welcome in Mankiller. Bustling—*hic!*—bustling community."

Scratch looked at Bo and shook his head. "We're wastin' our time talkin' to this fella. He's drunk as a skunk. You won't be able to get anything sensible outta him."

O'Brien leaned back in his chair and glared.

"Drunk as a skunk, am I?"

"That's the way it looks to me."

O'Brien pointed a trembling finger at Scratch.

"Don't you . . . disreshpect the office of . . . of sher'f, I'm the . . . the law around here——"

He stopped short, turned in his chair, and threw up all over the floor behind the desk.

Grimacing, Bo said, "Come on, let's get out of here. We'll ask somebody else about those men and that so-called toll bridge."

He and Scratch had started toward the door when O'Brien grabbed hold of the desk again and pulled himself up. "Wait a minute!" he called. "Did you say . . . toll bridge?"

Bo stopped and looked back. "That's right," He thought that the sheriff appeared slightly less drunk, probably because he had emptied his belly of all the rum he'd consumed earlier. "Two men stopped us at this end of the bridge over the river and demanded that we pay them a toll. Do they have a legal right to collect such a toll, Sheriff?"

O'Brien blinked rapidly. "You . . . you paid 'em, didn't you?"

Scratch smiled and shook his head. "No, we sorta persuaded them to let us pass without payin'. Some .44 caliber persuasion, if you know what I mean."

O'Brien looked even sicker than he had a moment earlier. "Oh, no. Godfrey Daniel and all his thrice-damned brethren! You didn't . . . you didn't *kill* them, did you?"

"It didn't come to shooting," Bo assured the lawman.

"Yeah," Scratch added, "they saw the light when they found themselves lookin' down the barrels of our guns."

O'Brien groaned. "Oh, this is bad, this is bad." He clawed his fingers through his hair in agitation. "Who was it? Did they tell you their names?"

"Luke and Thad," Bo supplied.

"Oh, my Lord. Luke Devery is his pa's firstborn son and right-hand man. Thad's his cousin, from the crazy side of the family. You made them back down?"

"They rubbed us the wrong way, I reckon you could say," Scratch replied.

Bo said, "I told them we'd check with the law, and if they have a legal right to collect a toll, we'd come back and pay them." He shrugged. "Then we made them toss their shotguns in the bushes and get out of our way."

O'Brien leaned his elbows on the desk and covered his face with his hands. "Lemme think, lemme think," he half-moaned. After a few seconds, he looked up at the Texans and went on, "Here's what you need to do. Go up to the next block and over a block. You'll see a place called Bradfield's. You go in there and . . . and talk to Sam Bradfield."

"Who's he?" Scratch asked.

"The undertaker. He's gonna need to size you boys up for coffins and find out what you want on your tombstones."

Bo and Scratch just looked at him for a moment, then Bo said, "You're telling us that Luke and Thad are going to kill us."

O'Brien nodded. "Oh, yeah. Sure as a pig shits in a pen. Them and their relatives, they won't let that pass."

"Well, no offense, Sheriff, but we'll have something to say about that. And if you don't want a lot of trouble in your town, you'd be wise to speak to those men and warn them."

"No, sir." O'Brien shook his head. "I'm not going near the Deverys. We have an arrangement. I leave them alone, and they leave me alone. Actually, they, uh . . . sort of pretend that I don't exist."

Bo bit back the words that sprang to his lips. He wanted to tell O'Brien that he was a not only a pathetic excuse for a lawman, but also a pathetic excuse for a man. Such a tongue lashing wouldn't accomplish anything, though.

"If anyone attacks us, Sheriff, we'll defend ourselves."

O'Brien held up a shaking hand, palm toward Bo. "Don't tell me. I don't want to know anything about it." He was frightened enough so that now he seemed half-sober, or only half-drunk, depending on how you wanted to look at it. "I suppose it's too much to hope that you boys are just passing through Mankiller?"

"We heard about the gold strike," Scratch said. "Figured to do some prospectin'."

O'Brien shook his head. "I was afraid you'd say that. Would you maybe . . . as a personal favor to me, maybe . . . consider riding on? Right now, maybe?"

"We're not going anywhere," Bo said, "except to get some rooms in one of the hotels and then maybe a good hot meal in one of the cafes."

Scratch smiled. "That sounds good to me, too."

"But you never did answer the question, Sheriff," Bo went on. "Do the Deverys have a legal right to collect that toll?"

"Some folks in town got together and built the bridge," O'Brien muttered. "Before that there was just a rope bridge."

"Then the answer is no."

O'Brien shrugged. "Depends on how you look at it. The Devery family owns a lot of land around here, including the part where the bridge ends."

"Well, then, in that case, maybe we should go back and pay them, like I said we would."

O'Brien gave Bo a bleak stare. "You really think that's going to do any good *now*? You insult a couple of the Deverys, pull guns on them . . . Do you really think paying a few dollars is going to change anything?"

Bo reached in his pocket, took out some coins, and counted out twelve dollars' worth. He put them on the desk in front of O'Brien and said, "If Luke and Thad show up to make a complaint, Sheriff, you give that to them, understand? And if that's not good enough to settle the debt . . ."

"Then I reckon they'll have to come find us," Scratch finished in an equally grim voice.

The two Texans turned and walked out of the sheriff's office, leaving the badly shaken O'Brien behind them.

When they reached the street, they paused. Now that they were out of earshot of the lawman, Scratch asked quietly, "You don't reckon we ought to ride on like the man suggested, just to save ourselves some trouble, do you, Bo?"

"I suppose it would have been a lot less trouble if you and I and Sam Houston and all those other fellas had just let Santa Anna go on about his business that day at Buffalo Bayou, wouldn't it?"

Scratch laughed. "Yeah, that's about what I figured you'd say. The Good Lord seemed to be out of cut-and-run the day He made us, didn't He?"

"I'd say so." Bo pointed diagonally across the street toward a building with a sign on it announcing BONNER'S CAFÉ. "That looks like a good place to eat. What say we get a surrounding before we go find a hotel?"

"Lead the way," Scratch said.

CHAPTER 8

They untied their horses and took the animals with them, threading their way through the crowds in the street. The hitch rail in front of the café was crowded, but there was just enough room left for the Texans' horses.

A pair of doors with curtained windows in their upper halves led into the building. When Bo opened one of them, a mixture of delicious aromas floated out and washed over him and Scratch.

Scratch paused to take a deep breath. He sighed and then asked, "Are you sure this is Mankiller and not heaven, Bo?"

"I don't reckon El Señor Dios would have a couple of mangy varmints like those Deverys trying to charge a toll to get into heaven, do you?"

"Probably not," Scratch agreed.

They went inside and closed the door behind them. The place was busy, which testified that the flavor of the food matched its aroma. Most of the tables covered with blue-checked tablecloths were occupied, and every one of the stools at the counter running along the right side of the room was occupied. A couple of pretty waitresses in gingham dresses and white aprons were hurrying from table to table, delivering platters of food and taking orders. An older but still very attractive woman behind the counter refilled coffee cups for the men who sat there.

Bo spotted an empty table. He pointed it out to Scratch, and they hustled to take it before anybody else could come into the café behind them and steal it out from under them.

As they sat down and removed their hats, one of the fresh-faced waitresses came over to them. "Coffee and the special, gents?" she asked.

Bo glanced at the chalkboard hung on the wall behind the counter. The special, written in lovely, flowing script, was roast beef, potatoes, carrots, peas, biscuits, and apple pie.

"Oh, my, yes, ma'am," Bo said, his mouth already watering. The prospect of such a meal after living on what he and Scratch could eat on the trail for a couple of weeks was very appetizing.

"And keep the coffee comin'," Scratch added.

The brown-haired waitress smiled at them. "I sure will," she promised. "Be right back with your cups."

Scratch watched her walk back to the counter to turn in the order. "Mighty friendly folks in this place," he commented.

"In the café, you mean," Bo said. "The rest of the town didn't strike me as being all that friendly."

"Well, no, I reckon not," Scratch paused. "You think those Devery boys will really come after us?"

Bo shrugged. "The sheriff seemed to think so. I'm not sure how reliable he is, but Luke and Thad didn't seem to be the sort who'd give up a grudge easily."

"In other words, we may be in for trouble." Scratch chuckled. "It's not like that'll be a big change for us, will it?"

Bo shook his head. Unfortunately, what Scratch said was true. All they wanted was peace and quiet, and in this case, the opportunity to do a little prospecting. It seemed that those things might be denied to them, at least for a while.

But for the time being, they had a good meal to look forward to, so they pushed those other thoughts away. Neither of them had been the sort to let worry consume them. They took things as they came.

The waitress came back a couple of minutes later, expertly balancing two cups and saucers and a coffeepot, the handle of which she held with a thick leather pad. She set the cups down, filled them, and said, "Your food will be along in just a few minutes, gents."

"Thanks, miss," Bo told her. He had been looking back and forth between the waitress and the woman at the counter and had noted the resemblance between them. "Begging your pardon if I'm too nosy, but is that your mother behind the counter?"

The waitress smiled. "That's right. And the other waitress is my sister."

"Family business, is it?" Scratch asked. "Is your pa back in the kitchen doin' the cookin'?"

The young woman's smile went away. "No,

I'm afraid not. I wish he was. He passed away a while back."

Scratch instantly looked apologetic. "I'm sure sorry, miss," he said. "Didn't mean to bring up any bad memories."

"No, that's all right. You didn't know. But to answer your question, my Uncle Charley is the cook." She smiled again. "And he's a really good one."

"I'm sure he is," Bo said. He took a sip of the strong black coffee. "He brews a good cup of coffee, too."

Customers at other tables were clamoring for attention. The waitress gave Bo and Scratch a friendly nod, then went back to work.

Scratch sighed. "It's downright amazin' how far in my mouth I can shove this big ol' foot of mine sometimes."

"I wouldn't worry about it," Bo said. "Like the girl told you, you didn't know about her pa."

Scratch cast an interested look at the counter and the woman working behind it. "That means the lady's a widow. Wonder exactly how long it's been since her husband passed on." There was nothing Scratch found more intriguing than a good-looking widow lady.

Bo laughed. "I get a feeling that if we wind up staying in Mankiller for very long, we'll be eating here a lot."

"We might be," Scratch said. "We just might be."

If they did, the quality of the food would justify it, Bo discovered as their meals arrived a few minutes later, delivered by the same waitress. The roast beef was tender, bursting with juices and flavor, and the rest of the food was almost as good. The biscuits were light and fluffy, a far cry from what a fella could cook on the trail. The apple pie topped off the meal perfectly, with its sweet filling and light, flaky crust. All of it was washed down with several cups of coffee, which the pretty brunette kept refilling.

The lunch rush died down a little while the Texans were eating. By the time they were finished, only about half the tables were occupied, and there were a few empty stools at the counter. The woman working there, the mother of the two waitresses, was able to pause and catch her breath. She pushed back a strand of brown hair that had come loose and fallen over her forehead. There were some threads of gray in that hair, but not many, Bo noted. He had to agree with what he knew Scratch was thinking . . . the woman had a mature beauty that made her very attractive.

In all their years of traveling together, the two of them had seldom if ever paid court to the same woman. One always deferred to the other out of the deep friendship they had developed. Since Scratch had expressed an interest in this lady first, Bo didn't intend to interfere.

He didn't expect anything lasting to come from it, anyway. Scratch had never been the sort to settle down. If such thoughts even began to crop up in his head, he tended to skedaddle as quickly as possible.

Now, however, Scratch stood up and, holding his hat in front of him, went over to the counter. He smiled at the woman and said, "Ma'am, I just wanted to tell you that was the best meal I've had in a month of Sundays."

She returned the smile. "Why, thank you, Mister...?"

"Morton, ma'am. They call me Scratch."

"Well, thank you again, Mr. Morton, but I can't take credit for the food. My brother is the cook."

"If you'd pass along my compliments to him, I'd sure appreciate it. And I can promise you, my partner and I will be back to eat here again."

"I hope so. Are you planning to be in Mankiller for long?"

"Depends on how we do once we start prospectin'."

The woman's smile went away. "You came here looking for gold?"

"Yes, ma'am. We read all about the big strike." Scratch saw something like disapproval lurking in her eyes. "You don't like the gold strike, ma'am? Seems like it'd help your business a lot."

"Of course it does," she said, "and I don't begrudge anyone who wants to seek their fortune. But I'd like to see more people come here who'd like to put down roots and help the town grow once this boom is over, as sooner or later it will be."

Scratch nodded. "I reckon you're right about that, ma'am. My partner and me, we ain't really the putting-down-roots sort of hombres, though."

"I see. Well, you're welcome here while you're in town, Mr. Morton, however long that may be."

"Thank you most kindly, ma'am. I didn't catch your name...?"

"It's Mrs. Bonner." For a second it seemed like that was all she was going to give him. Then she relented a little and added, "Lucinda Bonner."

"That's a mighty pretty name, Mrs. Bonner. It suits you."

Bo figured he'd let Scratch flirt with the woman long enough. He came up to the counter as well and asked, "How much do we owe you for the coffee and two specials, ma'am?" The price wasn't written on the chalkboard.

She turned to look at Bo. "That'll be ten dollars."

The eyes of both Texans widened in surprise. Scratch's shock overcame his interest in Lucinda Bonner, and he blurted, "Ten bucks? Ain't that kinda steep?"

"Of course it is," she replied. "But in Mankiller, five dollars isn't bad for a meal like that. You can go over to the hash house and get a bowl of greasy stew that isn't nearly as good, and it will set you back four dollars."

"Why are the prices so high?"

"Because the price of supplies is so high. I promise you, Mr. Morton, we're not gouging our customers. Even charging what we do, the café is barely getting by, if you want to know."

Bo said, "It's a boomtown. Supply and demand. Demand is high, and supplies are limited. We've seen it before, Scratch."

"Yeah, I reckon so." Scratch shook his head. "Still, it's mighty dear."

Bo slid a half-eagle across the counter to Lucinda Bonner. He kept a few coins in his pocket, and so did Scratch, but the rest of their stake was split up between a pair of money belts, one worn by each of them.

"There you go, ma'am," he told her. As he touched

a finger to the brim of his black hat, he added, "Best of luck to you and your daughters and brother."

"Thank you." Her hand moved, and the coin disappeared.

Bo and Scratch left the café. As they paused outside, Bo said, "I've got a feeling that if you intended to court that woman, Scratch, you may have ruined those plans by accusing her of overcharging us for those meals."

"Now, that ain't exactly what I said," Scratch protested.

"Close enough."

Scratch sighed. "You may be right about that, Bo. I was just surprised, that's all, and you know sometimes my talkin' is a few steps ahead of my thinkin'. I should've knowed better. We've been in enough boomtowns to know how it is."

"Yeah, we sure have," Bo untied the reins of his dun and the packhorse from the hitch rail. "I hope we can find room in a stable for these animals."

They led the horses along the street and were turned away at a couple of livery stables that were already full up. When they came to a ramshackle barn with a crudely lettered sign that read EDGAR'S LIVERY, Bo shrugged and said, "This may be the best we can do."

"Or maybe we ain't hit bottom yet," Scratch said. "Reckon all we can do is go in and ask."

They found the liveryman inside, mucking out a stall. That brought back unpleasant memories of Socorro and Johnny Burford.

"Are you Edgar?" Bo asked the thickset proprietor.

"That's right. You boys lookin' for a place to stable them cayuses?"

"Do you have room for them?"

The man nodded. "Yeah, I do. Be four dollars a day for each of 'em."

Scratch let out a whistle. "There's nothin' cheap in this town, is there?"

"Not right now there ain't," Edgar agreed. "Not in the middle of a gold boom." He rubbed at his grizzled jaw. "Tell you want I'll do, though . . . you got three hosses, so we'll call it ten bucks a day for all three. How's that sound?"

"Still a mite like highway robbery," Scratch grumbled.

"But we'll take it," Bo added. "Thanks."

He handed over a double eagle to pay for two days. At the rate their money was going, he hoped they would be able to find gold soon. Otherwise their stake would be gone and they'd have to move on.

Of course, that wouldn't necessarily be such a bad thing. They had gambled before and lost, and the good thing about being drifters was they could always ride away and leave those troubles behind them, as long as they had enough money left for a few supplies.

Edgar showed them the empty stalls. As they were unsaddling their mounts, Bo asked the liveryman, "Do you know a family named Devery?"

Edgar looked surprised. "Yeah, I know 'em. Why do you ask?"

Scratch said, "We had a run-in with a couple of 'em at the bridge leadin' into town."

"Is that so?"

"Yeah. Had to pull iron on 'em."

Bo said, "Sheriff O'Brien told us the Devery family owns a lot of the land hereabouts."

Edgar laughed. "Still seems strange to me that ol' Biscuits wears a law badge. Wasn't that long ago he was the one bein' locked up all the time." The liveryman lowered his voice to a conspiratorial tone. "Biscuits drinks a mite, you know."

Bo nodded. "We got that idea. We don't want any hard feelings with the Deverys. We just didn't think they had any right to charge us a toll. From what the sheriff said, though, maybe we should have paid."

"It was mighty high," Scratch put in, "but then, so's everything else around here."

"You know where we can find them?" Bo asked.

Edgar stroked his chin and nodded. "When you rode in, did you see that big ol' house up at the head o' Main Street?"

"We did."

"Well, that's the old Devery house. Jackson Devery—Pa Devery, some call him—lives there with his brood. You don't need to go all the way up there to see Luke and Thad, though."

"Why not?" Scratch asked, but Bo had already tumbled to something his partner hadn't.

"We didn't mention their names," he snapped as he started to reach for his gun.

It was too late. With a rush of footsteps, several people charged them from behind. The Texans tried to turn and draw their guns, but before they could manage that, crashing blows fell on their heads. They were driven forward, tackled, brought down on the hard-packed dirt of the barn's center aisle. Fists and booted feet and, for all they knew, gun butts thudded into them. Bo and Scratch struggled to throw off their attackers and get up, but there was too much weight pinning them down. Their heads spun wildly from blow after vicious blow.

Bo didn't know who lost consciousness first, him or Scratch, and it didn't matter one damned bit, anyway.

CHAPTER 9

"Shit! Wake up, Bo, wake up!"

As awareness seeped back into Bo's brain, he recognized Scratch's voice as the silver-haired Texan spoke urgently to him. A terrible stench filled his nostrils, and he wondered if that stink was what prompted Scratch's exclamation. It sure smelled like they were rolling around in some sort of dung.

Something wet and slobbery prodded his face. Bo forced his eyes open and found himself staring at close range into the beady little eyes of a massive hog. He yelled as he jerked away from the beast. Then someone grabbed his arm and hauled him up and out of a sticky, stinking morass that tried to drag him back down.

As he staggered to his feet, he looked over and saw that it was Scratch who had hold of him. At least, he thought it was Scratch. He couldn't be sure, because the hombre appeared to have been smeared from head to foot with a mixture of mud and other foul substances. Bo wondered suddenly if he looked the same way. He considered the likelihood to be pretty strong.

His eyesight was blurry because of gunk dripping over his eyes. He tried to wipe it away, but his hand was even filthier and just made things worse. Scratch tugged at his arm and said, "They threw us in a damn hog pen! We gotta get outta here 'fore those blasted porkers get us, Bo!"

Bo knew his friend was right. He saw a number of huge, muddy, bloated shapes around them. A bunch of hogs like that could consume anybody unlucky enough to fall in among them, and nothing would be left of the poor son of a bitch.

With the mud of the hog wallow dragging at their feet, Bo and Scratch fought their way toward the pole fence that surrounded the pen. They didn't know where they were, other than in a heap of trouble, but they could figure that out later, after they made it over that fence, away from the hogs. They reached it and began climbing, a task made more difficult by the slippery mud that coated their hands, and everything else.

Hogs snuffling hungrily around their legs added urgency to their actions. They struggled to the top of the fence and swung over it, but both Texans lost their grip as they did so and fell hard to the ground on the outside of the pen. At least now they were where the hogs couldn't get at them, so they were able to lie there and catch their breath for a few moments.

Not that they wanted to breathe much of that stinking air. Bo coughed and gasped and tried not to think about how much of the mud must have gotten in his mouth. As he and Scratch pushed themselves to their hands and knees and began to crawl away from the pen, both of them started spitting as hard as they could.

They made it about twenty yards before they collapsed. That was far enough so that the smell wasn't quite so bad. They could still smell themselves, though, and that was a terrible reek.

"We gotta . . . we gotta find some place to wash off," Scratch said.

Bo lifted his head to look around. He heard the bubbling, chuckling sound of running water, and after a moment he located what appeared to be the Animas River. He and Scratch were lying on a hillside. The stream was at the bottom of the slope, about fifty yards away.

Bo's eyes followed the river back along its course. He saw the sturdy wooden bridge in the distance, maybe a quarter of a mile way. That meant they weren't far out of Mankiller. They could walk back to the settlement.

But not looking and smelling like this. They had to clean themselves up first. Then they could take stock of the situation and figure out what to do next.

"Let's see if we can . . . make it to the river," he suggested to Scratch.

They fought their way to their feet and began stumbling down the hill. The rocky banks of the Animas were about eight feet high, but they weren't so steep that the Texans couldn't slide down them. That's what they did, coming to a stop on a narrow strip of grass at the edge of the water.

They were about to lean forward and plunge their mud-caked heads into the chilly, fast-flowing stream, when a rifle shot blasted somewhere nearby and a bullet kicked up dirt and gravel just a few feet away. As Bo and Scratch froze, a voice ordered harshly, "Don't move, you filthy bastards!"

Bo turned his head and saw a man coming toward them along the riverbank. He was a little below medium height and seemed to be almost as wide as he was tall. He wasn't fat, though. Instead, he bulged with muscle all over. A derby was pushed down on his bald head, and a red handlebar mustache curled over his mouth. He had a short, black cigar clenched between his teeth in one corner of that mouth.

He kept Bo and Scratch covered with the Spencer repeating carbine he had fired a moment earlier. He jerked the barrel a little and said, "Get away from that water!"

"Mister, we just want to clean up," Bo said.

"I know what you want to do. My claim's downstream, and I don't want you fouling the water with all that pig shit."

"You can't expect us to just stay like this!" Scratch protested.

The man shrugged wide shoulders. "It'll dry and crack off after a while."

"By then we'll be dead from the stink!"

"Yeah, well, you should count yourself lucky that you're not filling up the belly of some hog by now." The man's face became even more grim. "You wouldn't be the first fellas to wind up disappearing in the Devery hog pen."

"The Deverys own those hogs, do they?" Bo

asked. Somehow that idea didn't come as any surprise to him.

"Before I answer that, tell me . . . your last name wouldn't happen to be Devery, would it?"

The man's face darkened with anger. The tips of his mustache seemed to bristle with outrage.

"It would not," he said. "My name is O'Hanrahan, Francis Xavier O'Hanrahan, and I'm no relation to those damned Deverys!"

"It would seem that you're no friend to them, either."

"You could say that."

"Well, neither are we," Bo said, "and like Scratch told you, if we don't get cleaned up, the smell of this stuff is likely to kill us."

Francis Xavier O'Hanrahan grunted. "It won't kill you, but it might make you so sick you'd wish you were dead." He lowered the rifle's barrel. "Maybe I can help you. Come with me, if you want. Just don't try any tricks."

"Mister," Scratch said, "we ain't got any tricks left to try, even if we wanted to."

That was the truth, Bo thought. He had already realized that his gun was gone, and so were Scratch's Remingtons, along with the gun belt and holsters. Bo could tell as well that the money belt that was supposed to be under his shirt was gone. He would have been willing to bet—if he'd had anything left to wager—that the part of their stake Scratch had been carrying had vanished, as well.

O'Hanrahan motioned again with the rifle barrel

and said, "Just walk on down the bank here. I'll be behind you with this Spencer, so don't get any funny ideas."

They did as the burly Irishman said, trudging along the bank until they rounded a bend and came in sight of a rough dugout sunk in the side of the hill. A hundred yards or so up the slope yawned the open mouth of a mine shaft. Bo knew this had to be O'Hanrahan's claim.

O'Hanrahan stopped them and said, "Wait right here." He went to the dugout, stepped inside, and came back a moment later carrying a bucket in one hand and the rifle in the other. He laid the rifle across the top of a barrel and went to the river with the bucket.

"You intend to dump that over our heads, Mr. O'Hanrahan?" Bo asked.

"Take it or leave it," O'Hanrahan said around the unlit cigar still clenched between his teeth. "It'll be cold, but it'll wash some of that muck off."

"We'll take it," Scratch said. "I reckon I'd rather freeze to death than keep on smellin' like this."

O'Hanrahan filled the bucket in the stream, then carried it over to the Texans. "Who's first?"

"It doesn't really matter," Bo said. "It's going to take several buckets for each of us, at the very least."

"You're right about that." With that, O'Hanrahan lifted the bucket and upended it over Bo's head. The river water poured down and washed over Bo, dislodging some of the mud. It was just a start, though.

By the time half an hour had gone by, both of the Texans were soaking wet and shivering. Their teeth chattered. The ground around them was muddy from all the water O'Hanrahan had poured over them.

As the man stepped back after dumping a bucket of water over Scratch, he motioned toward the Animas and said, "All right, I reckon you're clean enough now you can jump in the river and finish the job. Take those clothes off and leave them on the bank. They'll have to be soaked and scrubbed, and even that may not be enough to get them clean. When you're done, come inside. I'll have a fire going in the stove and some blankets ready for you."

"Th-th-thank you," Bo managed to say through chattering teeth. It wasn't all that cold. The sun was even a little warm as it shone down over the hillside. But the water from the snowmelt-fed stream had leached all the heat out of the Texans.

They hurried over to the river, stripping off their wet, filthy clothes, and dropped them on the bank before wading out into the stream. Scratch cursed as the cold water rose on his legs. Bo just took a deep breath and went under.

They scrubbed away at themselves for long minutes before they felt clean enough to come out again. Circling around the dirty clothes and dripping river water, they headed for the dugout.

O'Hanrahan met them at the doorway with blankets, which they gratefully wrapped around themselves as they stepped inside. The dugout was made of stone and logs and had a thatched roof. The floor was dirt. It was simply furnished with a potbellied stove, a rough-hewn table, a couple of chairs, and a low-slung bunk with a straw mattress. A man could eat and sleep here when he wasn't working on his mine, but that was about all.

"Sit down at the table," O'Hanrahan told Bo and Scratch. "I've got coffee on the stove. I imagine that sounds pretty good right about now."

"You don't know the half of it, Mr. O'Hanrahan," Scratch said.

"Call me Francis." He brought the coffee to them as they sat down. "If you're enemies of the Deverys, then you're friends with just about everybody else in this part of the country."

"'The enemy of my enemy is my friend,'" Bo quoted. "Is that about the size of it?"

Francis grinned. "Aye. The Deverys are well hated in these parts, except by some who try to curry favor with them. And if the truth be told, probably even they can't stand the Deverys, either. They're just more pragmatic about it."

"What makes that bunch so powerful?" Scratch asked. "Just the fact that they own some land around here?"

"Not just *some* land," Francis corrected. "They own the whole town and this whole side of the valley for a good five miles. In other words, all the land where that big vein of gold is located."

Scratch stared at their host for a second before he said, "Well, hell! Why aren't *they* gettin' rich by minin' the blasted stuff?"

Francis poured a tin cup of coffee for himself. "Because that would be too much hard work for the Deverys. They'd rather get rich by raking off fifty percent of everything the miners take out of the ground. That's not including the hefty cut they take from all the businesses in the settlement. That arrangement is in the lease of everybody who moved in there."

"Wait a minute," Bo said. "How in the world did they manage to get a jump on everybody else and claim all that land after the gold strike?"

Francis shook his head. "They didn't claim it after the gold strike. They already owned it. They'd been farming here for several years before anybody found any gold."

"Farmin'?" Scratch repeated. "This ain't good territory at all for farmin', I'd say. Of course, I wouldn't really know, not havin' done much of it in my life."

"Oh, it's not," Francis said. "Not at all. From what I've heard, the family just barely eked out a living, and I wouldn't be surprised if they did a little rustling and the like to help them get by. Jackson Devery and his sons came here from Kansas, and I've got a hunch they pulled up stakes and moved west because the law made it too hot for them back where they came from."

Bo had only seen Luke Devery and his cousin Thad, but he didn't doubt that Francis was right. Luke and Thad appeared to be brutal, vicious men, the sort who wouldn't be above committing a crime. For that matter, Bo was fairly certain that Luke and Thad had been among the men who'd attacked them at the livery stable and robbed them, and the others had probably been members of the Devery family, too.

He indulged his curiosity by asking, "The fella

who owns Edgar's Livery Stable in town . . . would Devery happen to be his last name?"

Francis nodded. "He's Jackson Devery's younger brother. He came out here right after the town got started. That was before the gold strike, too. Jackson and his boys built that big house at the top of Main Street. You've seen it?"

"Yeah," Scratch said.

"That may have been the last real work they did. After a while, Jackson sent word back to his kinfolks in Kansas, and some of them came out to join him. They started the town. Even now, you can tell an original Devery building."

"They look like they're about to fall down," Bo guessed.

Francis laughed. "I see you paid attention when you rode in." He sobered. "Then a cowboy who was just passing through here found a gold nugget where there'd been a rockslide not long before, and he told people about it, and, well, you know what happened next. There was a big rush, and not just miners, either. All the sort of folks who flock into every boomtown showed up, from the gamblers and whores and saloon owners to the honest businessmen. Didn't matter what they had in mind. When they got here, they found that if they wanted to go into business, they had to promise the Deverys a healthy share of the profits. Same was true for the prospectors, like me."

"You seem to know an awful lot about it," Scratch commented.

Francis shrugged. "I was a newspaperman at one time, and the habit of asking questions never got out of my blood. I talk to people, and they seem to want to talk to me. Most of them, anyway. Hard to get a word out of Jackson. He doesn't come out of that old house much. But Edgar likes to talk."

Bo sipped his coffee, relishing the warmth of it. The chill was mostly gone from his bones now. He said, "I don't imagine folks like it very much when the Deverys carve off half the pie for themselves without doing any work for it."

"No, of course they don't. But the Deverys own the ground, so what can they do?"

"You made it sound a while ago like the Deverys have committed crimes. You implied that they had killed people and thrown the bodies in that hog pen, the way they did with me and Scratch."

Francis frowned. "I don't know that for a fact. But I *do* know that some of the business owners who have complained too much about the Deverys' share have wound up missing. No one's ever seen them again."

Scratch said, "Down in Texas, folks'd call in the Rangers if things like that started happenin'."

"This isn't Texas. If the Deverys have broken any laws, they've covered it up." A bitter laugh came from Francis. "Anyway, if you'd met our local lawman, Biscuits O'Brien, you'd know it's not very likely he'd ever stand up to the likes of Jackson Devery and his sons and relatives. Biscuits is such a pathetic excuse for a human being that I hate to claim him as a fellow son of Ireland."

"We have met him. Why do they call him Biscuits?" Bo asked.

"I don't have any earthly idea. But it suits him, don't you think?"

Bo had to admit that Francis was right about that.

"So, how did you boys get on the wrong side of the Deverys? You must've done something to offend them to wind up in the hog pen like that."

Bo felt instinctively that they could trust the burly O'Harrahan, so he explained about the encounter at the bridge, with Scratch adding some of the details. By the time Bo got to the part about taking their horses into Edgar Devery's stable, Francis was shaking his head.

"You fellas really are lucky to be alive," he said. "I'm sure when they dumped you in the hog pen, they figured you'd be out cold until it was too late to stop the hogs from eating you. You must be tougher than they thought."

"They took our guns and our money," Scratch said. "Probably our horses and the rest of our gear, too."

Francis nodded. "Oh, yes, I think you can be pretty certain of that. I'd say that you boys don't own anything at the moment except those filthy clothes you left outside."

"That's not true," Bo said. "Those other things still belong to us, whether the Deverys have them or not."

Francis looked at them and frowned. "How do you figure that? You can't get them back."

"Sure we can," Scratch said. "All we have to do is kill all them damned Deverys first."

CHAPTER 10

Francis O'Hanrahan looked at them like he couldn't believe what he had just heard. After a long moment, he shook his head.

"I'm tempted to tell you to get the hell out of here, right now. I'm like just about everybody else around here who isn't named Devery. I spent what I had to get here, once I heard about that gold strike. I can't afford not to stay and try to make the best of it, no matter how bad things are."

Bo thought about Lucinda Bonner and her daughters running the café in town, as well as all the other honest business owners. No wonder prices were so high and yet folks were struggling anyway. They had to turn over half of what they made to the Deverys. The thought made anger well up in him. It might be legal, but it just wasn't right.

And if the Deverys had been getting their way through intimidation or even murder, it wasn't even legal.

"We can leave if you want," Bo said.

Francis sighed. "No, you can stay. You can wash

your clothes and let them dry, since they're all you've got. I'd loan you some of my duds, but I don't have anything that'll fit a couple of long-legged Texans like you!"

"We're obliged to you, Francis," Scratch said.

"Yeah, yeah. Just do me one favor."

"What's that?" Bo asked.

"When the Deverys try to kill you the next time, they're liable to ask you first if anybody helped you. Don't tell them it was me."

Bo nodded. "You've got a deal."

"Meanwhile, you can stay here tonight. I can feed you, help you get back on your feet before you go back to the settlement . . . to get slaughtered."

"Cheerful cuss, ain't you?" Scratch said.

"Just trying to be realistic."

Now that they were mostly dry and had warmed up some, Bo and Scratch tied the blankets around themselves like Roman togas and went outside to get their clothes. Francis had a washtub and a wash-board, as well as a chunk of lye soap. They filled the tub with water and built a fire under it, and using a couple of branches to pick up the filthy clothes, they soon had the garments soaking in the hot water. They let it build to a boil. That couldn't hurt, and the clothes were old enough and had been washed enough times that they wouldn't shrink.

It took the rest of the afternoon to get the clothes clean, and even then, they still had a few stains here and there and carried a faint odor of hog pen that would just have to wear off. Scratch took that philo-sophically, saying, "Oh, well, it ain't like we nor-mally smell like roses, anyway."

While their clothes were drying outside, the Texans shared the supper Francis had prepared. It was salt pork, potatoes, and wild greens, and while it was a far cry from the wonderful meal they'd had in Lucinda Bonner's café earlier that day, they were grateful for the food.

Out of idle curiosity as they were eating, Bo asked their host, "Do you know Mrs. Bonner who runs the café in town?"

"Lucinda?" A smile lit up Francis's ruddy face. "Aye. Every bachelor for twenty miles around knows the lovely Mrs. Bonner."

That brought a scowl to Scratch's face. He had entertained thoughts of courting Lucinda himself, Bo knew, but now it appeared that if he did, he would have a lot of competition.

Francis went on, "It was all they could do to wait a decent amount of time after her poor husband passed away before they started showing up on her doorstep, bouquets in hand. I, uh . . ." He cleared his throat. "I may have paid her a visit myself. But it didn't do any of us any good. She's devoted to her girls and her business and hasn't the time for anything else in her life."

"Maybe she just ain't found anything else worth makin' the time for," Scratch suggested.

Francis laughed. "Hope springs eternal, doesn't it? You're welcome to try your hand, my friend, but I doubt it'll do you any good. Besides, once the Deverys find out you're still alive, you'll be so busy dodging them you won't have much time for pitching woo."

"Dodging the Deverys isn't what we have in

mind," Bo said. "We want our horses and our gear back, and somebody around here needs to stand up to that bunch."

"A noble goal. The first thing you should do is talk to a man named Sam Bradfield."

"The undertaker," Bo said. "Yeah, we know. Sheriff O'Brien told us the same thing."

Francis frowned. "Good Lord. I didn't realize I'd be offering the same advice as Biscuits O'Brien. What a mortifying turn of events."

It would be morning before their clothes were dry enough to wear. Francis offered them the hospitality of the dugout floor. They made beds of pine boughs and covered them with blankets. They had slept on worse in their time, but still it wasn't a very comfortable night.

The smell that clung to their clothes had faded a little more by morning, so Bo and Scratch were able to get dressed without wrinkling their noses too much. "When we get some money, we'd best buy ourselves some lilac water," Scratch suggested.

"Yeah, that'll make us smell a lot better," Bo said dryly. "Because lilac water and hog droppings go together so well."

Francis O'Hanrahan sat on a stump in front of his dugout, chewing on another unlit cigar, and asked, "What are you fellas going to do when you get back to town?"

"I've been thinking about that," Bo said. "We can't just walk in and confront the Deverys."

"We can't?" Scratch asked.

Bo shook his head. "No, there are too many of them, and we're unarmed. If they're as casual about breaking the law as they seem to be, they'll just jump us and beat the hell out of us again, then throw us back in the hog pen. They'd probably take the time to make sure we were dead first, though."

Scratch looked like he wasn't happy about agreeing, but he said, "Yeah, I reckon you're right, Bo. Ten to one odds are too much when we don't have guns or even knives."

"We're going to have to bide our time," Bo went on. "We'll try to stay out of the Deverys' way, maybe get a job and earn some money so we can outfit ourselves a little before we confront them." He looked over at Francis. "If there are jobs to be had in Mankiller, that is."

"Oh, there are plenty of jobs," Francis said. "People who own businesses can't find enough men to work for them, because everybody who's able-bodied enough is up in the hills panning in the creeks or digging mine shafts, trying to find gold. You can probably get jobs in one of the saloons as bartenders or dishwashers. The livery stables need men to handle horses and keep the stalls clean, too."

Scratch shook his head. "We've done our share of livery stable work lately."

"I'd say most of the stores could use an extra clerk or two, as well," Francis said. "I know that's probably not the sort of job you're used to, but since you don't have any money to buy a prospecting outfit, you're not going to have much choice. You've got to make enough to eat."

"You wouldn't happen to be looking for a couple of partners in this mining claim, would you?" Bo asked.

"I'm afraid not. By the time I pay the Deverys their share, the gold I've been taking out of the ground barely pays for my supplies."

"That's what I figured you'd say."

Francis shrugged. "Sorry I can't be of more help."

"You've done plenty," Bo assured him, "and Scratch and I really appreciate it. At least we're alive and have reasonably clean clothes to wear. For a while there it didn't look like either of those things was going to be possible."

They shook hands with Francis, then started trudging upriver toward the settlement. It wouldn't take them long to reach it. While they were walking, Scratch said, "I don't much cotton to the idea of hidin' out from them Deverys."

"Neither do I," Bo said, "but we've got to be reasonable about the situation. We can't take them on like this, broke and unarmed."

"What if Edgar sells our horses? We've had those animals a long time."

Bo nodded. "And they've been mighty good mounts, too. But there are other horses out there. Anyway, I don't think he's likely to sell them. Nobody around here could afford them except some of the Deverys, which means they'll still be around Mankiller. We'll have a chance to get them back, I'm sure of it."

"I hope you're right. I'd like to get my hands on them Remingtons of mine again, too."

"They'll probably wind up in Devery hands. We'll just have to be patient and see what we can do."

When they got close to the settlement, they circled

up the slope a ways so they could enter Mankiller by one of the cross streets. They found an alley that ran behind several of the saloons fronting on Main Street.

"We'll make a start here," Bo decided. "Maybe one of these places can use a couple of dishwashers."

"I'd rather tend bar, myself," Scratch said.

"Yeah, but that would mean being out front where the Deverys could see you if they came in."

Scratch frowned. "Damn, I don't like this! We never run from trouble before, Bo."

"I'm not sure we've ever been broke and unarmed before, either," Bo pointed out.

"Maybe not, but I recollect a time when you wouldn't have worried so much about that. You used to be willin' to charge hell with a bucket of water."

Bo bristled a little. "Are you saying that I'm getting old?"

"We ain't neither one of us spring chickens no more. It's just that one of us seems more worried about that fact than the other."

They stood there in the alley glaring at each other for a second. This wasn't the first time friction had flared between the two trail partners. No two people with such strong personalities could travel together for years without rubbing each other the wrong way sometimes.

But after a moment, Bo shrugged and said, "Think whatever you want to. When the time comes, just hide and watch and you'll see how worried I am about being old."

"I'll do that," Scratch said. "For now, let's go see about gettin' those jobs as . . . dishwashers."

They entered the first of the saloons they came to through the rear door and found a door that probably led to the owner's office. A knock on that door brought a call to come in. As they stepped inside, a gaunt-faced man with a Vandyke beard looked up from a ledger open before him on a desk.

"What is it?" he asked in a voice as sharp and pointed as his beard.

"My friend and I are looking for jobs," Bo said.

The saloon keeper leaned back in his chair. His eyebrows rose in surprise. "Jobs?" he repeated. "Most men who come to Mankiller are looking for gold."

"Not us," Bo said. "We're willing to work at whatever chores you have."

The man stroked his beard. "I could use a couple of swampers. Usually I can hire an old drunk for that job, but even they're out prospecting these days."

"How much is the pay?"

"Fifty dollars a week for each of you. That's all I can afford."

"That sounds pretty good—" Scratch began, but Bo held up a hand to stop him.

"Wait a minute," Bo said. "Let me do some figuring. Do you have a place here we can sleep?"

The saloonkeeper shook his head. "Every bit of space in this building is being used. There's a storage room down here, but it's full. My quarters and a couple of other rooms are upstairs, but the girls who work here use those extra rooms . . . twenty-four hours a day if you know what I mean."

"How much is a room in a hotel, assuming we could get one?"

The man smiled. "You might be able to get an eight-hour shift in one, but it would cost you dearly. The flophouses are easier to get into. Eight hours in a bunk there will run about twenty-five dollars."

Bo figured rapidly, recalling what Lucinda Bonner had told them about the price of meals in Mankiller. When he finished his calculations, he said, "What you're offering us as a week's pay would only last us about three days."

The saloonkeeper shrugged. "I can't help that. It's all I can afford."

"We'd be losing money going to work for you. If we had any to lose, that is."

The man just shrugged again. "Sorry."

Bo turned to Scratch. "Let's get out of here."

"Maybe one of the other saloons will pay better," Scratch suggested.

The bearded man's laughter followed them out the door.

Over the next couple of hours, Bo and Scratch paid unobtrusive visits to every saloon, hash house, and mercantile they could find. Every business owner they talked to was eager to hire them, confirming what Francis had said about there being a shortage of able-bodied workers in Mankiller.

But no one was willing to offer more than fifty dollars a week in wages, and some offered even less. The Texans' frustration grew.

"This is sure a bad layout," Scratch said as they paused in an alley behind one of the general stores. "Everybody needs to hire some help, but they can't afford to because of havin' to pay that big cut to the Deverys. We need money, but if we take a job, we'll be just as broke as we are now, maybe even broker, if there is such a thing!"

"Yes, it just goes around and around in one of those vicious circles, doesn't it?" Bo said.

"Maybe we should mosey down to the bridge and jump whichever Deverys are on duty there collectin' tolls. We could get a couple of guns that way and start huntin' 'em down, one or two at a time."

"If we did that, we'd be the ones breaking the law," Bo said.

"Then, dadgummit, what *can* we do?"

"You can come with me," a woman's voice said from behind them.

CHAPTER 11

Bo and Scratch looked around in surprise. Lucinda Bonner stood there wearing a dark blue dress and looking as lovely as ever. She had taken off the apron she wore while working behind the counter in the café.

Out of habit, Bo started to reach up and touch the brim of his hat before he remembered that he wasn't wearing one. He settled for nodding and saying, "Ma'am. It's good to see you again."

"It sure is," Scratch added. "Best not come too close to us. We've still got a little, uh, aroma about us . . ."

Lucinda smiled. "Yes, I know. Francis O'Hanrahan told me what happened."

"Francis came to see you, did he?" Bo asked.

Lucinda nodded. "That's right. He had an idea, and he seemed to think he ought to discuss it with me. Owning the café means that I'm acquainted with most of the businessmen in town. I've done a little asking around, and it appears that you gentlemen have talked to just about all of those businessmen this morning, asking them for jobs. Why didn't you come to see me?"

"Well, for one thing, it didn't take us long to figure out that folks here in Mankiller can't afford to pay wages that'll let a man make a living," Bo said. "We didn't figure you'd be any different."

"And for another, we still sort of stink," Scratch added.

Lucinda said, "It's true, I can't pay you a living wage, but if you'll come with me back to the café, I have a proposition I'd like to discuss with you."

"We don't take charity," Bo said. "At least, not on a permanent basis."

"And that's not what I have in mind. I assure you, if the two of you go along with what I and some others have in mind, you'll earn every penny that you make."

The Texans looked at each other and frowned. Scratch shrugged and said, "I reckon we might as well hear the lady out."

"I don't see that it would do any harm," Bo agreed. "All right, Mrs. Bonner, we'll come with you. We'd better be careful that none of the Deverys see us with you, though. That would probably get you on their bad side."

"All right. We'll go in the back door."

She led them through the alleys to the rear entrance of the café. When they stepped into the roomy kitchen, which Bo and Scratch hadn't visited before, they were surprised to see that more than half a dozen people were waiting there. The Texans recognized some of them as owners of Mankiller's businesses that they had visited that morning. Lucinda's two daughters were also there, along with a grizzled, middle-aged man that Bo assumed was Lucinda's brother Charley, the café's cook, and Francis Xavier O'Hanrahan, the miner who had helped them out.

"I found them," Lucinda announced to the group.

"Probably none of you have been formally introduced except for Francis, so I'd like for you to meet Bo Creel and Scratch Morton." She turned to the Texans. "Gentlemen, you know Francis, of course, and my daughters Callie and Tess. This is my brother Charley Ellis . . . Lyle Rushford, who owns the Colorado Palace Saloon . . ."

Rushford was the man with the Vandyke beard, the first one Bo and Scratch had spoken to after they'd returned to Mankiller. He nodded to them now.

"Abner Malden, owner of Malden's Mercantile," Lucinda went on. "Ed Dabney, from Dabney's Livery. Wallace Kane, our local assayer. Lionel Gaines, from Gaines' General Merchandise and Hardware. And Sam Bradfield—"

"The undertaker," Bo finished with a smile.

"We've been advised on a couple of occasions that we ought to make your acquaintance, Mr. Bradfield."

"I just hope you won't need my services any time soon, Mr. Creel," Bradfield said, returning the smile.

Lyle Rushford, the saloon man, spoke up. "Do you have any idea why Lucinda brought you here?"

"She said something about a proposition," Bo replied. His brain was working swiftly. "I suppose it has something to do with all of you working together to accomplish something?"

"That's right," Rushford said. "You see, individually none of us can afford to pay you what you'd need to live on. But if we all chip in and get the other business owners in town to contribute, too, we can come up with enough money to hire you and make it worth your while to work for us."

"To work for all of you, you mean?" Bo asked with a frown.

Lucinda said, "For the town, actually . . . Wait a minute. I think I hear someone coming in. Callie, please go see if it's Reverend Schumacher."

Callie, the pretty brunette who had waited on Bo and Scratch the day before, nodded and ducked out through the door between the kitchen and the café's main room.

"There's a church in Mankiller?" Bo asked. "I didn't notice a steeple."

"That's because there isn't one up yet," Lucinda explained. "There isn't even an actual church building. The members meet in various businesses, moving from one to another every Sunday. When we decided to have this meeting, I offered my kitchen and closed up for the time being, but I gave the reverend a key to the front door. He offered to fetch the other person you need to see." She smiled. "Being a preacher, he can be very persuasive."

Callie pushed open the kitchen door and came in, trailed by two men. One of them was young, wearing a dark, sober suit and a string tie. He had hold of the second man's arm in a firm grip that both propelled him along and kept him from stumbling and falling.

The second man was Sheriff Biscuits O'Brien.

The lawman looked around at the gathering,

blinking in confusion. "What's goin' on here?" he demanded. His thick voice, red face, and bleary eyes testified to the fact that he had gotten an early start on the day's drinking. He'd probably had an eye-opener as soon as he crawled out of bed.

"Sheriff O'Brien," Lucinda said, "we asked you to come here for a reason. This is a meeting of some of the honest business owners in Mankiller. An unofficial town council, if you will."

O'Brien shook his head. "There ain't no town council. Jackson Devery says we don't . . . don't need one."

"Jackson Devery is *not* the law in this town, Sheriff," Lucinda told him sternly. "You are. And it's time you started acting like it and enforcing the law."

O'Brien turned toward the door. "I don't wanna hear this."

He found his way blocked by Reverend Schumacher and Francis O'Hanrahan. Francis put his hands on O'Brien's shoulders and turned him around.

"You're going to listen, whether you want to hear it or not, Biscuits," the miner said.

"Who pays your salary, Sheriff?" Lucinda asked.

O'Brien blinked and frowned in confusion. "Why . . . I reckon Mr. Devery does."

"Jackson Devery collects the money for your wages," Lucinda corrected. "He collects from all of us. That means *you* work for *us*."

O'Brien started shaking his head again. "No, no . . . Mr. Devery tells me what to do . . ."

"Not anymore. When you took office, you swore to uphold the law."

Wallace Kane, a balding man with spectacles, said, "And by God, you're going to do it whether you like it or not!" He glanced at Schumacher. "Sorry, Reverend."

Schumacher didn't seem to mind. He said, "Listen, Sheriff, you know as well as any of us that lawlessness is running rampant in Mankiller. The town lives up to its name, because there's at least one murder nearly every night! Men are robbed at gunpoint, crooked gamblers operate openly, and prostitutes ply their trade not only in brothels but in some of the alleys as well! All this has to stop if Mankiller is ever going to become any sort of decent, respectable community."

"It's a boomtown," O'Brien said. "It won't never be decent and respectable. It'll just go on boomin' until the gold dries up. Then it'll be a ghost town!"

"It doesn't have to be that way," Lucinda insisted. "If something can be done about the criminal elements, the settlement *might* grow into a real town, the sort of town that will last once the boom is over. But the lawless have to be rooted out, and that's your job, Sheriff."

O'Brien was bareheaded, and he ran his fingers through his already wild hair, jerking on it and making it go in every direction even more than it already was. "What do you expect me to do?" he asked miserably. "Even if I wanted to clean up the town, I couldn't do it. I'm just one man."

Lucinda smiled. "That's why we're going to provide you some help."

"Oh, shoot!" Scratch said suddenly. "You're gonna ask us to be deputies!"

Bo had figured out where the meeting was going a couple of minutes earlier, so he wasn't as surprised as Scratch. He didn't say anything as Lucinda turned and waved a hand toward them, saying, "That's right. Sheriff O'Brien, meet your new deputies."

O'Brien just stared, overcome for the moment. Moisture leaked from one corner of his mouth.

Bo said, "Don't you reckon you ought to ask us if we *want* the job?"

"What else are you going to do?" Rushford asked. "We all know what happened to you. The Deverys jumped you, stole everything you had, and left you for dead. You're broke and you need a job. You're not going to find one that pays better than this."

Lucinda looked at the Texans and said, "I'm sorry if it seems like we're railroading you into this, but the town needs help, and you two gentlemen are the only ones who have come along who seem capable of giving it."

"How do you know what we're capable of?" Bo asked.

Francis said, "I've seen tough hombres before. I know men who can take care of themselves when I see them. You two qualify . . . even if the first time I saw you, you *were* covered in . . . well, never mind. We all know what you were covered in."

The other businessmen chimed in, asking Bo and Scratch to take the job. Bo heard the desperation in their voices, and after a minute, he held up his hands for quiet.

"I don't reckon you can legally hire us without the sheriff going along with it," he said. He turned to O'Brien. "What about it, Sheriff? Do you want Scratch and me to be your deputies?"

A calculating look appeared in O'Brien's eyes. He might be drunk, but he was still cunning. "Does that mean that you two fellas would do all the work?"

"I expect we'd have to do most of it," Scratch answered, not bothering to keep the disgust out of his voice.

"But I'd still be the sheriff?"

"Technically, yes," Lucinda said. "At least until your term of office is up, and that's not until next year."

"Well . . . as long as I don't have to *do* anything . . ."

"Blast it, just say yes, Biscuits!" Sam Bradfield burst out.

O'Brien looked cowed. "All right, all right. You don't have to yell at me. I guess it'd be all right if these two gents were my deputies."

"Then it's done," Lyle Rushford said.

"You'll need guns," Abner Malden told Bo and Scratch. "Come on over to my store, and I'll outfit you. Free of charge."

Not to be outdone, Malden's competitor Lionel Gaines said, "And if there's anything else you need, come to *my* store. I carry everything."

While the two storekeepers glared at each other, Ed Dabney offered, "I can provide horses for you while you're working for the town."

"And of course you can take all your meals here," Lucinda added.

A grin stretched across Scratch's face. "That's a mighty powerful incentive right there."

"Your money's no good in the Colorado Palace, either," Rushford told them. "I can talk to Harlan Green at the hotel, and I'll bet he can find rooms for you."

Wallace Kane said, "I'd offer you my services, gentlemen, but I doubt that you'll need to have any ore assayed while you're serving as deputies. However, if the situation comes up, don't hesitate to come see me."

Sam Bradfield smiled. "And I don't figure you'll want to take advantage of my services any time soon."

"I wouldn't be so sure about that," Scratch said, drawing puzzled frowns from everyone in the room except Bo. "Not personal-like, you understand," the silver-haired Texan went on, "but I reckon once word gets around town about us bein' deputies, we'll be sendin' you some business, Mr. Bradfield."

"It's liable to be another boom," Bo added grimly.

CHAPTER 12

It was late in the morning, so Lucinda needed to reopen the café for the lunch rush. She needed every bit of profit she could make in order to pay off the Deverys and keep going. The meeting had served its purpose anyway.

As the businessmen filed out of the café, Bo spoke quietly to Lucinda. "You might want to see about forming a real town council, Mrs. Bonner, with a mayor and everything. That way you can pass local ordinances you want enforced. Right now, all Scratch and I can do is enforce the state laws."

"That's a good idea," Lucinda agreed. "I'll talk to everyone. In the meantime, enforcing the state laws will be a good start. That will cover murder and robbery, anyway."

Bo nodded. "Yes, ma'am, it will."

He and Scratch left with Biscuits O'Brien and Abner Malden. The storekeeper escorted them up the street to his establishment. It felt good to be walking openly along the street again, rather than slinking through alleys. That sort of furtiveness really went against the grain for the Texans.

It was entirely possible, even likely, that some of the men they passed in the crowded street were members of the Devery family. Some of them might have even been members of the group that had attacked the Texans in the livery stable.

Bo and Scratch couldn't worry about being recognized now. If they were going to function as deputies, they couldn't hide.

But both of them were going to feel better once they had loaded guns on their hips again.

They reached Malden's store and went inside. As they looked over the selection of guns the storekeeper had on display, Bo asked, "Have there ever been any deputies here in Mankiller before?"

Malden looked like he didn't want to answer that question, but finally he said, "Well, yes. And a couple of sheriffs before Biscuits—I mean Sheriff O'Brien—too."

"What happened to 'em?" Scratch asked. "And I got a feelin' I ain't gonna like the answer."

"Some of them quit," Malden said. "They were attacked . . . jumped in the night and roughed up. No one knows who was responsible for that."

"Or at least nobody wanted to admit knowing," Bo said.

Malden shrugged. "Around here, it amounts to the same thing."

"How about the ones who *didn't* quit?"

Again, Malden hesitated before saying, "No one really knows. Maybe they left in the middle of the night. All that's certain is that they weren't around anymore."

Scratch said, "What you mean is that the Deverys' hogs got 'em."

"If that was the case, there wouldn't be any proof left, would there?"

Bo said, "How do you know Scratch and I won't wind up the same way?"

"To be honest, we don't. But we're hoping that you and Mr. Morton will be able to take care of yourselves better than those other men."

"Yeah, we hope so, too," Scratch said.

Bo looked over at O'Brien, who had sat down on a cracker barrel and appeared to have dozed off. "How did Biscuits wind up being sheriff?"

"Well, as you can imagine, after everything that had happened, no one really wanted the job," Malden explained. "Then Pa Devery came up with the idea of giving it to Biscuits. I'm not sure why. Maybe he just thought it was funny."

"Yeah," Scratch said. "Hilarious."

"Anyway, Biscuits was living pretty much hand to mouth, at that point. He was glad to get the wages, plus a place to sleep." Malden's mouth tightened in disapproval. "He spends most nights in one of the cells, sleeping off his latest bender."

"Does he ever try to enforce the law?"

"Not really. Sometimes the Deverys will come and get him and take him along when they confront someone who hasn't paid them their share of the profits. I suppose they think it gives their actions an air of legitimacy, just in case any real law ever comes in here. Of course, Biscuits just does whatever the Deverys tell him."

Bo shook his head. "Sounds like a mighty sorry situation."

"It is," Malden agreed. "Why do you think we were so desperate to hire the two of you? Mankiller needs to have some real law, if it's ever going to be a real town."

Bo wasn't sure that goal was even possible as long as the Deverys were around. But he and Scratch would do their best, he thought as he spun the cylinder of a Colt he had picked up.

At the very least, the next time they confronted any of the Deverys, they would be armed again.

When they left the general store a few minutes later, Bo had a new Colt just like the one he had lost to the Deverys snugged in his holster. Malden didn't have any Remingtons like the ones Scratch carried, and he assured the silver-haired Texan that Lionel Gaines didn't carry them, either. Since Scratch couldn't get the sort of fancy smokepoles he preferred, he had also gotten a new gun belt and holster from Malden and carried the same model Colt that Bo had.

Each of the Texans wore a new hat similar to the ones they had lost, as well. Bo recalled that there was a rack in the sheriff's office with rifles and shotguns in it, so they had decided to wait until they could check out those weapons before deciding if they needed any more.

Biscuits O'Brien shambled along with them like some sort of drunken bear. "Still think this is a bad idea," he muttered. "Don't want no trouble with nobody, though."

"Leave the trouble to us," Bo said. "Do you know if there are any deputy badges in your desk?"

Biscuits shook his head. "Could be. I ain't ever looked through all the drawers."

They reached the office and went inside. Scratch went to the rifle rack right away and began checking the weapons. He found a couple of Winchesters that appeared to be in decent shape, although they really needed cleaning because they hadn't been used for a long time.

Meanwhile, Bo went through the desk, sitting in the chair behind it while Biscuits stretched out on a lumpy sofa under the front window. "Got boxes of .44-40s for those Winchesters," he told Scratch as he pawed through one of the drawers. He set one of the cardboard boxes of ammunition on top of the desk and resumed his search.

One of the other drawers was crammed so full of wanted posters that Bo had trouble getting it open. He pulled out the thick wads of paper and stacked the reward notices on top of the desk as well. They were turned every which direction. As Bo straightened them, he asked the sheriff, "Don't you ever go through these?"

"Huh?" Biscuits looked from the sofa and blinked at him in confusion. "Oh, you mean all them reward dodgers. No, they just keep sendin' 'em to me, and I shove 'em in the drawer. As long as folks behave theirselves in Mankiller, it ain't none o' my business what they might'a done somewheres else."

Bo sighed. Biscuits really was a sorry excuse for a lawman.

"We'll have to go through these later," he told Scratch. "There's a good chance some fugitives are in town."

Scratch was peering down the twin barrels of a shotgun he had broken open. He snapped the weapon closed, then said, "You're gonna take it seriously, aren't you?"

"Take what seriously?"

"This deputyin' job. Just like when we pinned on those badges in Whiskey Flats a while back, you think we ought to be act like real deputies."

"We *are* real deputies," Bo pointed out. "The town's going to pay us and everything."

"All I care about is settlin' the score with those damned Deverys."

Biscuits clapped his hands over his ears and moaned. "Oh, don't talk like that!" he said. "I don't wanna hear anything like that!"

Bo looked at his partner. "We've got a chance to do some real good here, not just get back at the Deverys."

"And since when do we owe this town anything?"

"We don't," Bo admitted. "But the people who live here are counting on us, and that's important. I don't want to let them down."

Scratch put the shotgun he'd been looking at back on the rack. "Well, I wouldn't want to disappoint Mrs. Bonner . . ."

"There you go. Look at it that way."

Scratch grinned. "All right, I will. Those Greeners

look all right. You run across any shotgun shells in there?"

"Not yet." Bo returned to his search of the desk. The next thing he found was a drawer full of empty whiskey bottles, along with one that was still half full. He looked in disapproval at Biscuits, who just ignored him. The sheriff had started to snore softly.

Under a welter of papers in another drawer, Bo found four deputy badges. He took out two of them and tossed one to Scratch, saying, "Here you go."

Scratch caught it and pinned it on to his shirt. "You reckon the sheriff ought to swear us in?"

"Probably," Bo said as he fastened on his own badge, "but I think we might have a hard time waking him up to do it. How about we swear each other in?"

"Fine by me. Hold up your hand."

Bo lifted his hand.

Scratch said, "You swear to uphold the law, arrest any varmints who break it, and ventilate every Devery who gives you a good excuse to do it?"

Bo chuckled. "I swear. How about you?"

Scratch raised his hand and said, "I swear the same thing. I reckon we're real lawmen now, Bo, or at least as close to it as this town is gonna get."

Bo came out from behind the desk. "Maybe we'd better get started on our first patrol. Seems like it's our duty to let the citizens of Mankiller know that there are a couple of new deputies looking out for them."

They left Biscuits snoring on the sofa. People had seen them walking from the café to the store and from the store to the sheriff's office, but at that time the Texans had just been a couple of strangers, and unarmed strangers at that, before visiting Abner Malden's establishment.

Now they were armed, and not only that, they had law badges pinned to their shirts. Sure, the law badges were just cheap tin stars on which someone had done a fairly crude job of engraving the words DEPUTY SHERIFF.

It wasn't the badges themselves, however, that were important, but what they represented. The badges were symbols of law, of progress, of civilization, and of human decency itself. It was as true on the frontier as elsewhere that some of the men who wore such badges were corrupt or incompetent or both, but that didn't mean that what they stood for was worthless. The badges just needed the right sort of men behind them.

Bo and Scratch hadn't gone very far down the street before they began to attract attention. They saw men staring at them and heard the increased buzz of conversation behind them. They were walking toward the river, and they hadn't quite reached the bottom of the slope and the eastern end of Main Street when several men who were in front of them suddenly got out of the way in a hurry. That alerted the Texans that something was wrong. They stopped, hands poised near their guns just in case.

Two men appeared in the gap that opened up in the crowded street. Bo recognized them instantly: red-bearded, bare-chested Luke Devery and his ugly, lantern-jawed cousin Thad. Both Deverys came to an abrupt halt, their hands tightening on the rifles they carried.

CHAPTER 13

A long moment of tense silence crawled by, punctuated by music drifting out of one of the saloons. The talk in the street had stopped, and most movement had, too, at least at this end of town. Everyone was watching the confrontation between the Deverys and the two new deputies.

Luke finally broke the silence. "Well, what do you know? My brother Reuben told me he seen you fellas walkin' around a little while ago, but I didn't believe him. Now here you are, big as life."

"Are you admitting that you thought we were dead?" Bo asked. "How would you know that if you didn't have something to do with the attack on us?"

"Ain't admittin' nothin'," Luke replied with a shake of his head. "I just figured that two fellas as proddy and troublesome as you would've wound up dead by now." A sneer twisted his face. "You got nerve, wearin' law badges when you refused to pay a legal and proper toll to cross the bridge yesterday, not to mention pullin' guns on me and Thad when we was just doin' our jobs."

"Well, I reckon you're right about that," Bo said. Scratch started to protest, but Bo stopped him with a gesture. Facing Luke again, Bo went on, "We promised to come back and pay you if we found out we were in the wrong. Unfortunately, since then some no-good, cowardly thieves stole all our money."

Luke's beard bristled, and Thad snarled like a dog that wanted to control himself. Luke motioned for his cousin to control himself.

"So we'll have to pay you that twelve dollars later," Bo continued. "Just wanted you to know that we haven't forgotten about it." He paused. "We haven't forgotten about anything that's happened since we came to Mankiller."

"Well, you're gonna owe interest," Luke blustered.

"We'll pay it . . . within reason. Now, is there anything we can do for you fellas?"

"What the hell do you mean?"

Bo touched his badge with his left hand. His right remained where it was, hovering near the butt of his gun. "As you can see, Scratch and I are now deputies under Sheriff O'Brien. If you have any trouble, any legal complaints, you can come see us."

Thad burst out, "We don't have to come see nobody! This is our town! Devery law is the only law around here!"

Bo shook his head. "Not anymore." He raised his voice so that it carried clearly to everyone gathered at this end of the street. "Mankiller has real law and order now. That goes for everyone. If *anybody* breaks the law, folks can come to us and report it, and we'll set things straight."

Luke glowered at the Texans as he said, "You hadn't ought to make promises you can't keep, old man."

"We'll keep that promise," Bo said. "You can count on it."

He knew that word of his comments would spread rapidly through the settlement and the hills where the mining claims were located. The Deverys were widely disliked around here, and he hoped that anyone who had legitimate grievances would come forward. If Bo and Scratch had proof that the family had committed crimes, they could not only bring the guilty parties to justice, but it would also give them some leverage to try to force the Deverys into treating people decently. Since the family actually did own the land, there was no legal way to stop them from claiming a portion of the proceeds. But they could be fair about it, and that was Bo's goal.

Scratch, on the other hand, just wanted to kill Deverys . . . and it might come to that, Bo knew.

"You're full of big talk," Luke said, still sneering. "One of these days, you'll have to back it up."

"Any time you're ready, Devery," Scratch said. "Any time."

Thad looked like he was ready right here and now. His eyes were wide and rolling like he was half out of his mind, and his teeth ground together as he worked his distinctive jaw back and forth. Luke put a hand on his arm and tugged him away, though.

"Come on," he muttered. "We got to go talk to Pa."

The crowd parted again to let the two of them stalk off toward the big old house at the top of the hill. Thad looked back over his shoulder at Bo and Scratch a couple of times with hatred gleaming in his eyes.

"That fella's just one step away from a hydrophobia skunk," Bo said.

"And it ain't a very long step, neither," Scratch agreed. "We're gonna need eyes in the back of our heads, Bo."

"I'm not so sure, at least not where Thad's concerned. If he comes at us, I think it'll be head-on, so he can see what he's doing."

"You could be right about that. I'm gonna keep an eye out behind me, anyway."

"Always a wise thing to do," Bo concurred.

They crossed the street and started back up the hill. The buzz of conversation behind them was even louder now, and the stares of the townspeople were more intense. The Texans gave friendly nods to the citizens they passed. Some of those nods were returned warily, others were ignored. Nobody was quite sure yet what to make of them.

After they had gone a couple of blocks, they came to the disreputable-looking barn that housed Edgar's Livery Stable. Bo and Scratch looked at each other but didn't have to say anything. They turned and went into the barn through the open double doors.

"Hello!" Bo called. "Edgar! Are you here?"

The stocky liveryman came out of the tack room carrying a pitchfork. He stopped short at the sight of the Texans and then started backing away. Lifting the pitchfork to point the razor-sharp tines at them, he said, "Now, you fellas stay away from me! What happened weren't my fault. You shouldn't'a come in here and started that trouble!"

Bo frowned at him. "What in blazes are you talking about? We didn't start any trouble."

"That's right," Scratch said. "Hell, it was them other hombres who jumped us!"

Edgar kept the pitchfork in front of him and shook his head stubbornly. "That ain't the way I seen it, and I'll testify to that in any court of law I have to! You fellas came in here and got mad about the price I quoted you for takin' care o' your horses. Then you started raisin' a ruckus about it, and it was just pure luck my boy and some o' his cousins were passin' by and, uh, come to my assistance. Yeah, that's it. They come to my assistance. I don't know what happened to you after that, and it ain't none of my business."

The rehearsed sound of Edgar's speech told Bo that Luke and Thad must have stopped here on their way to the Devery house and told him what to say in case the Texans showed up.

"You know damn well that ain't the way it was," Scratch said angrily.

"I'll swear that I'm tellin' the truth, and so will Luke and Thad and the rest of them boys," Edgar insisted.

Bo put a hand on his partner's arm. "Let it go, Scratch," he said. "They've worked out their story, and we won't be able to budge them on it. It's their word against ours."

"Maybe so, but it ain't right," Scratch said. "This varmint's lyin'."

"You best be careful," Edgar warned. He jabbed at the air with the pitchfork for emphasis. "I'll swear out a complaint agin you for talkin' bad about me."

"Where are our horses?" Bo asked.

"You left 'em here without payin'. I had a perfect right to sell 'em—"

"You sold our horses?" Scratch roared.

Edgar cringed. "The packhorse is still here. But my brother Jackson seen the bay and the dun and took a likin' to 'em. I had a right to do it, I tell you. That ruckus you started caused some damage. I had a right—"

"Shut up," Bo said. He wanted to do things legal and proper, but he was having a hard time keeping a rein on his temper. Besides, being a Texan, he came from a long heritage of doing things illegal and improper when it was necessary to right a wrong. "Where are the horses?"

Edgar swallowed hard. "Up in my brother's barn."

"Go up there, refund whatever he paid for them, and bring them back here."

"I can't do that. Jackson'd never go along with it!"

"Convince him," Bo said. "Otherwise, we're going to arrest you and hold you for trial on charges of horse stealing."

"And you know what usually happens to horse thieves," Scratch said with a savage grin. He made a motion like he was tugging on a hang rope around his neck.

Edgar moaned in dismay. "You don't know what you're askin'. Jackson won't take kindly to—"

"We don't care," Bo cut in. "If you want to stick to that loco story of yours, go ahead and swear out a complaint against us for disturbing the peace. We'll be glad to answer those charges the next time the circuit judge comes through. Until there's a legal ruling, though, you had no right to sell our horses, so you'd better get them back. Understand?"

"I understand," Edgar said grimly. "Do you boys understand what you're gettin' yourselves into? You're just askin' for trouble!" A sly gleam appeared in the man's eyes. "How's about this? I'll get your horses back, and I'll even stake you to some money for grub and other supplies. Then you can take off them blamed badges and forget all about bein' deputies. Just ride on somewheres else and forget that you ever set foot in Mankiller, Colorado."

Bo shook his head. "I don't think so."

"We like it here," Scratch added. "And we ain't leavin' any time soon."

"Then God help you," Edgar said, "because you'll find out that when all hell breaks loose, nobody else around here will!"

As they started on up the street, leaving the livery stable behind them, Scratch said, "You believe that? That old son of a bitch lyin' and sayin' that all the trouble was our fault?"

"From what I've seen of them and heard about them, the Deverys are pretty cunning," Bo said. "The last thing they want around here is any real law. That's why they ran off or murdered the previous sheriffs and deputies, then finally put Biscuits O'Brien in the job. They knew he'd never try to stop them from doing anything they wanted to do, and yet if there were ever any questions from outside, they could point to him and claim that Mankiller has a lawman. If anything too bad happened, they could make it look like everything was his fault."

"I'll bet Biscuits don't realize that."

Bo grunted. "Biscuits doesn't realize much of anything except that he's thirsty. What he needs is to stop drinking, clean up a mite, and start acting like a real sheriff."

Scratch stopped and looked over at his old friend. "And you wouldn't be thinkin' about tryin' to wrestle him into doin' that, now would you, Bo?"

"What could it hurt?"

"It could hurt because you always see the good in folks and think you can help make 'em better, and then you get to dependin' on them. But then most of the time they'll let you down when you really need 'em. Ol' Edgar was right about one thing—we can't count on anybody but ourselves."

Bo shrugged. "Maybe you're right. But I don't think it would hurt to have a talk with Biscuits."

"If you want to waste your time, go right on ahead. But I ain't gonna count on that drunk for anything."

They resumed their walk up the street. After a moment, Scratch asked, "Did you know what you were talkin' about when you said that about the circuit judge?"

"Not really, no. I was just making a guess. But nothing's been said about Mankiller having any sort of judge or court. There must be a circuit judge who comes around. I'll talk to Mrs. Bonner and find out for sure. If there's not, we need to ask her to write to the governor and request that Mankiller be added to the circuit."

"Why's the governor gonna pay attention to a widow woman who runs a café?"

"Because by then, I expect she's going to be the mayor," Bo said with a smile.

Scratch shook his head. "That brain of yours is just brimmin' over with ideas today, ain't it?"

"Mankiller needs a real mayor and a real town council if we're going to be able to get anything done around here."

"That means havin' an election," Scratch pointed out.

"That's right."

"You think Pa Devery's gonna stand for that?"

"He'll have to unless he wants to draw more attention to the town, which wouldn't be a good thing for him and his family. They've had things their own way for long enough. They need to realize that they're going to have to give up some of their power."

"That's liable to bust things wide open."

"Well," Bo said with a smile, "that might not be such a bad thing."

Scratch chuckled. "I can't argue with that."

"One more thing we need to do is see if we can get a small advance on our wages," Bo went on. "If we're being provided with room and board, we won't need much money, but there might be times when a little cash would come in handy."

"Yeah. You haven't forgot that we came here to hunt for gold, have you? This whole business of takin' the deputy jobs was just so's we could build up a stake for prospectin', ain't it?"

"Oh, sure," Bo agreed easily. "There's no reason we can't try to do a little good for the town while we're at it, though."

Scratch looked a little dubious, but he didn't say anything else.

They were far enough up the street now that they could get their best look so far at the old Devery house. It was a sprawling, two-story structure built of unpainted boards that had faded and warped from time and weather. Several one-story additions had been built onto it, probably as more family members arrived from Kansas. Bo wondered idly if all the Deverys in Mankiller lived there, or if some of them had houses of their own. It didn't really matter, but he was curious.

The roof over the verandah sagged a little in places. The beams that held it up were crumbling. Weeds grew wild in front of the house, with a narrow path hacked through the briars. Clearly, the people who lived there didn't believe in taking care of their home. Folks could get away with that for a while, but sooner or later it always caught up to them, Bo thought. It was a good indicator of just what sort of people the Deverys were, too.

There were two gables with windows on the second floor, above the verandah. Ratty curtains hung inside the windows. As Bo watched the curtains in the window on the left moved a little, as if someone in the room had twitched them aside. He caught a glimpse of a pale face peering out, and even though he couldn't see the person's eyes at this distance, the gaze seemed to hold a peculiar intensity. He was about to ask Scratch if he saw the same thing, when the curtains dropped back into place and the face was gone.

"Looks like the sort of house all the kids would stay away from when we was young'uns," Scratch commented. "Like there were ghosts or monsters livin' there."

"If they were ghosts, they wouldn't actually be *living* there, would they?" Bo asked.

Scratch chuckled. "I reckon not. Monsters, then. Is that all right?"

Bo thought about the Deverys and said, "Yeah. That's a pretty good description."

They crossed the street again and turned downslope, heading back toward the sheriff's office. They hadn't gone even a block when they got a vivid reminder of the fact that the Deverys weren't the only troublemakers around here. Mankiller was a boomtown, after all, and had all sorts of vice and iniquity competing for the attention of a couple of newly minted star packers.

In other words, a man came crashing through the batwings of a saloon, sailed across the boardwalk in front of it, and landed in the street. He had nearly knocked down a couple of miners who were walking past.

Raucous laughter followed the luckless hombre who obviously had not left the saloon of his own volition. He had been tossed out. Several men emerged onto the boardwalk. One of them stepped to the edge and silenced the laughter of the others by pulling his gun. He looped a thumb over the hammer and cocked the revolver, saying with brutal amusement, "We've seen you fly. Now we're gonna see just how good you can jump, Peckham!"

CHAPTER 14

"Hold it!" Bo called, his voice ringing with command.

The man paused and turned a sneering, rawboned face toward the Texans. He was medium sized but powerfully muscled, wearing a leather vest over a faded blue shirt and gray wool pants tucked into high-topped boots with big spurs strapped to them. A flat-crowned black hat was thumbed back on his thatch of equally black hair.

"Who the hell are you?" he asked in flat, dangerous tones.

"Reckon that ought to be obvious," Bo said. "We're the law in Mankiller. Part of it, anyway." He inclined his head toward Scratch. "He's Deputy Morton. I'm Deputy Creel."

"Well, I'm Finn Murdock, and I don't give a damn. You old geezers run along now, and me and my friends won't teach you a lesson for interferin' with our fun."

The three men who had followed Murdock out of the saloon had the same sort of lean, wolfish faces. They wore their guns low and looked like dangerous men. Bo had no doubt that they were.

But he wasn't going to let that keep him from doing his job, and neither was Scratch. The silver-haired Texan drawled, "You fellas leave that hombre alone and run along now, and *we won't throw you in* jail for disturbin' the peace."

Murdock and the other gunmen stared at Scratch as if they couldn't believe what they had just heard. After a couple of seconds, Murdock said, "I've already got my gun in my hand, you old fool. I can kill you quicker'n you can blink, damn it!"

"You might be able to get lead in me," Scratch allowed, "but you'll be stone-cold dead before I hit the ground. I can guaran-damn-tee that."

People in the street and on the boardwalks began to scatter, sensing that bullets were going to be flying any second now. Bo and Scratch hadn't really wanted such a dramatic confrontation so soon, but on the other hand, it would help the word get around town that Mankiller had itself a couple of real lawmen now.

Assuming, of course, that the Texans lived through the next few minutes.

The man who had been thrown out of the saloon to start this scrambled to his feet. "Stop it!" he said in a choked voice. "Nobody has to die over this. You and your friends can have my claim, Murdock. I'll find another one."

Bo said, "So you're claim jumpers. Can't say as I'm really surprised. What is it, you let Peckham here do all the work, and then you take it over and cash in on it?"

"None of your business, that's what it is," Murdock snapped. "And you shut your damn mouth, Peckham."

One of the other men spoke up. "Finn, are we gonna let these old mossbacks talk to us like that, or are we gonna do something about it?"

"We're gonna do something about it," Murdock said between gritted teeth. *"Right now!"*

The barrel of the gun in his hand was still pointed up, as it had been when he cocked it. Now, as the sharp words came out of his mouth, it snapped down and gouted flame.

Bo and Scratch were already moving, though. Bo went left, Scratch went right, and as they darted aside, their Colts leaped into their hands. Scratch took Murdock first, triggering at the sneering gunman as he felt the tug of a bullet plucking at the shoulder of his shirt. The slug came close enough so that he felt the heat of its passage, but it didn't actually touch his flesh.

Murdock couldn't make the same claim. The .44 caliber round from Scratch's gun punched into his midsection and doubled him over. Murdock's gun went off again as his finger jerked the trigger, but it was pointing down now and the bullet tore into the boardwalk at his feet, throwing splinters in the air.

At the same time, Bo lined his Colt on the closest of the other three men and fired as they clawed at their guns. His first shot drove into the target's chest and knocked the man back through the batwings, which swung back and forth wildly from the impact.

A slug kicked up splinters at Bo's feet as he

shifted his aim. With the cool, steady nerves of long experience, he aimed and fired, sending another man spinning off his feet. Speed mattered in a gun-fight, but so did accuracy and steadiness.

A second shot blasted out from Scratch's gun. The steel-jacketed round ripped through the fourth man's body, puncturing his left lung. He crumpled, bloody froth bubbling from his mouth as he sprawled just in front of the saloon's entrance.

All four of the gunmen were down, but at least some of them were still alive and therefore still dangerous. The Texans moved quickly, striding forward to kick guns out of the reach of clawing fingers.

Finn Murdock stared up at Scratch from pain-wracked eyes and gasped out, "How . . . how did you . . ."

"Think about it, mister," Scratch said. "For fellas to get as old as we are, they have to be damn good or damn lucky . . . or both."

Understanding dawned in Murdock's eyes, but that was the last emotion to register there. They widened into a glassy stare as death claimed him.

The man who had fallen back through the bat-wings was dead, too, shot through the heart. The other two were unconscious and clearly not long for this world. Bo asked one of the bystanders to fetch the doctor anyway, then he and Scratch thumbed fresh cartridges into their guns to replace the rounds they had fired.

The miner, Peckham, stared at them from the street, where he had stood transfixed during the whole shoot-out. He seemed to have trouble finding his voice, but finally he was able to say, "You . . .

you killed all of them. Four against two . . . and you're not even wounded, either of you!"

"Murdock came close," Scratch said, fingering the tear in his shirt where the gunman's bullet had nearly tagged him. "This ain't horseshoes, though. Close don't count."

Peckham stumbled over to the boardwalk. He was a stocky, middle-aged man with a broad, friendly face and curly brown hair. He shook his head in amazement as he looked at the bodies.

"Never saw anything like it in my life."

That sentiment was echoed by numerous bystanders in the crowd that formed around the front of the saloon now that the shooting was over. Everybody wanted to take a gander at the bloody corpses.

A man pushed his way through the press of people. Bo recognized him as Sam Bradfield, the undertaker. Bradfield looked at him and Scratch and exclaimed, "Good Lord! When you said there'd be more business for me, I didn't figure you meant this soon!"

"Wasn't our choice," Bo said.

"Those hombres called the tune," Scratch added. "We just danced to it."

Peckham said, "They were trying to force me to sign over my claim to them."

"Is it a good one?" Bo asked.

A rueful laugh came from the stocky miner. "That's just it. I've found some color, but not all that much. By the time I give the Deverys their share, I'm just barely making enough to keep going. I found a good-sized nugget yesterday, though, and brought it into town today. I guess Murdock saw it and thought my claim was a lot richer than it really is. That's why I would have let them have it, especially if they hadn't started roughing me up."

Bradfield said, "I've seen this bunch hanging around town for several days. I had a feeling they were up to no good. They were just waiting for a chance to swoop in on somebody, like vultures. You were unlucky enough to be the one they picked, Tobias."

Peckham nodded. "I reckon so. Thing is, that claim's not really worth dying over."

"That's not what they died over," Bo said. "They died because Deputy Morton and I stood up to them, and their pride couldn't stand that."

Bradfield frowned at the Texans. "And you risked dying, too, Deputy. You've barely pinned on those badges. You haven't even had a chance to do the job we hired you for."

"This *is* the job you hired us for," Bo said, his voice hardening slightly. "Keeping the peace in Mankiller, no matter who threatens it. No offense, Mr. Bradfield, but if you want hired guns just to go after the Deverys, you'd best look for somebody else."

The undertaker shook his head. "No, no, don't get me wrong, Deputy. Absolutely, you should keep the peace and enforce the law. I just didn't expect that there would be gunplay involved so soon."

"Before we get this town cleaned up, I expect there'll be more," Bo said.

When they came into the sheriff's office a short time later, after Bradfield hauled off the bodies in his wagon, the Texans found Biscuits O'Brien sitting at the desk, a puzzled frown on his face.

"I thought I heard shootin' a little while ago," Biscuits said. "You fellas know anything about that?"

"A little," Scratch said dryly. "We had to gun down some hardcases who were attackin' a citizen and tryin' to steal his claim."

The sheriff's bloodshot eyes widened in surprise. "Did you say . . . gun down?"

Bo nodded. "I'm afraid so. We gave them a chance to back off, but they weren't having any of it."

"You . . . you killed them? How many were there?"

"Four," Scratch said. "Two of 'em died pretty quick, and the other two crossed the divide a few minutes later. We sent somebody to fetch the doc, but by the time he got there, it was too late."

Biscuits scrubbed his hands over his face and rocked back and forth in his chair. "This is bad, this is really bad," he said. "Who was it you killed?"

"The leader of the bunch called himself Finn Murdock," Bo said. "We never got the names of the other three, but I reckon we can try to find out."

Biscuits shook his head. "No, no, that's all right. Doesn't really matter, I guess. But people are gonna hear about this. It's liable to cause more trouble."

Bo propped a hip on the corner of the desk and nodded. "It's possible. Any time there's a gunfight, there's somebody out there who hears about it and thinks that he ought to challenge the winner, just to find out if he's faster."

"But there'll be other hombres who hear about it and decide that they'd better behave themselves while they're in Mankiller," Scratch pointed out.

"So it sort of evens out in the long run, if you look at it that way."

"What if the men you killed had friends who'll want to even the score for them?"

"We'll deal with that when and if the time comes," Bo said. "If you heard the shooting, Sheriff, why didn't you come to see what was going on?"

"Didn't figure it was any of my business," Biscuits replied. Then, as if realizing how that sounded, he added, "Anyway, I knew I had two deputies out on patrol to handle anything that happened."

"Yeah, you could look at it like that," Scratch said dryly.

"One thing lawmen do is watch each other's back," Bo said. "We're not professional star packers, but we've worn law badges before and know a little bit about it. Have you ever worn a badge before, Sheriff?"

Biscuits shook his head and reached up to touch the tin star pinned to his vest. He looked at it like he had never seen it before and couldn't figure out how it got there.

"Maybe you should be the sheriff instead of me, uh . . . what was your name again?"

"Bo Creel!"

"Yeah, that's right. Bo." Biscuits looked at Scratch. "And you're Scratch, right?"

"Yep."

Biscuits started fumbling with the badge in an attempt to unpin it and take it off. "I'll just resign," he said, "and one of you can have the job, I don't care which——"

Bo reached over and took hold of Biscuits's wrist, guiding his hand gently away from the badge. "You're the duly elected sheriff," Bo said. "There's no reason for you to resign."

"Duly elected," Biscuits repeated, then gave a hollow laugh. "I don't think anybody even voted in that election 'cept for Deverys and their friends and relatives. I can't be sure about that because, well, I was drunk all day Election Day. And just about every day since, for that matter."

He seemed sober at the moment. Bo knew that looks could be deceptive. Somebody like Biscuits who drank all the time could stay drunk, even when they didn't look it.

"It doesn't matter who voted for you. You're the sheriff, and you swore to do your duty and uphold the law."

"Oh, hell," Biscuits muttered. "Those are just words."

"And words mean something," Bo said. "So do actions. You can still be a good sheriff. You just have to act like one."

Biscuits looked up at him and laughed again. "You ain't gonna try to reform me, are you, Bo? I warn you, it's been tried before. Ask Reverend Schumacher. Hell, ask anybody in Mankiller. They'll all tell you how worthless I am."

"We'll see about that."

"You'll get yourself killed. I warn you about that right now. You go to dependin' on me, you're takin' your life in your hands," Biscuits shoved to his feet.

"Now, I got to go."

Bo stood up. "You mean go and get a drink?"

"If I do, that's my business." Biscuits came out from behind the desk and stumbled toward the door.

Scratch moved to get in his way, but Bo shook his head and said, "Let him go."

"Yeah, lemme go," Biscuits said. "Don't waste your breath tryin' to save me, Scratch."

When Biscuits was gone, Scratch looked at the door that had closed behind the sheriff and said, "That is one sorry-ass son of a bitch."

"Right now, maybe."

"He's right, Bo. You can't save everybody. Some folks are too far gone, and some just flat-out ain't worth it. I reckon Sheriff Biscuits O'Brien may fall into both them categories."

"We'll see," Bo said.

He sat down at the desk and spent the next few minutes going through the stack of reward posters he had gotten out of the drawer earlier, thinking that he might find a reward dodger on Finn Murdock or one of Murdock's companions. There was nothing on Murdock, however, and none of the drawings on the other posters matched the three men who were now keeping Murdock company down at the undertaking parlor.

It was well after noon by now, and the Texans hadn't eaten since breakfast at Francis O'Hanrahan's dugout that morning. They left the office and walked over to the café. The lunch rush had cleared out a little, so they went to the counter and sat down on stools there. Lucinda Bonner came over to them, a slight frown on her face.

"What's wrong, Mrs. Bonner?" Bo asked.

"I heard about that gunfight," she said. "You killed four men?"

Scratch shrugged. "Seemed like the thing to do at the time, since they were tryin' to kill us."

"Oh, I know, you had to defend yourselves. I don't fault you for that. I just hate to hear about more violence, and so soon after we hired you."

"You hired us to clean up the town," Bo pointed out.

"Yes, of course. But Mankiller already has a reputation for being a dangerous place. I mean, even that name . . . ! I just wish there was some way to get rid of the troublemakers without having to . . . to . . ."

"Shoot 'em?" Scratch suggested.

"Well, yes."

"We'll settle things peacefully with anybody who'll let us," Bo said. "We would have let those four gunmen walk away a while ago. It was their choice not to. I reckon you've seen enough of life on the frontier, Mrs. Bonner, to know that sometimes the only way to deal with trouble is to meet it head-on."

Lucinda nodded. "Unfortunately, that's true. And you certainly didn't waste any time letting everyone in town know that law and order has returned. I suppose that's a good thing."

"Have you thought any more about what we discussed earlier, about electing a town council and a mayor?"

"Yes, I spoke to Wallace Kane when he came back in for lunch, as well as Mr. Malden and Mr. Gaines. They're all for the idea. I think we can get all the men who were here earlier for the meeting to run for town council, except for Francis O'Hanrahan, of course. He doesn't live in the town limits. I suppose we can just pick one of them to be the mayor."

Bo smiled. "Actually, I had something else in mind. I think *you* ought to be mayor."

Lucinda looked shocked. "Me? But I'm a woman. I can't even vote!"

"Maybe not, but I don't see why that would keep folks from voting *for* you. You must know just about everybody in town, Mrs. Bonner. Most of them have probably eaten here at one time or another, and I would think the food here would be a good incentive for them to vote for you."

"That's hardly a reason to elect someone mayor," Lucinda protested.

"Who came up with the idea of hiring Scratch and me as deputies?"

"Well . . . Francis really thought of it, but he and I discussed it before we brought in the other businessmen."

"There's proof that you're devoted to improving the town and making Mankiller a better place to live," Bo said.

Scratch grinned as he leaned his elbows on the counter. "You're wastin' your time arguin' with this old varmint, ma'am. Once Bo gets an idea in his head, you can't blast it out with dynamite."

"That's because I'm right most of the time," Bo said.

"Well, there's one thing you're forgetting, Mr. Creel," Lucinda said as her face grew solemn. "If we have an election, Jackson Devery won't like it. He's not going to just sit back and accept any threat to his power in this town. He'll try to put a stop to it, and if he can't do that, he'll do the next best thing. He'll run for mayor himself and try to get his relatives elected as the town council!"

Bo shrugged. "That's his right. You and the others will just have to out-campaign him."

"Problem is," Scratch drawled, "if it looks like they're fixin' to lose, Devery and his bunch are liable to vote with bullets, not ballots!"

CHAPTER 15

The special was beef stew, and it was as good as the food they'd had here the day before. Bo and Scratch enjoyed the meal and mopped the last drops of stew from their bowls with pieces of sweet cornbread.

Lucinda had had to tend to the needs of other customers seated at the counter, but as the Texans finished their food, she came back over to them and said quietly, "I've been thinking about what we talked about. I'll discuss it with the others, and with my daughters, and if we're all in agreement, I'll run for mayor."

"It could be dangerous," Bo pointed out. "Especially if you wind up running against Jackson Devery."

She laughed. "It was your idea, Mr. Creel. Are you trying to talk me out of it now?"

Bo shook his head. "No, ma'am. I still think you'd make a fine mayor. I just want to be sure you know what you're getting into."

"I promise you, I know. It'll be worth a little risk

if we can work together and make Mankiller a decent place to live."

"There's one other thing you can talk to the business owners about, if you don't mind. If it's possible, Scratch and I could use a little advance on our wages." Bo grunted and shook his head. "After that run-in at the livery stable, we're flat broke."

"I'll see what I can do. We should be able to get a little money together." Lucinda frowned. "If you know it was the Deverys who attacked and robbed you, can't you arrest them for that?"

"Edgar Devery claims that we started the fight and that his son and the others just came in to help him. He says he doesn't know anything about what happened after we were dragged out of the barn."

"What about Luke and Thad and the others?"

Bo stroked his jaw as he thought. "We saw Luke and Thad on the street, but we didn't question them about what happened." He looked over at Scratch. "We ought to do that, just to see what they'll say."

"Whatever it is, I reckon there's a good chance it'll be a lie," Scratch replied.

"I wouldn't mind getting a look at this Jackson Devery, too. He's the leader of that bunch, so we're going to have to deal with him sooner or later."

Lucinda's eyes widened. "You're going up to the Devery house?"

"I think it'd be a good idea."

"Be careful. Those people are vicious."

"We've stepped plumb into a den of rattlers before, ma'am," Scratch said. "I reckon we'll be all right."

They left the café and turned toward the big house at the top of the hill. As they walked in that direction,

Bo asked, "When we were looking at the Devery place before, did you notice someone watching us from one of the second-story windows?"

Scratch shook his head. "Can't say as I did. You see somebody up there?"

"I thought I did," said Bo, "but I'm not sure."

The shoot-out with Finn Murdock and his friends was the talk of the town. Bo heard the low-voiced comments behind them as they passed knots of townspeople but paid little attention to them. As he and Scratch continued toward the house, people began to follow them. It was obvious that they were heading for the old Devery place, and the citizens of Mankiller were curious to see what was going to happen.

"Appears we're drawin' a crowd," Scratch said quietly after glancing over his shoulder.

"I know. I don't much like it, either, but I'm not sure what we can do about it. Folks have a right to walk where they want to."

It wasn't just pedestrians following them. Men on horseback fell in with the followers, and a couple of wagons joined the procession, too.

"Dang it, it's startin' to look like we're leadin' a parade!"

Bo sighed. "If there's any gunplay, they don't want to miss it."

"You reckon there will be? Any gunplay, that is?"

"That depends on how hotheaded Jackson Devery is. I've got a hunch the rest of his family will follow his lead."

They had almost reached the house. An un-painted picket fence enclosed the weed-grown yard in front of the place. The pickets had been nailed on carelessly, so some of them stood at angles, and the gate sagged loosely on its hinges. There was no walk inside, only a narrow path beaten down by the feet of those who lived here.

Bo was reaching for the gate when Scratch said, "Hold on. Look up yonder on the porch."

Bo looked and saw movement in the shadows cast by the porch roof. Two huge black dogs were lying there, their heads raised now as they stared at the Texans.

"If we set foot in there, them hounds are liable to come after us," Scratch warned. "They got a mean look about 'em."

"What else would you expect, considering who their masters are?" Bo asked. He raised his voice, calling, "Hello, in the house!"

There was no response except a pricking forward of the dogs' ears.

"Devery!" Bo shouted. "Jackson Devery! Come on out here!"

He glanced toward the second-story windows, halfway expecting to see the curtains move again, but they hung motionless behind the glass.

"Devery! Come on out in the name of the law!"

After another long, tense moment ticked by, the front door opened with a squall of rusted hinges. The man who stepped out onto the porch regarded Bo and Scratch with such a powerful, visceral hatred that they could feel it like a physical blow, clear across the front yard.

"I'm Jackson Devery," the man said. "What do you want?"

He was tall, broad-shouldered, a man still vital and fit despite his obvious age. Like the farmer he had once been, he wore overalls and a white shirt. His brown, leathery face was as sharp as the blade of an ax. Long white hair swept back in wings from his high forehead. Bushy side whiskers of the same snowy shade crawled down onto his strong jaw. He was clean shaven other than that and had the piercing eyes and arrogant confidence of an Old Testament prophet.

"I'm Deputy Creel, Mr. Devery," Bo said. "This is Deputy Morton."

"I'm Deputy Creel, Mr. Devery," Bo said. "This is Deputy Morton."

"I know who you are," Devery rumbled. "My brother came crawlin' up here beggin' me to let him take those horses back. I asked what you want."

"We came to talk to your son Luke and your nephew Thad. Are they here?"

"What business is it of yours?"

"Law business," Scratch snapped. "Better trot 'em out here, Devery."

The patriarch's eyes narrowed. "By what authority? You can't just pin on a badge and call yourself a deputy. Who hired you?"

"Sheriff O'Brien swore us in," Bo said, dodging the question a little. "It was legal and proper."

Devery's upper lip curled. "I'm not sure anything that drunken fool does has any legal standing."

"He's the duly elected sheriff," Bo pointed out.

"From what I've heard, you even backed him for the position."

"Well, if he hired a couple of mossbacked saddle tramps for deputies, I'm not sure he's fit to hold the office. Maybe *we* need to have ourselves another election around here."

Bo smiled. "Now that's not a bad idea," he said, and saw the frown that the words put on Devery's hatchet face. "Right now, though, O'Brien's the sheriff, we're legally appointed deputies, and we want to talk to Luke and Thad."

"You don't want to obstruct justice, now do you, Mr. Devery?" Scratch added in a mocking drawl.

Devery's already florid face turned an even darker shade of red as blood and fury rushed into it. But he kept a visibly tight rein on his temper and turned his head to shout into the house, "Luke! Thad! Get your sorry asses out here!"

Bo and Scratch kept their hands on their guns, just in case Luke and Thad came out shooting. After a minute, the two younger men shuffled out onto the porch and cast baleful looks at the Texans. Neither of them appeared to be armed.

Jackson Devery waved a knobby-knuckled hand at Bo and Scratch. "These here *deputies*—" He let scorn drip from the word. "—want to talk to you boys."

"Why do we have to talk to 'em?" Luke asked in a surly voice. "They're just a couple of troublemakin' drifters. They ain't *real* deputies."

"They claim they are," Devery said. "Just humor 'em . . . for now." That last was added with a tone of definite menace.

Luke and Thad stepped to the edge of the porch. "What the hell do you want?" Luke demanded. The big dogs stood up and flanked him, growling low in their throats and looking at Bo and Scratch as if thinking that the Texans would make tasty little snacks.

"All our money and gear back would be a good start," Scratch said.

Luke sneered and shook his head. "I don't know what the hell you're talkin' about, mister."

"The two of you and some of your relatives attacked us at the livery stable yesterday," Bo said.

"No, we didn't. We went in there to help my Uncle Edgar after you two saddle tramps started tearin' up the place. *That's* what happened."

"That's a damned lie," Scratch said. "You jumped us from behind when we weren't doin' anything except talkin' to Edgar."

Luke's face turned almost as red as his beard. "You'd best watch who you're callin' a liar, old man. The way I told it is the way it happened, and I got half a dozen witnesses to back it up."

"The men who helped you try to kill us, you mean? The ones who beat us senseless, stole everything we had, and dumped us in a damn mudhole for the hogs to eat?" Scratch's voice shook with anger as he spoke, and Bo knew that his old friend was barely holding in the rage he felt.

Luke shook his head. "If that really happened, we didn't have nothin' to do with it. We just dragged you outta Uncle Edgar's barn and left you in the alley beside it." He laughed coldly. "There's lots of shady characters in Mankiller these days. Ain't no tellin' who did those other things . . . if they really happened."

"Yes, you've made it plain you don't believe us," Bo said.

"And you can't prove a damned thing otherwise," Luke gloated.

"Why, you——" Scratch began.

Bo put a hand on his arm. "Take it easy. His word against ours, remember? And we swore to uphold the law."

Scratch drew in a deep breath and let it out in a sigh of frustration. "All right," he said. "For now."

Bo looked at Luke and Thad and went on, "If you boys happen to come across any of our belongings, we'd really appreciate it if they were returned."

Luke laughed again. "Yeah, sure. We'll do that, won't we, Thad?"

Thad just sneered and didn't say anything.

"In the meantime—and this goes for you, too, Mr. Devery—Deputy Morton and I want you all to know that we'll be helping Sheriff O'Brien enforce the law and keep the peace around here. If you have any problems, you come to us and let us handle them. Nobody takes the law into their own hands in Mankiller anymore."

"Is that so?" Jackson Devery demanded. "You know who founded this town, don't you, Deputy?"

"I do," Bo said, "but that doesn't make any difference. The founder of a town isn't above the law."

"For a long time, *I* was the only law in Mankiller!" Devery thundered.

Calmly, but loudly enough that the whole crowd could hear, Bo said, "Well, sir, those days are over."

Devery glared at the Texans for a moment, then snapped, "Is there anything else you want?"

"Not right now," Bo replied.

"Then get the hell away from my house. I'm done talkin'."

With that, Devery turned on his heel and stalked back into the house. Luke and Thad went inside, too, sneering and glowering at Bo and Scratch along the way, slamming the door violently behind them.

"Well, that didn't do us a damn bit of good," Scratch said quietly.

"Oh, I don't know," Bo said. "We got a look at the old man, and we know now that Luke and Thad aren't going to tell the truth about what happened yesterday."

Scratch snorted. "Hell, we knew that anyway." He paused. "You see those dogs on the porch?"

"It'd be hard to miss them."

"They're damn near as big as horses!"

"Bull mastiffs," Bo said. "They have hungry looks in their eyes, too. I'll bet they'd come after anybody who walked through that gate. But there are other ways in, if it comes to that." He smiled. "And who knows, maybe we can make friends with them."

Scratch just looked doubtful about that idea.

As they turned away from the old house, they saw that the crowd that had followed them up the street was still there, at least for the most part. Folks were lingering, as if they were waiting to see what the Texans would do.

Bo smiled at them and said, "You folks go on about your business now. There's nothing to see here."

One man with a balding head and a prominent Adam's apple stared at them and asked, "Are you fellas really deputies?"

Bo nodded. "Duly appointed and legally sworn."

"And you're gonna stand up to the Deverys?"

"We're going to enforce the law and keep the peace," Bo said. "That applies to the Deverys the same as it does anyone else."

The man looked at them for a moment longer, then asked, "Have you met Sam Bradfield?"

"Move along!" Scratch growled. "Or we won't be the ones needin' the undertaker."

The crowd started to break up as Bo and Scratch strode through it, heading back down the hill. They went to the sheriff's office and found that Biscuits O'Brien had not returned. He was probably in one of the saloons guzzling down rotgut, and he might even be passed out somewhere.

The Texans spent the rest of the afternoon organizing and cleaning up the office, which looked like it hadn't been swept out in months. There were two cells in the back. Bo took the mattresses from each bunk outside and gave them a good shaking to get rid of as much dust and as many bedbugs as he could. Scratch found a ratty broom in a closet and swept the place, then they both tried to wipe the grime off the windows. By the time they finished, the office and jail didn't look exactly clean, but at least they weren't filthy anymore, either.

Late in the afternoon, a man came in and introduced himself as Harlan Green, the owner of the Rocky Mountain Hotel. "Mankiller's best," he added with a wry smile, "which doesn't mean quite as much when you realize that there are only two hotels in town."

"Plus some flophouses," Bo said as he returned the smile. "Or so we've heard."

"What can we do for you, Mr. Green?" Scratch asked.

Green, who had graying, pomaded hair parted in the middle and a mustache, drew a couple of keys from the pocket of his coat and held them out. "It's more a matter of what I can do for you, gentlemen. Two rooms in the hotel, for you to use free of charge as long as you're working as deputies."

"Lyle Rushford talked to you, didn't he?" Bo asked, remembering what the saloon keeper had said that morning.

"Actually, Lyle and Wallace Kane both paid visits to me and explained the situation. I want to be part of the little group of concerned citizens that Mrs. Bonner has put together, and so does Jessie Haynesworth, who owns the other hotel in town." Green paused. "I'll be honest with you. I don't see how two men can clean up the lawless elements in this town and also stand up to Pa Devery and his clan, but if there's any chance of you being successful, I want to help as much as I can. Mankiller has the potential to grow into a fine town, but that'll never happen like it is now."

"We're obliged to you, Mr. Green," Bo said as he and Scratch took the keys.

"Now, those aren't fancy rooms," Green warned them. "And they're on the ground floor, in the rear, as well as being rather small."

"They'll be fine," Bo assured him.

"All we need's a place to lay our heads at night," Scratch added. He grinned. "Anyway, if Mankiller's as wild a place as we've heard it is, we may not be doin' much sleepin' for a while."

"It's wild, all right," Green said. "In spades."

A short time later, after Green had returned to the hotel, the Texans walked across the street to have supper at Lucinda Bonner's café. When they came in, all the tables were full, and so were the stools at the counter. But Lucinda's daughter Callie met them with a smile and said, "Ma told me to tell you if you came in just to go around back. She and Uncle Charley are in the kitchen, and you can eat back there if you don't mind."

"We don't mind at all," Bo told her. He and Scratch did as Callie said, knocking on the back door they had gone in through for the meeting earlier in the day. Lucinda called, "Come in."

They stepped into an atmosphere of warmth and delicious aromas. The room had two stoves in it, and both of them were going, Lucinda working at one of them and her brother Charley Ellis at the other. Lucinda smiled over her shoulder at Bo and Scratch and said, "Just sit down at the table. We'll have food ready in a minute."

Scratch returned the smile as he pulled back a chair. "Just like bein' back home," he said.

"And this way we don't take up valuable table or counter space," Bo added.

A few minutes later Lucinda brought them platters of thick steaks, fried potatos, biscuits, and gravy. After she had put the food on the table in front of the appreciative Texans, she reached into a pocket on her apron and brought out a small roll of bills.

"That's the best we can do in the way of an advance," she said as she handed the money to Bo.

"That'll be fine, ma'am," he told her. "What with Mr. Green giving us places to sleep in the hotel and the way you've been feeding us, I feel a little bad about taking wages from you folks as well."

Lucinda shook her head. "Don't feel bad about it, Mr. Creel."

"Might as well call me Bo."

"And I'm Scratch," the silver-haired Texan put in.

"All right," Lucinda said. "Bo and Scratch. I like those names." She grew sober again. "But like I said, don't worry about taking the wages we'll pay you."

"Why not?" Bo asked.

"Because if you stay in Mankiller for very long, I know good and well that you're going to earn every penny of them!"

CHAPTER 16

Despite Lucinda's pessimistic prediction, Bo and Scratch thoroughly enjoyed the meal, washing down the excellent food with several cups of coffee. When they were finished, they got to their feet and thanked Lucinda and Charley.

"What are you going to do now?" she asked.

"Well, I suppose we'll go back over to the sheriff's office and make sure nobody's been looking for us," Bo said. "Then I reckon we'll get started on our evening rounds."

"Where's Biscuits?"

Scratch shook his head. "No idea."

"You two are going to have to go it alone, you know that, don't you? You can't count on him for any help."

"Never thought we could," Bo said. "But maybe we can be a good influence on him and he'll straighten up."

Scratch snorted, showing just how much he believed *that*.

They left the café's kitchen as they had entered it,

through the back door. Full night had fallen while they were eating, so the alley behind the building was dark. The blackness was relieved slightly by the glow that came through the narrow passages between buildings from Main Street.

Even so, the shadows were thick back here, and Bo and Scratch were both wary and alert for trouble. Bushwhackers or some other threat could be lurking in the stygian gloom.

Nothing happened, though, as they made their way through the passage beside the café and came out on the boardwalk that lined the street. The settlement appeared to be as busy as ever. The boardwalks were crowded, and riders and wagons passed back and forth in the street. A blend of talk, laughter, and music filled the air. It should have been jarringly unmelodic, but somehow it wasn't. It was the sound of life.

Bo listened for screams and gunshots, because those would have been the sounds of death, but he didn't hear any. For the moment, at least, Mankiller was noisy but peaceful.

The sheriff's office was still empty, with no sign that Biscuits O'Brien had even been there since the Texans left. Scratch looked around the place with disgust written on his weatherbeaten face and said, "You know, sooner or later we're gonna have to go look for that sorry excuse for a lawman."

Bo nodded. "I know. He's probably somewhere either soaking up more booze or passed out from it, but I suppose he could be in real trouble."

As if his words were a stage cue, the office door opened hurriedly and a short man in work clothes stuck his head in. "Are you fellas the deputies?" he asked in an excited voice.

"That's right," Bo said as he turned toward the door.

"Well, you'd better get down to Bella's pronto! It looks like all hell's gonna bust loose down there!"

"Hold on a minute," Scratch said sharply to the townie. "What's Bella's, and where is it?"

The man looked at them like he couldn't believe what he was hearing, but he said, "Bella's is the biggest whorehouse in town. It's a block over and two down on Grand Street."

"Grand is the one that parallels Main on the north?" Bo asked as he and Scratch started toward the door.

The townsman nodded. "Yeah. You better hurry. Thad Devery's on a rampage, and he's got some of his cousins there to back him up."

Bo and Scratch exchanged a glance as they went out the door. An urgent summons like this, with the Deverys involved, smacked of a trap of some sort. As lawmen, though, the Texans couldn't just ignore it. It was possible that the madam and the girls who worked at Bella's really did need their help.

Bo caught hold of the shoulder of the man who'd come to the office and turned him so that his face was in the light. "Your name wouldn't happen to be Devery, too, would it?" Bo asked in a hard voice.

"Devery? Hell, no! My name's Ernie Bond. I drive a freight wagon. I don't have anything to do with the Deverys, other than the fact that I don't like 'em much."

The man seemed to be telling the truth. Bo

figured that he and Scratch would have to accept it for now and check out the situation at Bella's.

"Then lead the way," Bo ordered.

Ernie Bond gulped and looked like he would have rather done just about anything other than head back to the whorehouse, but he nodded and said, "Sure." He took off trotting along the boardwalk.

Bo and Scratch followed, their long legs allowing them to keep up with the smaller Ernie without much trouble.

They took the first cross street and cut over to Grand. The word must have gotten around town that there was some sort of trouble developing over at Bella's, because quite a few men were hurrying in that direction besides Bo, Scratch, and Ernie Bond. The ones who were slower got out of the way of the lawmen.

Ernie had said that Bella's was the biggest whorehouse in Mankiller. It lived up to that billing, Bo saw as they approached. The building took up half a block. Its windows were covered with thick curtains. The bottom half of the heavy front door featured elaborate woodworking, while the upper half had a pane of leaded glass surrounded by gold trim set into it. Painted on the glass in gold leaf was the simple legend BELLA'S PLACE. That was the only explanation anybody in Mankiller needed. Everybody knew what went on here.

Men clustered on the porch, pressing their faces to the glass as they tried to catch a glimpse through any tiny gaps in the curtains. More men were gathered in front of the door. Bo raised his voice and said, "All right, everybody step back. Let us through."

Some of the men started guiltily and got out of the way. Others were slower and more sullen about it, but they stepped aside after a moment.

Bo nodded to Ernie Bond and said, "All right, thanks for bringing us here. You don't have to go in."

"I won't, then," the little townie said. "There's liable to be bullets flyin' around in there before it's over!"

Bo hoped not, but he was prepared for anything as he opened the door and he and Scratch stepped into the whorehouse. They had their hands on their guns as they entered.

They found themselves in a foyer with a polished hardwood floor and fancy wallpaper. An oil lamp in a brass sconce lit the place up, revealing an arched entrance that led into a parlor to the left. A beaded curtain hung over the entrance. Straight ahead was a wide staircase with a carved banister.

Several women were clustered at the bottom of the stairs. The one in front was middle-aged but still quite attractive, with bright red hair piled high on her head in an elaborate arrangement of curls. She wore a sea-green gown cut low enough to reveal the pale swells of her breasts. The women behind her on the stairs were all considerably younger and skimpier dressed, so Bo pegged the redhead as Bella and the others as the soiled doves who worked here.

That thought was all he had time for before a loud crash came from inside the parlor.

"Thank God you're here!" the redhead exclaimed. She waved a handkerchief that she had clutched in one hand toward the parlor. "They've gone loco! They're going to tear the whole place up!"

"No, ma'am, they won't," Bo said. "Not if we can do anything about it. Is that Thad Devery in there?"

"Yes, and his cousins Reuben and Simeon. George tried to settle them down when they got upset, but I'm afraid they've killed him!"

That accusation made things even more serious. Bo and Scratch drew their guns as they turned toward the parlor.

"You and your gals better get upstairs, ma'am," Scratch said.

Bella turned and began shooing the whores up the stairs like a mother hen chasing a bunch of chicks across a barnyard.

"I'm sure smellin' a trap," Scratch went on as he and Bo paused at the beaded curtain.

"Me, too," Bo agreed, "but we've got to go in there anyway." Sounds of destruction continued to come from the parlor.

There was a splintering crash just as the Texans stepped into the room. Bo saw a man holding two of the legs of a chair he had just smashed against the floor. A glance around the room revealed furniture overturned and broken, paintings ripped down from the walls and torn to pieces, and shards of glass scattered across the floor where glasses had been shattered. It looked almost like a cyclone had hit the place.

In addition to the man holding the busted chair, two more men were in the room. They had hold of a piano, and from the looks of it, they were about to try to tip it over. Bo leveled his gun at them while Scratch covered the other man.

"Hold it!" Bo snapped. He recognized one of the men at the piano as Thad Devery. The other two shared a family resemblance. They would be Luke's brothers Reuben and Simeon.

"Drop those chair legs," Scratch ordered the man he was covering.

"Go to hell!" the man yelled. "Nobody tells a Devery what to do!"

"You better listen to me, boy," Scratch warned. "I'll blow your legs right out from under you if I have to, and you'll never walk right again."

Thad took his hands off the piano and stepped back from the instrument. "Do what he says, Sim," he told his cousin. "That old bastard's crazy enough to do it."

Glaring murderously at Scratch, Simeon Devery dropped the chair legs.

"What in blazes is going on here?" Bo asked.

"That's none of your business," Thad snapped at him.

"I reckon it is. You fellas are disturbing the peace if I ever saw it. This is wanton destruction of property, too. If you don't have a mighty good explanation for all this, I'd say you're facing some serious charges, Thad."

"We had a right," Reuben Devery said. "We paid our money, and then the gal said no. A whore can't say no. It ain't fittin'."

"Yeah, it's Bella you ought be threatenin' to arrest," Simeon added. "She tried to cheat us. Said she wasn't gonna make the gal do what we wanted, and she wasn't gonna give us our money back, neither!"

"Wait a minute," Bo said as his eyes narrowed. "Are you talking about one girl?"

"One whore, you mean," Thad said with his customary sneer that made his almost deformed face even uglier.

"And the three of you . . ."

"That's right. You got a problem with that, lawman?"

"I do, you damned degenerate," Scratch said. "I ought to do the world a favor and just gun down the three of you here and now."

"Take it easy," Bo told his old friend. "We'll do this according to the law." He motioned with his Colt. "The three of you take out your guns, nice and easy, and put them on the floor. Don't make any sudden moves, and don't try anything funny."

"Reckon they already did that with the whore," Scratch muttered.

"You got no right," Thad insisted. "Deverys don't answer to the law. Deverys *are* the law."

"Not anymore," Bo said. "Not after today."

A groan came from behind an overturned sofa. A husky figure started to rise into view. Bo glanced in that direction and saw a bald-headed black man with blood dripping down his face from an ugly cut on his forehead. He recalled Bella's comment about the Deverys killing somebody called George and figured this man was the house's bouncer and bodyguard. One of the troublemakers must have walloped him and knocked him out, and now he had come to.

Taking his attention off Thad Devery was a mistake. Scratch shouted, "Watch it, Bo!"

Bo's eyes flicked back to Thad and saw the young man dragging his gun from its holster. Thad was reasonably fast, although no one was ever going to mistake him for a real shootist like Smoke Jensen or Matt Bodine.

That was the kind of speed it would have taken to outdraw an already drawn gun. Bo didn't have to hurry his shot. Thad had barely cleared leather when Bo's Colt roared.

Because he'd had a chance to take aim, Bo didn't have to kill Thad. He drilled Thad's gun arm instead, the bullet breaking the bone about halfway between elbow and shoulder. Thad dropped his revolver, screamed in pain, and grabbed his arm as he slumped against the piano.

Bo switched his aim to Reuben while Scratch kept Simeon covered. "Either of you boys want to take cards in this game?" Bo asked in a hard, dangerous voice.

They shook their heads, eyes wide with shock as they looked at their cousin, who had slipped down to a sitting position on the floor. Thad whimpered and rocked back and forth as he clutched his wounded arm.

"You're damned lucky you ain't dead," Scratch told him. "Bo could've put that round right through your ticker."

Bo wiggled the barrel of his .44. "Guns, gents. On the floor."

Reuben and Simeon hastened to follow the order this time. When they had put their irons on the floor and kicked them away, Bo said, "All right, give your cousin a hand. We'll take him over to the jail and let the doctor have a look at him there."

"You're really arrestin' us?" Reuben asked. "But we're *Deverys*."

"Get used to it," Scratch said.

CHAPTER 17

As the Texans ushered their prisoners out of the parlor at gunpoint, Bella rushed down the stairs and asked, "Where's George? Is he alive?"

The bouncer came out of the parlor behind Bo and Scratch, stumbling a little because he was still unsteady on his feet from the blow on the head. "I'm all right, Miz Bella," he told her as he rubbed his forehead.

"Oh, good Lord!" Bella exclaimed. "You're hurt. What'd they do to you?"

"One of 'em snuck up on me and walloped me with somethin'. A gun barrel, I think."

"Better have the doctor look at that cut," Bo advised. "It might need some sewing up."

"The sawbones'll be over at the jail for a while," Scratch added. "Got a prisoner here with an arm that needs patchin' up."

Bella stared. "One of you *shot* Thad Devery?"

"I did," Bo said. "He was fixing to shoot me at the time, so I figured it was best to stop him."

George shook his head ponderously. "You done

brought the wrath o' that whole clan down on your head now, mister. They ain't never gonna forgive nor forget this."

"Well, the Deverys weren't exactly our *amigos* to start with," Scratch said with a grin. He prodded Simeon in the back with the barrel of his gun. "Go on now, get movin'."

A stunned silence fell over the crowd gathered outside the whorehouse as the three prisoners emerged with Bo and Scratch behind them. The citizens of Mankiller had grown accustomed to the idea that the Deverys did whatever they damn well pleased and got away with it.

Now, here was vivid, indisputable evidence that things had changed, at least for the time being.

"You folks get out of the way," Scratch called. "Let us through."

"And somebody please fetch the doctor and have him come up to the jail," Bo added. "We have a man here who needs medical attention."

He didn't add that the wounded prisoner was Thad Devery. Everybody could see that with their own eyes. Several men took off at a run, each evidently determined to be the first to reach the doctor and give him the summons.

An ambush seemed unlikely with so many people around, but on the other hand, a crowd made a good hiding place for would-be killers, Bo thought. Gunmen could open fire on him and Scratch, and in this mob it would be hard to tell where the shots were coming from.

Bo didn't believe the other Deverys would risk it, though, with Thad, Reuben, and Simeon right there in the line of fire, too. He had suspected a trap all along, but he was starting to lean toward the idea that it was purely a coincidence the three men had gone on a rampage at Bella's when their perverted desires were thwarted.

No one tried to ventilate the Texans as they marched the prisoners over to Main Street and up to the sheriff's office and jail. Most of the crowd followed them, looking on this incident as part of the evening's entertainment.

Not all of the bystanders came along. Bo was confident that some of them had already slipped away to pay a visit to the old house at the top of the hill and give Jackson Devery the shocking news that two of his sons and his nephew had been arrested.

As they came into the office, Bo saw that Biscuits O'Brien had returned at last. The sheriff sat behind the desk. He was slumped forward with his head turned so that his cheek rested on the blotter. Loud snores issued from his mouth. He didn't wake up or even budge as the five men tramped through the office and into the cell block.

"Help Thad onto the bunk in that cell," Bo told Reuben and Simeon, "and then you two take the other cell."

They did as he said, and when Thad was stretched out groaning on the bunk in one cell and his cousins were in the other one, Scratch slammed the barred doors. He wasn't gentle about it, either, making quite a racket.

Biscuits kept snoring in the front room.

"I reckon it'd take the angel Gabriel blowin' the last trump to wake that varmint, and I ain't sure about that," Scratch said disgustedly. "You figure he's got any actual blood left in him, Bo, or is rotgut the only thing flowin' in his veins anymore?"

Bo smiled and shook his head. "I don't know, but when he does wake up, I'll bet he's surprised to find that he's got some prisoners in his jail."

"Especially *these* prisoners."

A few minutes later, a middle-aged man with a bristly white mustache came into the office. "I'm Dr. Jason Weathers," he announced. "I hear you've got a wounded man here."

"That's right," Bo said. "We saw you earlier today, after that shoot-out, but nobody introduced us. I'm Bo Creel, and this is Scratch Morton."

"Texan, by the sound of your voice."

Scratch grinned. "Born, bred, and forever. Some things don't go away."

"I'd better get to work," Weathers said. "I hear my patient moaning and cussing back there." He started for the cell block, then paused and lowered his voice to ask, "Is it true? You really shot Thad Devery and arrested him and two of his cousins?"

"It's the truth," Bo assured the doctor.

"Well, all I can say is . . . it's about time." Weathers gave them a curt nod and went into the cell block.

Bo followed with the key ring that had been hanging on a nail in the wall behind the desk. He unlocked the cell where Thad lay on the bunk and then stepped back to let Weathers go in. Keeping his hand on his gun, Bo stood in the little hallway between the cells and watched as the doctor cleaned the wound.

Thad carried on even more while that was going on, and screamed like a little girl when Weathers set the broken bone. The doctor put splints in place on both sides of the arm and then wrapped it securely. By the time that was finished, Thad's head had fallen back on the bunk, and he appeared to have passed out.

"Good work, Doctor," Bo said as he closed the cell door behind Weathers. "Fella called George down at Bella's place is in need of your services, too."

Weathers nodded and said, "So I've heard. That's where I'm going now."

The two of them went out into the office. Bo closed the cell block door. Weathers paused beside the desk to look down at the still-snoring Biscuits and shake his head.

"He never should have been made the sheriff. As long as he didn't have a regular job, he never had enough money to drink constantly, like he does now. And I'm convinced that Jackson Devery slips him some extra, just to make sure that he never sobers up and tries to actually enforce the law."

"Well, that's changed now, ain't it?" Scratch said.

"Yes . . . for now. But if I was you, I'd be sure to make the acquaintance of—"

"Sam Bradfield," Bo and Scratch said in unison.

Weathers didn't smile, but grim amusement twinkled in his pale blue eyes. "I see I'm not the only one who's given you that particular bit of advice." He nodded to them as he went to the door. "Good night, gentlemen. I hope you're still alive come morning."

"What do you mean by that?" Bo asked.

"I mean that when Jackson Devery hears that his boys are behind bars, he may not wait until the sun comes up to declare open war on you two."

When the doctor was gone, Bo went over to the desk and gripped Biscuits's shoulder. Giving it a good hard shake, he said, "Sheriff! Sheriff, wake up!"

Biscuits's head lolled back and forth while Bo was shaking him, but as soon as Bo stopped, a particularly loud snore issued from the mouth of the sleeping man. Scratch laughed.

"You've got a real chore in front of you, Bo, if you figure on wakin' him any time soon. What's wrong with just lettin' him sleep it off right where he is?"

"Nothing, I suppose," Bo said. "But if there's trouble, we'll have to worry about him getting hit by a stray bullet."

"There's a cot in the back room, right? Why don't we pick him up and put him back there? At least he'd be out of the way."

Bo nodded. "I reckon that's the best thing we can do. You want his feet or his head?"

"I'll take his feet. There's probably so much whiskey on his breath it'd make a man tipsy just to get too close to him."

They pulled the chair back and took hold of Biscuits. He was dead weight as they lifted him and carried him into the back room, which was so narrow there was room for the cot but not much more. When they lowered him onto it, Biscuits stirred slightly and muttered something completely unintelligible, then started sawing wood again.

"And that's our boss," Scratch said.

As they went into the front room, they heard a rising tide of loud voices in the street outside. The Texans looked at each other, and Scratch said, "That don't sound good."

"We'd better see what it's all about," Bo said.

Scratch went to the gun rack and took down one of the Greeners. "Don't open that door yet," he advised. "Not until I load up this street-sweeper."

He brought the shotgun to the desk, broke it open, and took shells from a drawer to load it. Bo said, "That's a good idea," and followed suit, lifting down one of the scatterguns for himself. No matter how arrogant and angry a man might be, facing the double barrels of a shotgun would make him stop and think twice about doing anything foolish.

When the Texans were well armed, Bo nodded to Scratch, who grasped the doorknob and turned it. They stepped out onto the porch, and a sudden hush fell over the street.

A man stood with his back turned toward the jail, facing the crowd. His arms were raised as if he had been haranguing the onlookers. Now he lowered them and turned slowly.

Bo had already recognized the man from his size and white hair as Jackson Devery, so he wasn't surprised to see the hatchet face of the clan's patriarch. A quick scan of the crowd didn't reveal Luke or anyone else Bo recognized as a Devery. Their leader appeared to have come alone to the jail.

"What do you want, Devery?" Bo asked curtly.

A muscle in Devery's tightly clenched jaw jumped a little as he pointed at the jail and said, "You got two of my boys and my nephew locked up in there."

"That's right, we do."

"Well, what the hell's wrong with you?" Devery thundered. "Let 'em out!"

Bo shook his head. "We can't do that. They're under arrest for assault, destruction of property, and attempted murder."

"Murder?" Devery roared.

"They pistol-whipped a fella who works in the establishment they tore up."

Devery waved that away. "You mean a darky who works in a damn whorehouse! Nobody cares about that!"

"The law does," Bo said. "For that matter, your nephew Thad drew on me, so that probably counts as attempted murder, too."

"I hear you shot him! Shot him like a dog!"

"Bo could've killed him, easy," Scratch said. "Thad's lucky to be alive, considerin' the stunt he pulled, and that's the truth."

Devery shook his head. "I don't care about any of that. You can't hold 'em. You can't put Deverys behind bars. Not in this town!"

"Sorry. They'll have to stay locked up until we figure out what to do about a trial."

A gleam of triumph suddenly appeared in Devery's eyes. "There ain't gonna be no trial!" he trumpeted. "Because there ain't no judge! It'll be six months before the circuit judge comes through again, if he ever comes at all!"

Bo didn't know if that was true or not, but if it was, it was a blow to his hopes. On the other hand, maybe it was an opening . . .

He raised his voice so that it carried clearly to everybody in the street and said, "If that's the case, then it sounds to me like what the citizens of Mankiller need to do is elect their own judge, so they won't have to wait for somebody to come in from outside in order to see justice done!"

A surprised silence hung over the street for a moment, before someone in the back of the crowd called, "Hell, yeah! We need our own judge!"

Other people took up the cry, and as the cheers of support for the idea grew, Jackson Devery's face flushed darker and darker with rage.

Scratch caught on to what Bo was doing. He held up a hand for silence, and when the crowd quieted enough for him to be heard, he said, "While you're electin' a judge, you might as well go ahead and elect a mayor and a town council, too! Then this town can be run like a real town ought to be!"

That declaration brought even more thunderous cheers. Devery suddenly swung around and jabbed a shaking finger at the crowd.

"Shut up! Shut the hell up, all of you! There ain't gonna be no election, not for a judge, not for a town council, and not for no damned mayor! I founded this town! I own the land all up and down this valley! I run things around here, by God!"

"Not anymore, Devery," Bo said quietly to the man's back.

Devery stood there for a long moment, trembling with fury. Then he turned to glare at the Texans again and said in a low voice, "You two bastards are gonna regret this, and so are the fools who put you up to it. I'll burn this town to the ground before I let anybody take it away from me."

"Why would you do a stupid thing like that?" Bo asked. "You're making a fortune off the gold rush. It's unfair, but it's legal. Why can't you just sit back and collect your money?"

Devery's breath hissed between his clenched teeth. "You sons o' bitches always look down your noses at me and my kin. I seen it all my life. Think you're better than me and mine."

"Mister, you don't know what you're talkin' about," Scratch said. "Bo and me, we're just a couple of hombres who been driftin' most of our lives, never ownin' much but our horses and saddles and the clothes on our backs. We don't think we're better than anybody, you can damn well bet a hat on that."

Devery ignored him. He swung around and waved his hands at the crowd again. "All of you!" he shouted. "All of you will be sorry you crossed Jackson Devery! You hear me?"

With that, he turned and stalked off along the boardwalk, slashing his arms at the bystanders who didn't get out of his way fast enough. Jeers and catcalls followed him.

Bo said, "I understand why they feel the way they do about Devery, but those folks aren't making things any better."

"Yeah, he's full of pride and plumb loco to start with," Scratch agreed. "That ain't a good combination.

Mix that together with anger over his boys bein' locked up and fear that he's gonna lose somethin' he thought he never could lose——"

"And it's liable to turn into something dangerous enough to blow up this whole town," Bo said.

CHAPTER 18

Now that they had prisoners locked up in the jail cells, Bo and Scratch knew they couldn't leave things in the hands of Biscuits O'Brien. Someone would have to stay there all night and guard the place.

"We'll take turns," Scratch suggested. "One of us can stay, and the other can go over to the hotel and get some sleep. I'll flip you for the first shift."

"With what?" Bo asked. "We don't have any coins, just those few bills Mrs. Bonner was able to give us as an advance."

Scratch rubbed his jaw. "Oh, yeah. Dadgummit. I don't even have my lucky silver dollar no more."

"Your two-headed silver dollar, you mean?"

Scratch put his hand over his heart. "Why, Bo, are you accusin' me of cheatin' in the past whenever we'd flip for somethin'? And us havin' been saddle pards for so long! I can't believe you don't trust me."

Bo grinned and jerked a thumb toward the door. "Go get some sleep. I'll take the first shift. I'm not that sleepy right now, anyway."

"Well, if that's the way you want it . . ." Scratch tucked one of the scatterguns under his arm and then left the office.

Bo turned the flame on the lamp a little lower, made sure all the blinds were down over the windows, and placed the other shotgun on the desk so it would be within easy reach when he sat down. The front door opened inward and had brackets on either side of it so that a bar could be lowered into them. Bo found the bar in the back room where Biscuits continued to snore. He put it in place, blocking the door.

He checked the back door. It was locked but didn't have a bar. If he and Scratch were going to stay on here for very long, they could add a bar to make that door more secure, Bo thought. The front window could use some iron bars mounted in them, too. A lawman sometimes needed to be able to fort up in his office and withstand a siege. Bo could see such a situation developing here in Mankiller, definitely.

Satisfied that he had done what he could to prepare for trouble, Bo sat down behind the desk. He tipped the chair back a little and raised one booted foot, propping it on the corner of the desk. He wasn't comfortable enough that he was in any danger of dozing off, but at least the stance was a little restful.

Meanwhile, Scratch found that there were still quite a few people standing around in the street, watching the jail in amazement as if they couldn't quite believe that three of the Deverys were actually locked up in there. They stepped aside and gave him respectful nods as he walked toward the desk in the lobby.

"Deputy Morton," he greeted Scratch. "Where's Deputy Creel?"

Harlan Green was behind the desk in the lobby.

"Bo's stayin' over at the jail for now," Scratch replied. "You might've heard tell about how we got some prisoners that need guardin' tonight."

Green nodded. "Thad, Reuben, and Simeon Devery. It's all anyone's been able to talk about. You and Deputy Creel are famous, at least in Mankiller."

"Famous for bein' dumb enough to take on the Deverys, you mean," Scratch said with a shake of his head.

"Not at all. Everyone I've talked to admires the two of you. It's just that . . ."

"You ain't sure if we'll live long enough to do any real good, right?"

Green shrugged eloquently. "Men have tried to oppose the Deverys before. None of them are still around."

"I know what you mean. Bo and me are pretty doggone stubborn, though, and we been around long enough to know a few things about takin' care of ourselves."

"I hope so. I certainly wish you the best. Is there anything I can do for you? Have a tub and some hot water brought up, anything like that?"

Scratch shook his head again. "No, I'm just gonna turn in and get some shuteye for a while, then go over and relieve Bo. See you later." He headed for the hallway that ran toward the back of the hotel, right next to the stairway to the second floor. The rooms Green was providing for them were down that corridor, near the back door.

Scratch found his room and used the key to let himself in. The glow from the dimly lit hallway showed him a small room containing a narrow bed, a rug on the floor beside it, and a night table with a lamp, a basin, and a pitcher of water on it. A porcelain thundermug peeked out from under the bed. A single window had the curtains pulled over it. There was no chair, but Scratch didn't intend to do any entertaining here, only sleeping.

A packet of lucifers lay on the table beside the lamp. He snapped one of them to life with his thumbnail and held the flame to the wick, then lowered the chimney and let the yellow glow fill the room. He closed the door and turned the key in the lock, then leaned the shotgun in a corner. The air in the room was a little stuffy, so he pushed the curtain aside to raise the window a couple of inches.

As he lifted the pane, Colt flame bloomed like a crimson flower in the thick darkness of the alley outside. The glass shattered in front of Scratch's face. He felt a sting on his cheek where a flying shard nicked him, and at the same time he felt a heated disturbance in the air only inches from his right ear and knew it was a bullet whipping past his head.

Instinct sent both hands stabbing toward his hips as he ducked away from the broken window, even though he wore only one gun at the moment. That Colt came swiftly and smoothly from its holster and roared as flame licked from its barrel. The window was already busted, so Scratch didn't worry about that. He just triggered three fast shots at the spot where he had seen the muzzle flash.

More shots thundered in the alley, sending Scratch diving to the floor. As he rolled over, he caught a glimpse of a shotgun's twin barrels being thrust through the window. Surging up onto his hands and knees, he dived behind the bed, which was the only cover in the room.

The Greener's double blast was so loud in the close confines of the little room that it pounded against Scratch's eardrums like giant fists. Both loads of buckshot ripped into the bed, shredding the mattress and throwing chopped feathers into the air so that they filled the room and floated down like abnormally large snowflakes.

With the feathers falling around him, Scratch heaved up from behind the ruined bed and slammed two more shots through the window into the alley. That emptied his Colt, so he ducked down again and grabbed fresh cartridges from his pocket so he could start thumbing them into the cylinder.

The shotgun's roar had deafened him, so he couldn't hear much of anything. When he had the revolver reloaded, he ventured a look and didn't see anything except the last of the feathers from the mattress drifting to the floor. He reached over and turned the lamp down until the flame guttered out. Darkness washed over the room.

Crouched there in the shadows, Scratch waited to see if anybody was going to shoot at him again. No more flashes came from the alley, but maybe the bushwhacking skalleyhooters were just biding their time.

A heavy pounding on the door made Scratch aware that his hearing had returned. Urgent shouts followed it. "Deputy Morton! Deputy Morton! Are you all right?"

Scratch recognized the voice. It belonged to Harlan Green.

After checking himself over for wounds and not finding any other than the little cut on his cheek from the flying glass, Scratch called, "Yeah, I'm fine! Best say outta here, though, Mr. Green. Those varmints could still be out there!"

"Should I send for Deputy Creel?"

Scratch hesitated. In addition to wiping him out, the attempt on his life could have been a ploy to lure Bo away from the jail, so that the other Deverys could go in and free the ones who were locked up.

"No, just keep everybody away from this room!" Scratch called back to Green. "Might still be some lead flyin' around!"

He didn't think the bushwhackers would linger very long after their ambush failed, but he couldn't rule out the possibility that they were still lurking out there. Since the bedspread was already ruined because the shotgun blast had blown a big hole in it, he pulled it off the bed and balled it up. Then he reached up, found the lamp and the matches on the table, and brought them down. He dumped the oil from the lamp's reservoir onto the spread.

Taking the oil-soaked ball of cloth with him, Scratch crawled around the bed and over to the window. Being careful not to get it too close to the bedspread, he lit another lucifer. He held the match to the spread, which *whooshed!* into flame. Scratch heaved the blazing makeshift torch through the window into the alley and lunged up after it. He kicked out the last of the frame and leaned through the opening, confident that he had taken by surprise anybody who was still skulking out there.

As he swept the Colt and his eyes from side to side, Scratch saw that the alley was deserted. He climbed through the window and dropped to the ground, then stomped out the burning bedspread. Men clustered on the boardwalk at the mouth of the alley, calling questions to him. Scratch walked up to them with the gun still in his hand, ready if he needed it.

"Settle down," he told the men. In the light that came through the windows of the buildings around them, he looked them over, pegging them as miners and townsmen. He didn't see anybody who looked like a Devery.

"What happened, Deputy?" one of the men asked.

"Nothin' much," Scratch said. "Some fellas took a few potshots at me through the window of my hotel room, but they missed. Did any of you folks see anybody runnin' away from this alley?"

He got head shakes and shrugged shoulders in response to the question. Either nobody had seen anything . . . or they were still scared to buck the Deverys. Of course, it was possible that the bushwhackers had fled the alley in the other direction.

Harlan Green came out onto the hotel porch, carrying a rifle. "Deputy Morton, is that you?" he asked. Scratch stepped up onto the porch. "Yeah. Anybody hurt in there? The lead was really flyin' around there for a minute."

"Everyone's fine, as far as I know."

"Good. Can't say the same for the window in that room, though. It's busted all to pieces. Bed's torn up, too. It caught both barrels of a shotgun blast that was intended for me."

"Window glass and a bed can be replaced," Green said. "I'm not sure an honest lawman can."

Scratch grinned. "Sorry about the damage, anyway. I reckon you could send Pa Devery a bill for it, but I got a hunch he wouldn't pay up."

"You think he's responsible for what happened?"

"I'm pert' near sure of it."

Not a hundred percent, though, Scratch thought. While the odds were mighty high that Jackson Devery was behind the ambush, Scratch couldn't forget the deadly dustup he and Bo had had earlier that day with Finn Murdock and the other three hardcases they'd been forced to kill. It was still possible that some of Murdock's friends had tried to even the score.

"I'll send for a carpenter to board up that broken window," Green said, "and of course I'll find another room for you."

Scratch shook his head. "I appreciate the offer, but I don't reckon it's necessary. Think I'll get my gear and mosey back on over to the jail. Probably better if both of us spend the nights there as long as we've got prisoners locked up. Especially those particular prisoners."

"You might be right. Good luck, Deputy."

"Much obliged," Scratch said.

With the odds lined up against them, he and Bo were liable to need all the luck they could get.

CHAPTER 19

Bo had barely gotten settled down in the office when he heard the gun-thunder from somewhere not too far away. He bolted up from the chair, grabbing the shotgun from the desk. He was certain that the shots had come from the direction of the hotel, and Scratch had gone over there just a few minutes earlier. It was possible that somebody had been laying in wait to ambush him.

Bo took a couple of steps toward the door of the sheriff's office, then stopped short. A grimace pulled at his mouth. Every instinct in his body called out for him to go to the aid of his old friend, but at the same time, alarm bells rang loudly in his brain.

Someone might be waiting in the darkness for him to yank the door open and rush out of the office, making a perfect target of himself as he was silhouetted by the light behind him. Or it might not be a lone rifleman lurking, but rather several killers armed with shotguns, ready to blast him out of existence. And with him out of the way, Bo thought, it would be an easy matter for Jackson Devery to waltz in here and let his sons and nephew out of jail.

Bo knew he couldn't allow that to happen. Deep trenches appeared in his cheeks as he heard a Greener roar, followed by more shots from a handgun. All he could do was pray that Scratch was all right.

Maybe the ruckus didn't have anything to do with Scratch, Bo told himself. Mankiller was known far and wide as a boomtown, the sort of town where hell was in session nearly twenty-four hours a day. True, the settlement had been surprisingly peaceful today, but Bo suspected that was because everybody was sort of in a state of shock over the idea that somebody would actually stand up to the Deverys. That attitude would wear off, probably sooner rather than later, and Mankiller would return to its wild, wicked ways.

But even though Bo knew that made sense, he couldn't bring himself to believe. The same instincts that wanted to send him charging out the door told him that Scratch was right in the middle of all that flying lead.

The shooting had stopped now, Bo realized grimly. But what that meant, he didn't know.

"Hey! Hey, Creel! You hear them shots?"

That was Thad Devery's voice coming from the cell block, through the barred window in the door between the two parts of the building. Bo's head turned in that direction. His lips pulled back from his teeth in a savage snarl.

"That was the other old fool dyin'! You know

that, don't you, Creel? Why don't you go and try to help him? See what that gets you! Haw haw haw!"

The donkeylike bray of laughter was all Bo could stand. He strode across the room, grabbing the key ring along the way, and unlocked the cell block door. The other two Deverys were laughing now, too, but Bo didn't pay any attention to them.

Instead he stopped and swung the shotgun up, leveling the twin barrels as he aimed through the bars at Thad's face. The laughter stopped like it had been chopped off by an ax. Thad's eyes widened so much the whites showed all the way around the pupils. He had been standing beside the bunk. Now, he collapsed onto it as all the color washed from his face. His wounded arm bumped the wall and it must have hurt like blazes, but he didn't seem to notice.

Bo squinted over the barrels and slowly cocked both hammers on the weapon, one and then the other. Thad panted in terror. A dark stain began to spread over the crotch of his jeans.

"Please," he moaned. "Please don't."

"Damn it, deputy, no!" one of the other Deverys said behind Bo. "You can't just shoot him down like a dog!"

"Yeah," Bo said through gritted teeth. "Yeah, I could. It'd be easy."

"You . . . you'd n-never forgive yourself!" Thad stammered in desperation.

A smile as cold as a blue norther blowing through the Texas Panhandle spread across Bo's face. "You stupid little chickenshit," he said. "I could blow your brains out and never lose a minute's sleep over it the rest of my life."

Thad must have known that Bo was telling the truth. He covered his eyes with a trembling hand and sat there shaking as he started to cry. Neither of the other prisoners said anything now, as if they were afraid that the slightest sound would cause Bo's finger to tighten just a little more on those triggers. That was all it would take. Just a little squeeze . . .

A fist pounded on the office door. "Bo! Bo, it's me! Lemme in!"

Bo dragged a deep breath into his lungs, slowly as if a great weight was pressing against his chest. Then he lowered the shotgun and carefully put the hammers back down.

"You're a lucky man, Thad," he said.

Thad continued to cry. The stink in the room was ample evidence that he had done more than piss himself in his terror.

Bo swung around, glanced at the other prisoners. They drew back like they'd unexpectedly found themselves standing on the brink of a long drop. Bo walked out of the cell block and slammed the door behind him.

"Hang on," he called through the door to Scratch as he set the Greener on the desk. "I'll take the bar off the door. Are you all right?"

"Yeah," Scratch replied. "Open up and I'll tell you about it."

Bo grunted as he lifted the bar from its brackets and set it aside. He unlocked the door and swung it open. Scratch came in, not wasting any time in doing it. He knew as well as Bo did what a good target a man made when he was standing in a lighted doorway.

Bo shut the door, turned the key in the lock, and set the bar back in place. Scratch said, "I reckon you heard the shots?"

"I did. I knew you had to be right in the middle of them, too."

"Damn straight. There were bushwhackers waitin' in the alley outside the window of my hotel room. They made a mess of the place, but the only thing that got me was a piece of flyin' glass when the window broke." Scratch touched a small smear of dried blood on his tanned, leathery cheek. "Reckon I made things hot enough for 'em that they gave up and lit a shuck."

"Did you get a look at them?"

Scratch shook his head. "Nope. Never saw anything except muzzle flashes."

"Bound to have been the Deverys, though."

"Bound to," the silver-haired Texan agreed. "Unless it was friends of that fella Murdock and those other hombres we had to shoot."

Bo ran a thumbnail along his jawline as he frowned in thought. "Yeah, I suppose it could've been something like that. My money's on the Deverys, though."

"Yeah, mine, too. When you heard the shootin', your first impulse was go chargin' out there, wasn't it?"

Bo grunted. "Well, sure. I figured you were in trouble."

"And that old man Devery's cunnin' enough to know that. You done the right thing by stayin' forted up in here, Bo."

"Yeah," Bo said with a hint of bitterness in his

voice. "I know that, but it wouldn't have helped much if it turned out you were dead."

Scratch grinned. "But I ain't. I'm hale and hearty as ever. So don't lose no sleep over it."

"I don't intend to. I reckon you're planning to stay here the rest of the night?"

Scratch pointed at the sofa with his thumb. "It's probably a mite lumpy, but one of us can sleep there while the other stays awake and on guard. Sound like a good idea to you?"

"It does," Bo agreed. "And we'd better get used to it, too. We may have to keep it up until everything is settled." He looked toward the back room, where the sound of Biscuits O'Brien's snores continued unabated. "Because I don't think we're going to be getting any help any time soon."

The rest of the night passed quietly. With the impending war between the Texans and the Deverys, it seemed that the rest of the troublemakers in the settlement were content to hold their hell-raising in abeyance, at least for the time being. Bo knew that wouldn't last, but he was grateful for any break that he and Scratch could get.

Early the next morning, while Bo was brewing a pot of coffee, Biscuits O'Brien stumbled out of the back room groaning and holding his head. Scratch pulled out the chair at the desk and let Biscuits slump into it. The sheriff rested his elbows on the desk and ran his fingers through his tangled hair.

"Damn it, somebody make the room stop spinnin'!"

"The room's still, Sheriff, I'm afraid it's your head,"

Bo told him. "I'll have the coffee ready in a minute, if you'd like a cup."

Biscuits groaned again. "I don't want any coffee. Damn it, I'm already too sober!" He yanked a drawer open and started to paw through it. "Where's my bottle?" His voice grew more desperate. "Where's my bottle? Where's it gone?"

"Take it easy," Bo said. "It's still there."

"Ah!" Biscuits snatched at something in the drawer and brought up the half-full bottle of whiskey. "Thank the Lord!"

Scratch reached over and took the bottle out of his hand before Biscuits could pull the cork. Biscuits let out a startled yelp and stared at Scratch as if the silver-haired Texan had just grown a second head.

"What the hell are you doin'? Gimme that back!"

Biscuits tried to lunge up out of the chair and reach for the bottle, but he moaned and fell back. His hands clutched the edge of the desk in a death grip like the world was about to throw him off if he didn't hang on for dear life.

"I'm gonna be sick. Oh, hell, I'm gonna be sick. Help me into one of the cells. I gotta lay down."

"You can't go in the cells," Bo said. "They're occupied."

"That's what we wanted to tell you," Scratch added. "That's why you need to wait on that eye-opener. Your brain don't need to be all muddled up right now."

"Occupied?" Biscuits muttered. "You mean . . . we got prisoners locked up?"

"That's right," Bo said.

Biscuits pulled at his hair again. "I wondered why I woke up on that cot. The bunks in the cells are comfort . . . comfortabler."

"That ain't a word," Scratch said.

"Shut up and gimme that damn bottle! Who's the sheriff here?"

Scratch held the bottle out of reach. Bo said, "You're the sheriff, Biscuits. That's why you need to think straight. We have prisoners. Important prisoners."

Biscuits stared at him out of bleary eyes. "Who?"

"Thad, Reuben, and Simeon Devery."

The sheriff's eyes got wide, although not as wide as Thad's had been the night before when Bo pointed the shotgun at him. "Deverys!" Biscuits exploded. "You can't lock up any of the Deverys!"

"Too late," Scratch said with a grin. "We already went and done it."

"But . . . but why?"

"They went loco—or just crazy mean—and started wrecking one of the whorehouses," Bo explained. "Bella's Place."

Biscuits panted. Sweat coated his face. "That . . . that ain't no reason to arrest 'em. Pa Devery would've made good the damages."

"Really?" Scratch asked doubtfully.

"Well . . . no, prob'ly not. He prob'ly would've told Bella to go suck an egg."

"That's not all," Bo went on. "They pistol-whipped a man who works for Bella—"

"George? Good ol' George?" Biscuits interrupted.

"That's right."

"Is he hurt bad?"

"I reckon he'll be all right, but what they did to him is assault and attempted murder. They could've killed him easy enough. And then Thad drew on me, which is attempted murder of a peace officer."

"He didn't shoot you, did he?"

"Nope." Bo took a sip of the coffee he had just poured in a cup. "Because I shot him first."

"Son of a bitch! You shot a Devery?"

"Yep."

"Is he . . ." Biscuits swallowed and had to force himself to finish the question with a visible effort. "Is he dead?"

"No, he's just got a busted wing. But he won't be wrecking a whorehouse or trying to shoot a lawman, or anybody else, for that matter, any time soon."

Biscuits closed his eyes and breathed heavily for a moment. Then he said, "I didn't think things could get any worse, but I reckon they have. We got to let those boys go right now."

Scratch shook his head. "Can't do that, Sheriff. They're under arrest. A judge'll have to rule before we can release 'em."

"Judge?" Biscuits shrilled. "What judge? There ain't no judge around here but the circuit rider, and he won't be back for weeks!"

Bo said, "There's going to be an election. Mankiller's going to elect a judge, along with a mayor and a town council. Things are going to be run properly around here from now on."

Biscuits stared at him for a few seconds, then said, "I get it now. You're crazier'n I am! Just a couple of crazy old coots who think you're real lawmen! There ain't no such thing in these parts. There's only the Deverys."

"Not anymore," Bo said. "The decent people in town—and there are enough of them to make a difference, whether you believe that or not—have had enough. There may not be anything we can do right now about the Deverys collecting half of what everybody makes, but at least we can stop them from running roughshod over the whole settlement and everybody else in these parts."

"And while we're puttin' a stop to the Deverys' shenanigans, we'll clean up the rest of the hellholes around here, too," Scratch added. "Mankiller's gonna be a safe place to live."

"You two really have been chewin' locoweed, haven't you?" Biscuits muttered.

Bo smiled. "I'll tell you something even more loco, Biscuits . . . you're going to help us."

Biscuits started shaking his head. "Oh, no. No, you're in this mess on your own. I don't want any part of it!"

"It's too late for that. You're the sheriff. Thad and those other boys were arrested on your watch. Jackson Devery's going to blame you for what happened, too."

Biscuits shot up out of his chair, and this time he made it. "No!" he cried. He pawed at the badge pinned to his vest and finally succeeded in ripping it free. He threw it on the desk, where it bounced off and landed in the floor with a tinny clatter. "I won't be the sheriff anymore! I quit! I'm done, you hear me?"

Scratch bent and picked up the badge. He rubbed it against his shirt to get the dust off it. "Don't reckon you can do that, Biscuits," he said. "Least-ways, not yet."

Biscuits stared at him in disbelief. "You're sayin' I can't quit my job?"

"There's no one in authority to accept your resignation," Bo pointed out. "If you really want to quit, you'll have to wait until after the election. Then you can turn in your resignation to the town council."

It was a flimsy excuse and Bo knew it, but he was counting on Biscuits's head hurting too much for the sheriff to think it through.

That was what happened. Biscuits slumped back into the chair and pulled a little more hair out. By the time the Texans left Mankiller—if they lived to do so—he was liable to be bald as an egg, Bo thought.

"What am I gonna do?" Biscuits asked miserably. "What am I gonna do?"

"Is there any chance you can stay sober? If there is, you can stay here and guard the prisoners while Scratch and I deal with bringing law and order to the rest of the town. You'll have to keep a clear head, though. The Deverys are liable to try some tricks."

"Stay . . . sober?" Biscuits repeated, sounding so uncomprehending that he might as well have been speaking a foreign language.

"That's right. If you can do that, Biscuits, you've got a chance to be a real lawman, whether you think that's possible or not."

"I dunno." Biscuits licked his lips. "I could sure use a drink to help me think."

Scratch shook his head. "If you're gonna help us out, Biscuits, you've taken your last drink for a while."

"No! Oh, God . . . no, I can't, I just can't . . ."

Someone knocked on the front door and interrupted Biscuits's moaning.

Bo and Scratch turned quickly in that direction, their hands going to their guns. "Who's there?" Bo called.

"It's Lucinda Bonner," a pleasant female voice answered. "Harlan Green told me that you're living in there now, so I took the liberty of bringing your breakfast over to you. I have flapjacks and bacon and scrambled eggs——"

Biscuits made a gagging, choking sound and bolted out of the chair. He flung himself at the door to the back room and disappeared in there. Hideous sounds filled the office until Bo closed the door, muffling them somewhat. Scratch shook his head and said, "Hope he found a bucket in time."

"Goodness gracious," Lucinda said when Bo unlocked the door and opened it for her, so she could carry a large tray filled with covered plates into the office. "What was that racket?"

"Nothing for you to worry about, ma'am," Bo assured her. "Sheriff O'Brien's just, uh, not very hungry right now."

"But that's all right," Scratch added with a grin. "More for us that way!"

CHAPTER 20

Biscuits stubbornly refused to eat anything, but he did finally come out of the back room after Lucinda was gone and accept a cup of coffee. As he sat down at the desk to sip the strong black brew, he said with a bleak frown, "You know Devery's gonna kill all of us, don't you?"

"He might try," Scratch said. "That don't mean he'll succeed."

Biscuits shook his head. "I still don't see why you're doin' this. What do you hope to gain from it?"

"They stole our horses and all our gear," Bo said.

"We have to do something about that."

"So you're gonna try to take their town away from them?"

Scratch smiled. "Somethin' like that."

"Plus it's just the right thing to do," Bo added. "Folks around here deserve better than to have the Deverys taking advantage of them. There's a good chance they've gotten away with murder more than once, and that just can't stand."

"People get away with murder all the time,"

Biscuits said. "You gonna clean up the whole world, Creel?"

"Nope," Bo said. "Just this little corner of it."

Biscuits sighed. "You've put me in a hell of a bind. Devery's not gonna trust me now."

"He never trusted you. If he did, he wouldn't have tried to keep you drunk all the time by slipping you extra money for whiskey."

At the mention of drinking, Biscuits's tongue came out of his mouth and licked nervously over his lips. "Just a taste?" he asked. "Just one damned taste?"

"Not yet," Bo said. "You need to be away from the stuff for a while before you try to handle it again. You may not be able to, even then."

"You're meaner'n a damn Comanche."

"You'll thank me later," Bo said.

"Don't count on it."

It was time for Bo and Scratch to make the morning rounds, but before they left, they searched the sheriff's office for more bottles of whiskey that Biscuits might have stashed here and there. They found several, and Scratch gathered them up in his arms as the Texans prepared to leave.

"What're you gonna do with that stuff?" Biscuits asked. A pathetic whine came into his voice. "I paid for it with my own money. I need it. You got no right to steal it like this."

"We're not stealing it," Bo said. "We're just keeping it for you, for the time being. Maybe you'll get it back sometime."

"I'm your boss, you know," Biscuits blustered. "I give the orders around here, not you."

"If you have any orders concerning the law business, you go right ahead and tell us what they are. But we're taking this booze away because we're your friends, not your deputies."

"I don't remember askin' you to be my friends, damn it!"

"Well," Bo said, "sometimes friendship is forced upon us."

Biscuits slumped back in the chair and shook his head miserably. "Go on. Get out. And if you really want to do me a favor, get on your horses and ride out of Mankiller and don't ever come back!"

Scratch looked at Bo. "That reminds me. We'd best go talk to Edgar and make sure he got our horses back from his brother."

"Good idea," Bo said with a nod. To Biscuits, he added, "If the prisoners get restless, you can tell them that we'll bring back some breakfast for them in a little while."

Biscuits didn't look up. He just waved a trembling hand to acknowledge that he heard.

Once they were in the street and out of earshot, Scratch said, "You know, it's fixin' to get a lot worse for that gent. He'll be sicker the longer he's without his tonic."

Bo nodded. "I know. I wish one of those cells was empty. It would be better if we could just lock him up until he's over the worst of it. Unless we stay there and watch him every minute of the time, he can slip out and find something to drink. We may not be able to help him at all."

"But we can try, is that it?"

"I reckon it's worth it to try," Bo said. He nodded

toward the whiskey bottles in Scratch's arms. "What are you going to do with those?"

"Thought we might take 'em over to the hotel and see if Harlan'd lock 'em up in his safe for us," Scratch said with a smile. "They're valuables. At least, ol' Biscuits thinks they are."

"That's a good idea. Come on."

They went along the street to the Rocky Mountain Hotel, where Harlan Green was surprised but willing to lock up the whiskey for them.

"First time I've ever had bottles in my safe, I think," he commented. "I'm not supposed to give these back to Sheriff O'Brien, is that it?"

"He shouldn't even know that you have them, but if he comes asking about them, just deny knowing anything," Bo said. "We'll take the responsibility."

Green nodded. "Fine." He paused. "You know, after the attempt on Deputy Morton's life, last night was about as quiet as any we've had around here for a while. I think maybe the two of you have gotten the town so shaken up already that folks are more likely to behave themselves."

"Maybe," Bo said, "but I wouldn't count on that lasting."

From the hotel they walked up to Edgar's Livery Stable. Edgar Devery was standing in front of the barn as they approached. He cut his eyes back and forth as if wondering if he ought to go and hide from them, but in the end he stayed where he was and gave Bo and Scratch a curt nod as they came up to him.

"Your horses are back in their stalls," he told

them. "My brother didn't like it at all, but he went along with it."

"Good," Bo said. "We won't have to arrest you for horse theft, then."

"That trumped-up charge never would'a stuck," Edgar said.

"I don't reckon we'll ever know," Scratch said.

"Has any of our other gear shown up?"

"Now *that's* something I don't know a damned thing about. I didn't mess with anything except those horses. You'll have to take up the other with somebody else."

"Like Luke and Thad?" Bo suggested.

"Thad's already in jail," Scratch added. "Maybe we could convince him to talk."

Edgar glared at them. "You hurt that boy and you'll regret it. He's my son, and I won't stand for him bein' mistreated."

"Yeah, I can tell how concerned you are about him by the fact that you ain't even paid him a visit since he's been locked up."

Edgar looked uncomfortable, shifting his feet as he said, "I don't much cotton to jails. Fact is, them iron bars give me the fantods."

"Been on the wrong side of 'em before, have you?"

"That ain't none of your business," the liveryman snapped. "I'll be by to see Thad sometime. You just make sure he's fed and took care of proper-like, or you'll answer to me."

"He'll be taken care of," Bo said. "But it might go a little easier for him if he confessed to the other things he's done that he shouldn't have."

"Talk to him, not me," Edgar said, eyes downcast.

Bo took out one of the bills Lucinda had given them. He said, "Here, put this on our account, too. We'll be in Mankiller for a while, so I suppose we might as well leave our horses here."

Edgar stared in surprise at the money Bo was extending toward him. Without taking the bill, he said, "I figured you'd want to move them horses to one of the other stables."

"You'll feed and water them properly, won't you?"

"Well, sure. I never mistreated an animal, not in my whole life."

"There you go. Take the money, Edgar."

The liveryman still hesitated, but after a moment he lifted his hand and took the bill from Bo. As he tucked it into a pocket of his overalls, he gave the Texans a surly nod and muttered, "Obliged."

As they walked away, Scratch asked quietly, "What'd you do that for? I figured we'd take the horses down to Dabney's place. He'd probably take care of 'em for free, since he's one of the bunch who wanted us to be deputies."

"I'm sure he would have," Bo agreed. "But maybe by leaving them with Edgar, we've planted a seed that tells him we're not as bad as he thinks we are."

"We arrested his boy," Scratch pointed out. "And I don't reckon he's ever gone against his brother in his life. You ain't gonna turn him against Jackson, Bo."

"Maybe not, but it doesn't cost much to try."

Scratch didn't argue, but the way he shook his head made it clear that he thought Bo was wasting time and money on the effort.

They walked around the rest of the town. It was early enough in the day that the saloons, brothels, and gambling dens weren't doing much business, although none of them were actually closed. The general stores owned by Abner Malden and Lionel Gaines had plenty of customers, though, and the Texans saw several men going into Wallace Kane's assay office to have the ore they'd gouged out of the hillsides checked for gold.

Lyle Rushford stood on the porch of the Colorado Palace Saloon, smoking a cigar. He nodded to Bo and Scratch as they came along the boardwalk.

"Morning, deputies. Any more trouble last night after that shooting at the hotel?"

"No, it was quiet," Bo said.

Rushford nodded. "I'm not surprised. Nobody kicked up a ruckus in my place, and since it's the biggest saloon in Mankiller, some sort of hell-raising usually goes on. I haven't even heard about anybody being found in an alley with his throat cut and his poke gone this morning."

"Does that happen very often?" Scratch asked.

Rushford sighed and said, "More often than I'd like to think about. The murders here in town haven't averaged one a night . . . but the number is too close to that for comfort."

"I hope we can put a stop to that," Bo said, "but there's only two of us, and we can't watch every-where, all the time. What we may have to do is close some of the worst places down."

"That won't make you any friends," Rushford warned.

"Well . . . we didn't take the jobs to make friends."

They moved on to the café, where they met blond Tess Bonner coming out the door with a tray in her hands. She smiled at them and said, "My mother asked me to take this food over to the jail for the prisoners."

"Better let me go with you," Bo said. He didn't want Tess anywhere near the prisoners with only Biscuits O'Brien around to keep an eye on things.

Scratch jerked a thumb at the door. "I'll go on in and talk to Miz Bonner," he said.

Bo nodded. "That's fine. We need to start getting an election organized, and I'm sure she can be a big help with that."

He started across the street with Tess. When they reached the sheriff's office, he opened the door for her. As soon as it swung back, the sharp tang of whiskey hit Bo's nose. He stiffened in surprise.

"Oh, my goodness," the young woman said as she looked into the office.

Bo sighed. Biscuits was slumped forward on the desk again, out cold. An empty bottle lay near his hand. Obviously, they hadn't searched hard enough, Bo thought. Biscuits had had an extra bottle squirreled away somewhere.

"Is the sheriff . . . all right?" Tess asked hesitantly.

"No, but he will be," Bo replied, his voice grim with resolve. "Even if we have to kill him to make him that way."

CHAPTER 21

Lucinda greeted Scratch with a smile as he came up to the counter and rested his hands on it. "Good morning again, Deputy Morton," she said.

"Scratch," he reminded her.

"Of course. Scratch. How in the world did you wind up with that name, anyway? Surely it's not your real name."

"Well . . ." He frowned. "You know, it's been so long ago, I sort of disremember how come folks started called me Scratch. Seems like it's always been that way, ever since me and Bo were boys back in Texas."

"What about your real name?"

Scratch shook his head. "Nothin' I'd want to claim."

"Now you've made me curious," Lucinda said with a laugh. "I'll respect your privacy, though." She paused. "Tess just left here with some meals for the prisoners. I assumed that you'd want me to feed them."

Scratch grunted. "Your food's a heap better'n

what they deserve, ma'am. I reckon for now, though, that'll be fine. Maybe the town can make a deal with one of the hash houses to provide meals that ain't so good. You be sure and keep track of what you're owed, too. Once the town council's set up, maybe you can get paid back for it."

"I'll do that," Lucinda said. "And speaking of the town council, I talked it over with Dr. Weathers and several of the local businessmen when they came in to eat breakfast this morning. They all think that the sooner we hold an election, the better." A blush appeared on her face. "And I'm surprised to say that they were all in agreement with Bo's suggestion that I run for mayor, too."

Scratch grinned across the counter. "Those fellas know a good idea when they hear it. Got any idea who's gonna run for town council?"

"Wallace Kane and Dr. Weathers agreed to. I think they're good choices, because they don't have any actual competition in their lines of work. I think I can get Sam Bradfield to say yes, too. We'll need one more member. That way there'll be four councilmen, and as mayor, I can cast the deciding vote in case of a tie." Lucinda put her hand to her throat. "Oh, my. I just assumed that I'm going to be elected, didn't I? I didn't mean to sound so . . . so sure of myself. That's arrogant."

"Nothin' arrogant about it," Scratch assured her. "Havin' an election's just a formality, anyway. I don't reckon anybody's likely to run against any of you."

"We'll see. It wouldn't be a proper election unless it was open to anybody who wanted to run, would it?"

"Reckon not," Scratch agreed.

Lucinda half-turned to reach toward the coffeepot on the stove behind her. "Do you want a cup of coffee?"

"I sure——"

That was as far as Scratch got before he heard someone screaming outside.

"Why don't you wait here, Miss Bonner?" Bo suggested as he and Tess stood in the doorway of the sheriff's office. "I'll help Sheriff O'Brien lie down on the cot in the back room."

"That's not necessary on my account, Mr. Creel," Tess said. "You don't have to protect my delicate sensibilities. I've seen men passed out from drinking before. We've lived in Mankiller for a while, and it's really not that unusual a sight."

"I suppose not." Bo reached for the tray. "I'll just take this to the prisoners. I'll bring the tray and the plates back later. You don't have to come in."

"Again, not necessary." Tess marched into the office.

Bo shrugged and went around her to unlock the cell block door. As it swung open, one of the prisoners in the cell to the right said loudly, "Damn it, it's about time you bastards fed us!"

Bo stepped into the aisle between the cells and drew his Colt. He pointed it at Reuben and Simeon and said, "I don't know which of you men said that, but there's a lady present and you'll keep a civil tongue in your head. You understand?"

They flinched back from the menacing muzzle of

the gun. "Sure, Deputy," Reuben muttered. "Didn't mean nothin' by it."

The stink from Thad fouling himself the night before still lingered in the air. Bo looked over at the other cell and saw Thad sitting on the floor, leaning against the wall with a dull, dispirited look on his face. Bo knew they'd have to clean him up and get some clean clothes on him somehow. Thad's father ought to be the one to handle that, Bo decided, whether jails gave him the fantods or not.

"Miss Bonner, just put that tray down on the desk," Bo called into the front room. "You don't want to come back here, and I mean it."

Simeon Devery nudged his brother with an elbow, leered, and said, "They got one of them pretty Bonner girls to bring us breakfast."

Bo glanced sharply at him. "Forget it," he said under his breath. "She's not coming back here, and you're not going to say one word to her."

"You're a cruel man, Deputy," Simeon said.

Bo went out into the office, where Tess had placed the tray on the desk. "You're sure you don't want me to take it to them?" she asked.

"I'm positive," Bo said. "Thank you, though, and thank your mother for me as well for providing the food." He went to the still-open front door. "Now, if you want to head back over to the café——"

The sound of a terrified scream coming from somewhere down the street cut the suggestion short.

Bo bit back a surprised exclamation. He didn't know what was going on, but it occurred to him that Tess might be safer here in the sheriff's office than she would be out on the street. He looked back at her and snapped, "Stay here!" then stepped out onto the boardwalk and took off quickly toward the sound of the screaming, which hadn't stopped.

From the corner of his eye, he saw Scratch emerging from the café and knew that his old friend had heard the screams, too. The silver-haired Texan loped across the street to join Bo.

"Got any idea what that commotion's about?" Scratch asked.

Bo shook his head. "Not one." He drew his Colt. "I think it's coming from that alley up there, though."

The cries echoed from the walls of the buildings on either side of the narrow passage. As Bo and Scratch reached the alley mouth, they saw that it ran all the way through to Grand Street on the other end, where the unknown trouble was taking place. As the Texans started through the alley, Bo saw a woman on her knees next to a huddled, shapeless figure. She had her hands clamped to her cheeks and was swaying back and forth a little as she screamed.

Bo and Scratch came up to her as a crowd began to gather in Grand Street near the alley mouth. Bo saw that the shape on the ground was a man lying on his back. A dark pool of blood surrounded his head. The blood had come from his throat, which had been slashed deeply from one side to the other in a wound that resembled a hideous, grinning mouth.

Scratch reached down to take hold of the screaming woman's arms. "Ma'am, come on away from there," he told her, raising his voice to be heard over the cries. "You got to settle down now."

She tried to pull away from him, but he was too

strong. He lifted her to her feet. She turned abruptly and clutched at him, pressing her face against his chest as she began to sob.

Bo looked at the people in the street. "Anybody know who these folks are or what happened here?"

A man pointed at the corpse. "That . . . that's Duke Mayo. He's a gambler, plays at the Fan-Tan most of the time."

Bo nodded grimly. He and Scratch had passed by the Fan-Tan while they were making their rounds, and he'd heard about the place. It was a dive, a gambling den in a particularly squalid stretch of such establishments along Grand Street, which hardly lived up to its name in places.

"What about the woman?"

"I think she's a whore. Janey, Jenny, something like that," the townsman said. "I wouldn't know for sure. I don't have no truck with women like that."

Bo thought the fella was protesting a mite too much, but he didn't say anything about that. Instead, he asked the woman who was crying, "Ma'am, do you know anything about what happened here?"

She took her face away from Scratch's tear-streaked shirtfront and stopped wailing long enough to shake her head and say, "N-no. Duke and I . . . we were supposed to get together for breakfast . . . like we always do . . . before we turned in for the day."

Bo understood what she meant. Gamblers and soiled doves lived their lives mostly at night and slept away the days.

"But he . . . he didn't show up," the woman went on. "So I . . . I went looking for him . . ." Her voice trailed off in a series of sobs.

Bo gave her a moment, then said, "And I reckon you found him like this?"

Her head bobbed up and down wordlessly.

"You and him were . . . friends?"

"He was my . . . my . . . husband!"

She went back to wailing.

Bo and Scratch looked at each other, and Bo shrugged. Gamblers and prostitutes could be married just like anybody else, he supposed.

Bo said to the townie who had identified the dead man, "You say he played at the Fan-Tan?"

"Most of the time," the man replied, adding hastily, "Or so I've heard. I don't frequent places like that, either."

"Oh, stop worryin' so much," Scratch told him. "We're not gonna go tell your old lady what you been doin'."

The man started to edge away. "I better be going now . . ."

Bo let the man go. He said to the other bystanders, "Somebody needs to help this lady."

That caused the crowd to break up even faster. Bo muttered in disgust. He wasn't sure what they were going to do with Janey, or Jenny, or whatever her name was.

"Let me take her."

The Texans turned and looked back along the alley. They saw Lucinda Bonner standing there, trailed by her daughters. Holding out a hand, Lucinda came closer and went on, "We'll take her back over to the café and see if we can't calm her down."

"I don't know if you want to do that," Bo said.

"Don't tell me what I do or don't want to do, Bo

Creel," Lucinda said. "I'm sure that you and Scratch have business to attend to, so let me help."

Scratch gently disengaged himself from the soiled dove and turned her around, steering her toward Lucinda. He was obviously glad to be free from the responsibility. "We're much obliged, ma'am," he told Lucinda. "If you wouldn't mind, could you see to it that somebody fetches the undertaker? We got to find out what happened to this fella."

"We've got a pretty good idea what happened," Bo said. "What we need to do now is find out who did it."

Lucinda got an arm around the woman's shoulders and led her away, helped by Callie and Tess. Bo and Scratch went the other way, stepping out onto Grand Street.

"We gonna have a talk with folks at the Fan-Tan?" Scratch asked.

"That's where we'll start," Bo said grimly.

CHAPTER 22

The Fan-Tan was a smallish building made of chunks of red sandstone, with a red slate roof. It was located between a couple of larger buildings, a whorehouse much less fancy than Bella's Place to the right and a barn with a wagon yard behind it to the left. The door to the Fan-Tan was painted a surprising shade of green. It stood a couple of inches ajar, indicating that the place was open. There were no windows in the front wall. As far as Bo and Scratch could tell, it didn't have any windows at all, but that was all right because the people who frequented the gambling den weren't really interested in seeing the light of day.

Bo pushed the door back and went inside. Scratch followed close behind him. Both men had their hands near their guns, ready to hook and draw.

The air inside the Fan-Tan was stale with a mixture of smells. Tobacco smoke, beer, bay rum, and unwashed human flesh were dominant, underlaid with the mingled reek of vomit and piss. The place was dimly lit by a couple of hanging lanterns that flickered as the open door made the air stir sluggishly. Bo saw poker tables, a roulette wheel, faro and keno layouts. A short bar ran along the left wall. The chunky, bald-headed man behind the bar wore a dirty apron and stifled a yawn as he looked at the two newcomers.

"Somethin' I can do for you?" the bartender asked.

The poker tables were empty, except for one where a pair of men in seedy suits sat playing a desultory game of showdown. They weren't betting, just turning over cards, and neither man seemed to give a damn whether he won or lost each hand.

Scratch kept his eye on the two card players while Bo went over to the bar. "You know a man called Duke Mayo?" he asked.

The bartender shrugged beefy shoulders. "Sure, I know Duke. He plays in here sometimes."

"Seen him lately?"

"Why're you lookin' for him?" The bartender gazed pointedly at the badge pinned to Bo's shirt. "He in some kind of trouble?"

"Not a bit," Bo answered honestly. Duke Mayo was beyond ever being in trouble again. "Was he in here last night?"

"Yeah. He sat in on a game that lasted most of the night. Cashed in and left here maybe three hours ago."

"Won quite a bit, did he?"

The bartender shrugged again. "I'm busy servin' drinks most of the time. I don't keep up with how the games are goin'."

Bo's gut told him the man wasn't telling the truth. Not all of it, anyway.

Before he could ask any more questions, a door in the back of the room opened, and a man came out carrying a bucket and a mop. He was short and frail looking, with wispy gray hair and a face ravaged by time and liquor. He wore gray striped pants and a shirt that had once been white, and he kept his head down and muttered to himself as he set the bucket down and started mopping the floor.

Bo turned back to the bartender and asked, "Did anybody leave out of here right after Mayo?"

The man scowled. "Look, Deputy, I told you, I do my own work and mind my own business. I didn't see nothin' or hear nothin' and I don't know a damned thing except that I'm sleepy. I can't help you, understand?"

Bo inclined his head toward the two men at the poker table. "Were they part of the same game as Mayo?"

The bartender blew out an exasperated breath.

"Why don't you ask 'em yourself?"

"All right, I will," Bo said. "What's your name?"

"Ashton. Mike Ashton."

"You own this place?"

"That's right."

"Might be a good idea for you to start being a little more observant about what goes on in your business, Ashton."

The man shook his head. "That just shows how much you know, mister."

Bo turned away from the bar, stepped around the elderly swamper, and went over to the table where the game of showdown continued. The two gamblers deliberately ignored him and Scratch until Bo said, "We'd like to talk to you gents."

Without looking up, one of them said, "Go ahead and talk."

The other snickered. "That don't mean we'll listen, though."

Bo leaned forward and used his left hand to sweep the cards off the table, onto the floor. His right palmed out the Colt, and as he eased back the hammer, he said, "This means you'll listen . . . and that you'll talk, too."

Both men had reacted to Bo's sudden, unexpected action. They stiffened in their chairs and started reaching under their coats. The sound of Scratch's gun being cocked was loud in the smoky silence. Caught between the two weapons, the men froze, then slowly moved their hands back into plain sight.

"On the table," Bo ordered.

They placed their hands on the ratty green felt and glared up at the Texans with murderous hatred.

"What do they call you?" Bo asked.

"I'm Stansbridge," said the one who had spoken first.

"Keegan," the other man added.

"All right," Bo said. "Were either of you in the game Duke Mayo was playing in last night?"

"We both were," Stansbridge said.

"How did he do?"

"He cleaned up," Keegan replied with a sneer.

"Took your dinero, did he?" Scratch drawled.

Stansbridge's narrow shoulders rose and fell. "You win, you lose. That's the nature of the game."

"Did you take it unkindly when you lost?" Bo asked.

"Didn't bother us a bit," Keegan said.

"If you're accusing us of something, Deputy, why don't you just come right out with it?" Stansbridge said.

"All right, I will. Did you follow Mayo when he left here, cut his throat, and steal back the money he won?"

"Of course not," Stansbridge said in a cool, unruffled voice. "We've been right here. We haven't set foot out of the place in more than twelve hours." He raised his voice a little. "Isn't that right, Mike?"

Ashton ran a filthy rag over the scarred wood of the bar. "That's right," he said. "They been sittin' right there, Deputy."

Bo glanced over at the Fan-Tan's proprietor. "I thought you didn't pay any attention to what was going on in here."

"Some things I see, some things I don't," Ashton said. "But I know those two haven't left, just like they told you."

Bo didn't believe what the three men had said, but he couldn't disprove it, and he sensed that they wouldn't budge from their stories. He had a strong hunch that he was looking at the murderers of Duke Mayo. There was a matter of proof, though.

"All right," he said heavily as he lowered the hammer of his gun and then pouched the iron. "I'm putting you on notice, though, Ashton. If we hear about any trouble in this place, we'll shut it down. You understand?"

Ashton looked like he wanted to come over the

bar and tear into the Texans, but he controlled his anger. "I heard about you two. Comin' into town and actin' like you're runnin' things now. The Deverys'll settle your hash. You just hide and watch."

Bo ignored that. "Don't forget what I said."

As he and Scratch turned toward the door, the swamper's foot suddenly bumped against the bucket and upset it. Dirty, soapy water spilled out on the floor. The old man jumped back, crying out in alarm.

"You damned old fool!" Ashton bellowed at him. "Clean that mess up! Right now, you hear me?" He leaned forward over the bar and spat in disgust at the swamper's feet. "I don't know why I keep you around here in the first place."

"I'm sorry, Mike, I'm sorry! I'll go get another bucket of water and clean it up right now!"

The swamper grabbed the bucket and headed for the back door. Ashton swatted at him with the bar rag but missed.

Bo could tell that Scratch wanted to go to the old-timer's defense. He caught his friend's eye and shook his head. They had more important things to deal with at the moment.

Back out in the street, they paused in front of the Fan-Tan. Scratch said, "Bo, you know damned well those two killed that fella Mayo."

"I expect you're right," Bo admitted. "As long as Ashton backs their story, though——"

The sound of someone hissing at them caught the Texans' attention. They turned to see the old swamper standing at the corner of the building. He beckoned to them with a palsied hand.

Bo and Scratch looked at each other and frowned. Then Bo shrugged, and they went over to see what the swamper wanted.

"What can we do for you, mister?" Scratch asked.

The old man licked his lips nervously. "Are . . . you boys really lawmen?"

"Yeah, but I ain't sure you could call us boys," Scratch said. "Hell, I'll bet you ain't that much older than us."

The swamper shook his head. "It ain't the years so much as it is the miles."

"We've put plenty of those behind us, too," Bo said. "Now, what was it you wanted to tell us?"

The old man's fingertips rasped on the white beard stubble that poked from his chin. "I heard you askin' about Duke Mayo. I was in there when he cashed in from that game and left. It was just a couple o' minutes after that when them other two, Stansbridge and Keegan, left, too. They lied to you about that, and so did Ashton."

Bo felt his heart beat a little faster in anticipation. "You'd swear to that in court?" he asked.

The swamper hesitated. "I dunno . . . I knocked that bucket over a'purpose so's I could come tell you about it, but I don't like the idea of standin' up in court and sayin' the same thing."

"You don't have to worry about Ashton and those gamblers," Scratch told him. "They'd be arrested by then. They couldn't hurt you."

"Yeah, but what if they was to get loose for some reason? A jury might set 'em free, even though ever'body would know they was guilty."

Bo couldn't dispute that. It wasn't uncommon for

the members of a frontier jury to ignore the facts of a case and just do what they wanted to do, whether it was convicting an innocent man or acquitting a guilty one. He didn't want to let Stansbridge and Keegan get away with murdering Duke Mayo, though, and he was certain that was what had happened.

"Tell you what," he said. "We'll arrest the three of them and tell them we have a witness, but we won't say anything about who it is. Maybe once they're behind bars, they'll go ahead and confess."

"Maybe . . ." the swamper said, but he sounded doubtful.

"We'll do everything we can to protect you," Bo promised. "Sooner or later, somebody's got to stand up for what's right. That's the only way we can bring law and order to Mankiller."

The swamper took a deep breath, then nodded his head. "All right. Lemme get back in there before you come in, though, so's they won't have as much reason to think it was me you been talkin' to."

Bo nodded and said, "Sure, we can do that."

Scratch added, "How come you want to see them get what's comin' to them? They treat you bad?"

"Ashton's a jackass, and pizen-mean. The other two ain't much better. But Duke, he always had a kind word for me and slipped me a little dinero now and then. For a tinhorn gambler, he weren't a bad sort. He had a wife, too, a gal named Janey, and she was pretty nice for a whore." The swamper shook his head. "Folks go down some wrong trails sometimes—I done it myself, more often than I like to think about—but that don't mean they're bad sorts."

Bo put a hand on the man's shoulder. "You're right about that, amigo. Now get back in there with your bucket, and we'll wait a few minutes before we arrest those varmints."

The swamper nodded and turned to hurry toward the back of the building. He disappeared behind the Fan-Tan.

"I just thought of somethin'," Scratch said. "We've only got two cells in the jail, and they got prisoners in 'em already. If we arrest Ashton, Stansbridge, and Keegan, where're we gonna put 'em?"

Bo frowned. "That's a problem, all right. If we're going to clean up this town, we'll need more space for prisoners. I'll have to talk to Lucinda and some of the others about that. For now, though, I think I saw a smokehouse with a pretty sturdy door on it. We can put them in there and lock it up."

Scratch nodded and hitched up his gun belt. "Sounds good to me. Let's go educate those hombres about how they hadn't ought to go around cuttin' people's throats."

CHAPTER 23

Three out of the four men in the Fan-Tan looked surprised when Bo and Scratch came back into the gambling den. The swamper kept his eyes downcast and watched his mop making damp circles on the floor, but there was nothing unusual in that.

"Forget something?" Ashton asked from behind the bar. He didn't look the least bit happy to see the Texans again.

"Yeah, we did," Bo said as he came to a stop beside the table where Stansbridge and Keegan sat. "We forgot to arrest these two four-flushers for murdering and robbing Duke Mayo."

Stansbridge's face flushed with anger. "Damn it, we told you we haven't been out of here for hours."

"And Mike backed us up on that," Keegan added.

"Yeah, but we got a witness who says that all three of you are lyin'," Scratch said.

"Witness!" Ashton repeated. "What witness?"

"Never mind about that," Bo said. "You'll find out all about it later. We're taking these two to jail, and you're coming along, too, Ashton. You lied to a peace officer, and that's against the law."

Ashton shook his head and rumbled, "I'm not goin' anywhere." He looked and sounded like an angry old bull.

"We'd rather you came along peaceable-like," Bo said, "but one way or another, you're under arrest, too."

"The hell with this!" Keegan suddenly exclaimed. "You two are about to wind up dead in an alley just like Mayo!"

"Damn it!" Stansbridge exploded. He realized what his friend had just done.

A grim smile played over Bo's lips. "We didn't say anything about where Mayo's body was found. How would you know it was in an alley, Keegan, if you didn't have something to do with him dying there?"

Keegan cursed and sprang to his feet. His hand darted under his coat and came out with a pocket pistol. At the same time, Stansbridge surged up from his chair. He thrust his arms out, twisting his forearms as he did so, and a pair of derringers leaped into his hands from under his sleeves, where they had been concealed in spring-loaded sheaths.

Bo and Scratch were moving, too, splitting up and slapping leather at the same time. Colts blurred from their holsters. Muzzle flame stabbed through the dim interior of the Fan-Tan as gun-thunder echoed against the low ceiling.

Both shots that crashed out from Scratch's gun found their target. The slugs drove deep into Keegan's chest and knocked him back, off his feet.

The little pistol in his hand cracked wickedly, but the barrel had tilted up and the bullet went harmlessly into the ceiling.

At the same time, a bullet from Bo's gun punched into Stansbridge's midsection. He doubled over in agony, hunched above the table. His fingers tightened involuntarily on the triggers of the derringers, causing both weapons to fire. The bullets struck the cards that the men had picked up to resume their game of showdown. The pasteboards scattered again. A second later, Stansbridge collapsed on the table and began bleeding on the green felt.

"Look out!"

The shout from the swamper made both Texans swing around. They saw that Ashton had grabbed a sawed-off shotgun from under the bar and pointed it at them. Before Ashton could pull the triggers, the swamper brought his mop up and struck the barrels of the deadly scattergun with the handle. That knocked the weapon up enough so that the double load of buckshot went over the heads of Bo and Scratch and tore into the ceiling and the wall behind them instead.

Both Colts roared. Seeing the sawed-off pointed at them, Bo and Scratch had reacted instinctively and fired. Their slugs smashed into Ashton and sent him stumbling back against the shelves of liquor behind the bar. The bottles came crashing down, shattering and filling the room with the overpowering smell of spilled booze. It mingled with the acrid tang of gun smoke as Ashton dropped the shotgun, flopped forward onto the hardwood, and then slid off to land behind the bar.

Bo hurried to the end of the bar so that he could cover the man, although he had a hunch Ashton wasn't a threat anymore. Seeing the sightless eyes staring at the ceiling, he knew he was right. Ashton was dead.

So were Stansbridge and Keegan. Scratch made sure of that, then reported, "These tinhorns have crossed the divide, Bo."

"So has Ashton," Bo replied. He looked at the swamper. "Are you all right, mister?"

The old man ran trembling fingers through his wispy white hair. "Y-yeah, I reckon so. I didn't get hit by any of those shots." He leaned over the bar to look at Ashton's corpse. "You're sure he's dead?"

"I'm sure," Bo told him.

The old man licked his lips. "That's a lot of whiskey goin' to waste, soakin' into the floor like that."

"Yeah, but only a man with no dignity left at all would get down and try to lap it up like a dog. You're better than that, amigo. You proved it by telling us what you knew about Duke Mayo's murder."

The swamper sighed. "I reckon you're right. Still, it's a mortal shame to see all that whiskey spilled."

"I agree with you," Scratch said. "Nothin' we can do about it, though."

The shots had drawn some attention. Bo and Scratch had left the door standing halfway open when they came back in, and now a couple of curious townsmen poked their heads in.

"I'd be obliged if one of you gents would let Sam

Barfield know that his services are needed here, too," Bo said.

"What happened?" one of the men asked.

Bo snapped his gun's cylinder closed after replacing the round he had fired. "The men who murdered Duke Mayo got what was coming to them," he said. "And so did the man who tried to cover up for them and then threw down on a couple of lawmen."

"Take a good look, boys, and spread the word," Scratch invited. "That's what's gonna happen to hombres who figure on breakin' the law in Mankiller."

The two men looked at the corpses with big eyes, then disappeared. The sound of running footsteps came from outside. One of the men had probably gone to alert the undertaker that he was needed, as Bo had requested, and the other was probably going to be busy spreading the news about the shoot-out in the Fan-Tan.

As he finished reloading his Colt, Scratch said, "Well, this solves one problem."

"What's that?" Bo asked.

"Now we don't have to figure out where we're gonna lock up these varmints."

"True enough. We can't just kill *everybody* who breaks the law, though."

Scratch sighed. "No, I suppose not." He paused. "I'm glad Biscuits ain't here."

"Why's that?"

Scratch nodded toward the bar. "Because I got a hunch that no matter what you said, he'd be down on his knees behind that bar right now, lappin' up those puddles of who-hit-John like a dog!''

News of the shoot-out spread like wildfire from one end of Mankiller to the other. In less than twenty-four hours as deputies, the Texans had killed seven men, wounded another, and arrested three members of the most powerful family in town, plus the shoot-out Scratch had had with the bushwhackers at the hotel. People couldn't stop talking about how the new lawmen were going to either clean up Mankiller at last . . .

Or be dead before they had a chance to do anything else.

When they got back to the sheriff's office, Biscuits O'Brien was still asleep on the cot in the back room. Bo and Scratch got him up and forced him to drink black coffee until he was reasonably awake, if not sober. He refused to reveal where he'd had the extra bottle of whiskey hidden. Short of beating it out of him, the Texans didn't know what else to do.

Reuben and Simeon yelled complaints from the cell block, but Bo and Scratch ignored them. Bo left Scratch there to keep an eye on things and went to pay a visit to Edgar Devery.

"You need to come down to the jail," Bo began, and when Edgar started to shake his head, he went on, "Hear me out. Your boy Thad's in a bad way."

"Is that wound in his arm festerin' up?" Edgar asked with obvious concern in his voice. "Dang you, Deputy——"

"His arm's fine," Bo cut in. "But he messed himself last night, and he needs some clean clothes."

"That ain't my responsibility."

"He's your son, and nobody else is going to take care of him."

"His sister will," Edgar said with a scowl.

"His sister? You'd send a man's *sister* in to help him clean up after something like that?" Bo didn't bother trying to keep the contempt out of his voice. "What kind of man are you, Edgar?"

"All right, all right, damn it! Quit pesterin' me. I'll go up to the house and get him some clean clothes, then I'll be down to the jail after a while."

"Thanks," Bo said. "And I'm sure Thad will be grateful to you, too."

"I wouldn't count on it. Boy's as mean and surly as a bear with a toothache."

"I didn't know you had a daughter," Bo commented. "In fact, I haven't seen any female Deverys."

"Yeah. Name's Myra. She don't come out much. Mostly she stays in her room on the second floor." Edgar tapped the side of his head. "Poor gal ain't quite right. She'd rather be shut up readin' books and such-like. Seems sort of embarrassed about bein' a member of the family."

From what he had seen of them so far, Bo would have said that Myra Devery might just be the sanest one of them all, if she felt like that.

He wasn't sure if Edgar would live up to his promise or not, but true to his word, the liveryman showed up at the jail that afternoon with some clean clothes, a handful of rags, and a bucket of water. Scratch patted him down to make sure he wasn't trying to smuggle a weapon to the prisoners, then they let him go into the cell block. Scratch unlocked Thad's cell and then relocked the door behind Edgar. When the liveryman called to be let out half an hour later, he said, "Ought to smell better in there now."

"We can dang sure hope so," Scratch said.

The one drawback to having Edgar come in and help Thad clean up was that he got to take a good look at the jail and its defenses, such as they were. Bo still expected an attempt to free the prisoners, maybe as soon as that night.

However, the night passed quietly. The Texans took turns sleeping and standing guard, just as they had taken turns going across the street to the café for meals. Lucinda reported how everybody was talking about them and how there was a sense of law and order growing suddenly in Mankiller that the citizens had never experienced before.

The next night, the Texans were summoned to one of the town's saloons, where a couple of drunken miners were brawling. Bo left Scratch at the jail and answered the call for help, and as soon as he pushed the batwings aside and stepped into the saloon, silence fell like a hammer. The two men who'd been wrestling on the floor picked each other up and quickly started righting the tables and chairs they'd knocked over. They weren't completely sober, but they weren't nearly as drunk as they had been a few minutes earlier, either.

"We're sorry, Deputy Creel," one of them said.

"Yeah, don't know what came over us," the other

miner added. "We got to arguin' and just got carried away a mite."

"We'll pay for any damages," the first one offered.

"Well . . ." Bo looked at the proprietor, who nodded his agreement to the suggestion. "All right," he told the two men, "but next time find some way to settle your argument without causing any trouble."

"Yes, sir, Deputy, we sure will!" Both men nodded vehemently.

Outside the saloon, Bo paused, grunted in surprise, and shook his head. A reputation as a town-taming lawmen nobody wanted to cross was one thing he'd never figured on having. It seemed to be pretty effective, though.

Over the next week, he and Scratch found out just how effective. After the extraordinarily violent first twenty-four hours on the job, the next seven days were relatively trouble free. There were no murders, the first time in memory that an entire week had gone by without a killing, and only a few fights broke out that the Texans had to break up.

The Deverys also seemed to be lying low. Jackson Devery didn't make any more appearances demanding that his sons and nephew be released. The prisoners complained incessantly, but they seemed to be getting used to being behind bars. Edgar visited Thad a few times, which perked up the young man. He began to get some of his natural piss and vinegar back, which Bo wasn't sure was a good thing.

Thad's sister Myra came to visit him, too. She was a pale, blond young woman who spoke in a shy half-whisper when she said anything at all and kept her eyes downcast. Her visits seemed to lift Thad's spirits, too. Bo was convinced she was the person he'd seen peeking out through the curtains in the second-floor window of the old Devery house.

With one of the Texans keeping an eye on him nearly all the time, Biscuits O'Brien had suffered the torments of the damned. He had been sick at his stomach, he'd had the shakes, he had been drenched in a cold sweat. But by the time a week had gone past, he was sober . . . and mad as hell about that fact.

He was complaining about that very thing one afternoon when the office door opened and Lucinda Bonner came in. Bo and Scratch were straddling ladderback chairs, but they stood up instantly and nodded to her. "Ma'am," Scratch said.

"You boys are too polite," Lucinda said as she waved them back into their chairs, but her smile said that she liked the attention.

"That's our Texas upbringin'," Scratch told her. "My ma would'a kicked me from heck to Goliad if I didn't stand up when a lady entered a room."

"Mine, too," Bo agreed.

"Well, that's nice of you," Lucinda said, "but you can sit down and relax. I brought something I want you to see."

She had a stack of papers in her hand. They looked like handbills of some sort, Bo thought, and as Lucinda held one up, he saw that he was right.

The printing was big and bold and read:

MANKILLER, COLORADO

ELECTION, JUNE 5th
Colorado Palace Saloon

VOTE

Mrs. Lucinda Bonner *for* MAYOR

Dr. Jason Weathers • Harlan Green

Sam Bradfield • Wallace Kane

for TOWN COUNCIL

Col. Horace Macauley *for* JUDGE

VOTE for Progress

VOTE for <u>Law and Order</u>

VOTE for Mankiller's <u>Future</u>!

"Well," Bo said as he looked at the handbill and thought about how the Deverys might react to it, "that ought to do it."

CHAPTER 24

It didn't take long, either. Lucinda paid a couple of local boys to nail the handbills up around town, and as soon as they started appearing, folks began to talk. It was like a tidal wave of sensation washed over Mankiller. Everybody was talking about the impending election, which was only a week away.

Bo was in the café having a cup of coffee when the door opened and heavy footsteps sounded. The place was busy as usual, but silence fell as all the conversations abruptly ceased. Bo turned his head and saw Jackson Devery stalking toward the counter.

Devery didn't appear to be armed, but his face was flushed with barely contained rage, as usual. He slapped one of the handbills down on the counter in front of Lucinda, who had been talking to Bo. It was torn in the upper corners where it had been ripped down.

"What the hell is this?" Devery demanded.

"Keep a civil tongue in your head, Devery," Bo snapped. "There's no law against cussing in town, so I can't arrest you for it, but I can give you a thrashing if I have to."

Devery sneered at him. "You could try." He turned his attention back to Lucinda. A finger stabbed down on the handbill. "You can't do this. It ain't legal."

Lucinda was staying calm in the face of Devery's anger, and Bo admired her for it. She said, "Actually, it is legal, Mr. Devery. Colonel Macauley, who, as you may know, is an accomplished attorney, has advised us that the citizens of a town have the right to call an election. All it requires is that the majority of eligible voters sign a petition requesting that an election be held."

"Petition?" Devery repeated. "What petition?"

Lucinda reached below the counter and brought up a stack of papers which she set beside the handbill. "This one. People have been signing it all week. There are copies at the general store and the assay office, too. Once we had enough signatures, we could set the election date and candidates could declare."

The steady assurance with which she spoke took some of the wind out of Devery's sails. Bo could see it. It didn't take Devery long to recover, though.

"I can hire lawyers, too," he said. "I'll sue you. This has got to be illegal. Mankiller is my town."

"You may own the land, but that doesn't give you any sort of legal authority over the citizens. They have a right to determine their own local government. When Mankiller was awarded a post office, the State of Colorado recognized it as a town, which means everything about this election is legal, Mr. Devery."

"It won't stand." Devery thumped a fist on the counter. "It won't stand, I tell you!"

"Wait and see," Lucinda said softly.

Looking like fire and brimstone was about to explode from him, Devery turned and stomped out of the café. Stunned silence remained behind him for a moment, then the customers began to talk again, louder and more excited than before.

Lucinda must have put quite a bit of effort into maintaining her control. She looked and sounded a little shaky now as she asked Bo, "What do you think he's going to do?"

"There's nothing he can do to stop the election," Bo told her. "From what you've told me and what you just explained to Devery, the law's on your side. If he does try to interfere, the state could come in and arrest him. Might even get some U.S. marshals in here."

Lucinda shook her head. "He's too smart to attract much outside attention to what he's been doing. Not unless it was a last resort, anyway. But I can't imagine that he'll just allow this to happen without trying to stop it somehow."

Bo agreed with her. "We'll just have to keep our eyes open," he said. "When trouble comes, we'll be ready for it."

Bo wasn't ready for what happened bright and early the next morning, though. The sound of hammering drew his attention as he left the sheriff's office to start morning rounds. He looked along the boardwalk and saw Luke Devery standing next to one of the posts holding up the awning in front of the assay office. Luke had a hammer in one hand and a sheaf of papers in the other.

"What in blazes are you doing?" Bo asked as he walked up behind Luke.

Red beard jutting out belligerently, Luke turned to face him. "What's the matter, lawdog? Can't you read?"

Bo could read, all right, and he didn't like what he read on the piece of paper Luke had just nailed to the post. Somehow, the words on the hand-lettered notice didn't surprise him.

Vote JACKSON DEVERY For Mayor

LUKE DEVERY

REUBEN DEVERY

SIMEON DEVERY

GRANVILLE DEVERY

For Town Council

EDGAR DEVERY For Judge

Vote for THE DEVERYS

Founders Of Mankiller

"You got a problem with that, Deputy?" Luke's voice dripped scorn as he spoke.

"Well . . . I'm not sure your Uncle Edgar is qualified to be a judge."

"He's fair, and that's all a fella needs. And speakin' of fair, you don't intend to give me any trouble over puttin' up these posters when you let that Bonner woman have her handbills nailed up all over town, do you?"

Grim-faced, Bo made a gesture of dismissal and said, "Go ahead. Put them up on the boardwalk posts all you want. But you'd better get permission before you nail one onto the wall of somebody's business."

Luke grinned. "Don't you worry. If I need permission for anything, I'll get it."

Whistling a jaunty tune, he sauntered away along the boardwalk, pausing three or four posts farther down the street to take some nails from a pocket of his overalls and put up another poster. Bo looked at the first one and studied the writing, wondering who had done the lettering. It was nice work, and he suspected that Myra Devery was responsible for it. He wasn't sure any of the others in the family had a delicate enough touch to produce something like that.

By the time he got to the café to break the news to Lucinda, he found that she had already heard about this new development. Mankiller's grapevine was working efficiently this morning.

"Can the Deverys do that?" Bo asked. "Just up and run for election against you like that?"

Lucinda smiled ruefully. "Any citizen of Mankiller can declare himself a candidate."

"Or herself," Bo pointed out.

"That's probably the shakiest part of the whole proposition," she admitted. "Being a woman, I'm not an eligible voter. However, if I'm elected and it's set aside legally later on, the town council will have the power to appoint one of themselves as acting mayor until a special election can be held. That's what Colonel Macauley says, anyway, and he knows more law than anybody else around here. So we're going to carry on as planned. Now we just have to defeat Jackson Devery and his bunch."

Bo grunted. "That shouldn't be a problem."

"Maybe more so than you think," Lucinda said with a frown. "I don't think anyone in town actually *likes* the Deverys, but there are people who'd like to curry favor with them. And there are plenty of people who are *afraid* of them. They might think it would be safer to vote for the Deverys. I wouldn't be surprised if they did something to try to make more people feel that way before the election."

"Intimidate the voters, you mean."

Lucinda nodded. "Exactly."

"That would be against the law, wouldn't it?"

"I would think so."

Bo rubbed his jaw. "Let 'em try it, then. They might wind up with more trouble on their hands than they bargained for."

Bo had to get on with his rounds, so he said so long to Lucinda and left the café. As he walked along the street, he saw a number of people gathered around the handbills that Luke Devery had put up. The Deverys' entry into the election campaign had stirred up a lot of interest.

Other than that, the town was quiet this morning.

Another night had passed without a murder. The citizens of Mankiller might be starting to feel secure and safe for a change. Bo hoped that if that were the case, it wouldn't turn out to be a big mistake for them.

When he returned to the sheriff's office, he found Biscuits O'Brien saying to Scratch, "Tell me again how all that whiskey spilled on the floor in the Fan-Tan."

Scratch shook his head. "I ain't gonna do it. You know good and well it'll just give you nightmares, Biscuits."

"Yeah, I know. I can see it in my head. Haven't been able to stop thinkin' about it ever since you told me." Biscuits shuddered.

Scratch glanced at Bo, then looked again. "You appear to have somethin' on your mind, pard," he said. "What is it?"

Bo beckoned for them to follow him as he started toward the cell block door. "You're right," he told Scratch. "Come along back here so I'll only have to say it once."

Wearing puzzled expressions, Scratch and Biscuits followed Bo into the cell block. Reuben and Simeon immediately started to complain, but Bo held up a hand to silence them. Thad just glared from the cell across the aisle.

"I've got some news for you boys," Bo told the brothers. "You probably don't know it yet, but you're running for town council in the election."

"What?" The exclamation came from four people: Scratch, Biscuits, and the two candidates themselves. Thad was the only one who still didn't say anything.

"I said you're running for town council," Bo repeated. "Your brother Luke is, too. He's out nailing up handbills all over town about it right now."

"But that ain't possible," Scratch protested. "They're in jail!"

Bo shrugged. "That doesn't keep them from running. If they're elected, I figure the new judge will dismiss the charges against them."

"What new judge?"

"Their Uncle Edgar."

"That damn liveryman who tried to steal our horses?"

"One and the same," Bo replied with a nod.

"But he can't be a judge! He takes care of horses and mucks out stalls for a livin'."

"Evidently that doesn't disqualify him. And I'm sure that if these two get elected, it'll mean that the rest of the Devery slate won the election, too."

"The rest of the Devery slate?" Biscuits asked.

"The old man's running for mayor, and somebody named Granville Devery is running for the other spot on the town council."

Reuben said, "That's one of our cousins. Uncle Lester's boy."

"I don't recall hearing about a Lester Devery," Bo said.

"That's 'cause he's dead," Reuben explained. "Fever got him a little more'n a year ago."

Scratch grunted. "Sorry . . . I guess." He looked around at Thad in the other cell. "I notice they didn't put *you* up for election."

Thad sneered. "I'm not interested in bein' on any damn town council. The whole thing's loco anyway.

When I get outta here, I'll show all of you who the real law is in Mankiller."

"I reckon we'll see about that," Bo said, although he thought it was a foregone conclusion that if the Deverys got elected, Edgar would dismiss the charges against his own son. Bo went on, "It won't take long, either. The election's only six days away."

"A lot can happen in six days," Thad said.

Bo didn't like the sound of that. Didn't like it one damned bit.

CHAPTER 25

That evening, the group that had hired Bo and Scratch to be deputies in the first place met again. Lucinda sent word to Bo that they would like for him to be there.

"Are you sure you don't mind missing out on whatever they're going to talk about?" he asked Scratch before he left the sheriff's office to attend the meeting.

"You mean, would I rather sit in some stuffy room and listen to folks yammer about politics, or stay here and play dominoes with Biscuits?" In recent days, Scratch had been teaching Biscuits how to play the game. Like any good Texan, he was horrified by the thought of somebody not knowing how to play dominoes.

Bo smiled. "Yeah, I know how you feel about politics."

"It brings out the windbag in just about anybody, even good folks like the ones we're tryin' to help. When you get back, you can tell me what they said, Bo. The important stuff, anyway. That'll do me just fine."

"And I don't reckon I'd be welcome," Biscuits said. "It was Pa Devery who pinned this star on me, after all."

"That was when you were drinking," Bo pointed out. "You're sober now."

Biscuits heaved a sigh. "Don't I know it? And there ain't no tellin' how long that'll last."

"It'll last," Bo said, probably with more confidence than he actually felt. Biscuits was still pretty shaky at times, and more than once Bo had caught him sitting and staring into space as he licked his lips, the almost overpowering thirst for liquor easy to see on his whiskery face.

As Scratch began to shuffle the dominoes on top of the desk, Bo left the office and walked across the street to the café, where the meeting would take place. Night had fallen, although there was still a little bit of red in the western sky from the vanished sun. Music came from the saloons and there were still quite a few people on the boardwalks and in the street. Nobody seemed interested in making trouble, though.

Bo went into the café, which had closed early for this meeting. In addition to the group that had hired him and Scratch, Dr. Jason Weathers, Harlan Green, Colonel Horace Macauley, and several other business owners Bo had gotten to know were there. Some of them sat at the counter with their backs to the kitchen, while the others were grouped at a couple of the tables. Lucinda stood in the center of the meeting. She was the only one who didn't have coffee.

"Go behind the counter and help yourself to a cup if you'd like, Bo," she told him with a smile.

Bo returned the smile and said, "Don't mind if I do." When he was fortified with a cup of the strong, black brew, he thumbed his hat to the back of his head and sat down on one of the stools at the counter.

"We've gotten together here tonight to talk about what we're going to do about the Deverys running against our candidates," Lucinda began.

"We can't do anything about it except defeat them," Colonel Macauley said. He was a white-haired, white-mustachioed Virginian who tended toward expensive cigars, frock coats, and beaver top hats. A Southern drawl softened his voice. He had commanded a cavalry regiment during the Late Unpleasantness, as he referred to the war, and had left his ruined plantation behind afterward to come west and practice law.

He went on, "What they're doin' is perfectly legal, no matter how much of a consarned shame and fraud it may be. I think we all know that the Deverys aren't interested in establishin' any kind of legitimate local gov'ment. They just want to keep the reins of power in their own iron fists by any means possible."

"Colonel, if you're going to make a speech——" Lyle Rushford began, then the saloon keeper stopped short and looked around at the others. "That's it! We need to have a rally so that all of our candidates can get up and tell people why they should vote for our side."

"Nor have I," Wallace Kane added.

Lucinda looked uncomfortable. "I don't know," she said. "I've never been much of one for making speeches."

"They don't have to be fancy speeches like the colonel here, say, could make," Rushford said. Macauley looked pleased at that. "They can be simple, as long as they're sincere."

Dr. Weathers spoke up. "Well, I, for one, don't object to telling people how I feel. One of the things you learn as a doctor is how to give people a piece of your mind when you think they need it."

Harlan Green chimed in, "I reckon I could say a few words, if I need to. I'm not that crazy about the idea, but I guess it would be all right."

"I'm still not sure," Lucinda said. She looked at Bo. "What do you think, Bo?"

He shrugged. "Personally, I've never cared much for political rallies and all that speechifying. But they must work, or people wouldn't keep having them."

"Deputy Creel's got a point, Lucinda," Sam Bradfield said. "If we're going to beat the Deverys and finally break their hold on this town, we have to use whatever weapons are available to us, even speeches."

Lucinda sighed. "I suppose you're right, Sam." She looked around at the others. "All right, if we're all in agreement, we'll have a rally. When?"

"The night before the election," Abner Malden said. "You want what you say to be fresh in folks' minds when they go to vote the next day."

A chorus of agreement came from the other men. With the issue of whether or not to have a rally settled, they started hashing out the details, and after some discussion, they decided to hold the gathering in front of Rushford's Colorado Palace Saloon. They would build a speaker's platform at the edge of the street and hang red-white-and-blue bunting on the railing that ran along the edge of the second-floor balcony. Lanterns could be hung from that balcony, too, so that there would be plenty of light for the crowd to see the speakers.

When they started talking about the order in which the speeches would be presented, Bo drank the last of his coffee and eased off the stool. "If you'll pardon me, gents . . . and ma'am," he added with a nod to Lucinda, "I ought to get back to the sheriff's office. I think you're on the right track here, folks, but you don't really need me to help you figure out what you're going to do."

Lucinda put a hand on his arm and squeezed for a second. "Thank you, Bo."

He smiled, nodded, tugged on the brim of his hat, and left the café.

He wasn't quite back to the sheriff's office when he heard the sound of running footsteps approaching. A man came out of the darkness. He didn't seem to see Bo until the Texan reached out and grabbed his arm.

"Whoa there!" Bo said. "What's the matter, mister?"

"Deputy, is that you?"

"Yeah. What's wrong?"

The man was out of breath. "Some fellas are . . . bustin' up Bella's Place."

"Again?" Bo said, recalling how he and Scratch had been summoned when the three Devery boys were wrecking the brothel. He recognized the man as Ernie Bond, who had brought word of the trouble that other night. "Who is it this time?"

"A whole gang of . . . prospectors." The little townie puffed a couple of times as he tried to catch his breath. "I dunno . . . what set 'em off."

Bo said, "All right, thanks. We'll take care of it." He sent Ernie on his way and hurried into the office.

Scratch and Biscuits looked up from their domino game, clearly startled by the abruptness of Bo's entrance. "What's up, Bo?" Scratch asked.

"Trouble," Bo replied tightly. "Some sort of riot over at Bella's Place."

Scratch started to his feet. "More Deverys, you reckon? We don't have all o' 'em locked up yet."

"No, according to what I was told, it's a bunch of prospectors causing the ruckus this time." Bo looked hard at Biscuits. "Sheriff, can we leave you here to guard the prisoners?"

Biscuits swallowed nervously. "By myself?"

"Load all three shotguns and set them on the desk," Scratch suggested. "That'll give you six barrels full of buckshot to discourage anybody tries to get in and ain't supposed to."

"Well, I . . . I suppose so."

Bo and Scratch were thinking the same thing, that this might a trick to get them away from the jail so that the long-awaited attempt to break out the prisoners could take place. For some reason, though, Bo had his doubts this time. The Deverys, led by their patriarch, seemed to have their sights set on winning the election and solidifying their hold on the town that way. Bo wasn't sure they would risk that on a jailbreak at this point.

He also knew that so far, Biscuits hadn't been forced to take a real stand against the man who had put him in office. He might buckle if he had to face Jackson Devery. But sooner or later, the Texans had to find out where Biscuits stood, and now was as good a time as any, Bo decided.

"You'll do fine," he told the sheriff. "We'll be back as soon as he can."

"Load those shotguns," Scratch added as he clapped his hat on his head and started for the door with Bo.

"And bar the door behind us!" Bo called back through the entrance.

As they started over toward Grand Street, Scratch said, "Maybe we should'a brought a couple of shotguns with us. They don't call 'em riot guns for nothin', you know."

"We'll be all right," Bo said. "Probably just have to talk a little tough, and those miners will settle down."

They heard the yelling and commotion coming from Bella's before they even got there. Hurrying even more, they reached the building and had to duck as a chair came crashing out through a window just as they got there. Broken glass sprayed over the boardwalk around them.

"Son of a bitch!" Scratch said.

Bo drew his gun. "Reckon this might take more than a few harsh words."

He yanked open the elaborate front door and plunged into the whorehouse with Scratch right on his heels. Chaos surrounded them, filling both the foyer and the parlor. Punches flew as men battled feverishly with each other. At least a dozen combatants were involved. Racket filled the air, a mixture of curses from the battling men, screams from the frightened soiled doves caught in the middle of the violence, and splintering crashes as furniture was grabbed, broken up, and used as weapons.

George, who appeared to be fully recovered from the pistol-whipping he had received at the hands of the Deverys, stood at the edge of the action, obviously eager to plunge right into it. Bella was beside him, though, both hands gripped tightly around one of his muscular arms as she held him back.

"You'll just get yourself hurt!" she was saying.

"Let the damn fools fight it out of their system!"

Then she saw Bo and Scratch. "Deputies! Do something!"

So it was all right for the two of them to risk life and limb, Bo thought, but not George. That was how it should be, he told himself. After all, they were paid to take such risks. But George probably was, too.

Scratch leaned close to Bo. "If we fire a couple of shots into the ceilin', that might settle 'em down!"

Bo shook his head. "Yeah, but if any of them are packing irons, it might cause them to start shooting, too. Then we'd have a real mess here. Plus it'd leave some holes in Bella's ceiling."

Scratch shrugged and asked, "What do you think we ought to do, then?"

"Settle this down the hard way," Bo said. He holstered his gun, stepped forward, and grabbed the shoulder of a man who stumbled backward toward him after an opponent had landed a punch in his face. Bo hauled the man around and threw a punch of his own. His fist crashed into the surprised man's jaw and drove him off his feet.

The man who'd been fighting with the one Bo had just hit glared at the Texan. "He was mine!" the man yelled. He lunged forward, swinging a wild, roundhouse blow at Bo's head.

Bo ducked under the man's fist, stepped in close, and hooked a right into the man's belly. His fist sunk deep and made the man bend forward. That put him in position for the hard left hand that Bo brought almost straight up under the chin. The man's head jerked so far back it looked like his head was going to come right off his shoulders.

Scratch whooped, "Now you're talkin'!" and plunged into the melee.

George said, "Dadgummit, Miss Bella, I *got* to get in there!" He pulled loose from her and joined the Texans in hand-to-hand battle with the rioting miners.

For several hectic minutes, Bo, Scratch, and George waded through the thick mass of struggling men. Their fists shot out to the right and left, delivering punches that landed solidly and sent men sprawling on the floor. One of the fighters started trying to kick a man who had fallen, but he had landed only one kick when George grabbed him from behind by the belt and the shirt collar and lifted him off his feet. The man let out an alarmed yell that cut off abruptly as George rammed him face-first into a wall.

One of the men jumped on Bo's back from behind. Bo staggered a couple of steps before he caught his balance. He bent over, reached up, and grabbed the startled man by the hair. With a heave, Bo threw the man over his shoulder. The man came crashing down on his back, and Bo was left with a couple of handfuls of hair with bits of bloody scalp attached to them. He had pulled the hair out by its roots.

Scratch stood toe-to-toe with a husky miner and traded punches, each man giving as good as he got for several moments. Scratch's opponent had the advantage in just about everything: height, weight, reach, and age.

But Scratch had the wiliness that came from years of brawling. He feinted so skillfully that the man fell for it and left himself wide open for the hard left that Scratch planted on his nose. He bit on the next feint as well and let Scratch get close enough to lift a knee into his groin. It was a low blow, but effective. The man groaned and doubled over as he clutched at himself. Scratch clubbed his hands together and brought them down on the back of the man's neck. The impact hammered the man to the floor.

George grabbed two more men by their necks and banged their heads together. Their skulls met with a loud thud. When George let go of them, they collapsed bonelessly.

"That looks like all of them," Bo said.

It was true. Some of the men had knocked each other out, and the Texans and George had taken care of the others. A few of the men on the floor were moaning and semiconscious, but most of them were out cold. Bo checked for pulses and found that they were all still alive. He was grateful for that, anyway.

The three men weren't hurt except for some bumps, bruises, and scrapes. Bo and Scratch found their hats, which had come off during the fracas, and put them back on. Then Bo turned to Bella and asked, "What started this?"

"I don't know," the redheaded madam said helplessly. "About half a dozen of those men just came in and started fighting with some of my customers. There was no reason for it I could see unless they were carrying a grudge because of something that happened somewhere else."

That was possible, Bo thought. The two bunches could have been enemies, and one could have followed the other here to the brothel.

Bella's green eyes suddenly widened. "Unless . . ." she began.

"Unless what?" Bo asked when she paused.

"Can you come with me, Deputy? There's something in my office I want to tell you."

Bo looked over at Scratch and George. "Can you keep an eye on those varmints in case they start to wake up?"

Scratch grunted and drew his Colt. "If they start to wake up, I'm liable to give 'em a little love tap with my gun butt."

"Just don't bust any skulls permanent-like," Bo said.

He followed Bella back to her office in the rear of the building. It was a small but comfortably furnished room. She motioned Bo into a leather armchair and went behind the desk.

"Jackson Devery came to see me this afternoon, Deputy," she said as she sat down.

"Devery?" Bo repeated with a frown. "What did he want? I mean—"

Bella smiled and shook her head. "Devery's a lot of things, none of 'em good, but he's not a man who patronizes a whorehouse. No, he acted all friendly-like and asked a favor of me."

"A favor?"

"He said he wanted me and my girls to tell every man who comes in here to vote for him and the other Deverys in the election. Said we ought to tell them that if that bunch on the other side is elected, they'll shut down all the saloons and gambling dens and houses like this one."

"I doubt if that would happen," Bo said. "I haven't heard them say anything like that, and Lyle Rushford, the owner of the Colorado Palace, is a member of the group."

Bella nodded. "I know. It doesn't seem likely to me, either, and I said as much to Devery. I told him I wasn't going to mess with politics. When a man's here visiting one of my girls, the last thing he wants to hear is some damned political speech."

Bo figured that was probably true. He asked, "How did Devery react to that?"

"The same way he reacts to just about everything. He got mad," Bella leaned forward. "And he said that if I didn't go along with what he wanted, I'd be sorry, Deputy. Mighty sorry."

CHAPTER 26

Bo looked across the desk at Bella for a long moment, then said, "You think Devery had something to do with what happened here tonight?"

"He threatened me, Deputy. There's no other way to look at it. It can't be a coincidence that he came to see me today, and this fight broke out tonight after I wouldn't go along with what he wanted."

Bo scraped a thumbnail along his jaw. "You might be right. You said those miners came in and started the fight for no reason. Maybe Devery paid them to do it, or forced them in some other way."

Bella nodded. "That's what I'm thinking. You know he owns all the claims around here and demands a share from the miners. Maybe he told them he'd take a bigger cut if they didn't do what he said."

"Or bribed them by promising that he'd take a smaller cut," Bo speculated. "Either way, sending them here to start a fight is crooked."

"What about trying to get me and my girls to tell people how to vote?"

Bo shook his head. "That's just electioneering.

A mite dirty, maybe, but not against the law. The threatening and the fighting, that's what's crossed the line."

"What are you going to do about it?"

"First things first," Bo said as he put his hands on his knees and pushed himself to his feet. "We have to get some proof that Devery had anything to do with this ruckus."

He and Bella went back to the parlor. Bo told Scratch what Bella had said, then asked the madam to point out which of the unconscious men had started the fight. When she had done so, Scratch and George dragged the men to one side of the room.

Bella's soiled doves started fussing over the men who'd been the victims in the attack. Those hombres might have headaches when they came to, Bo thought, but other than that it would probably be a pretty pleasant awakening.

Not so for the ones who'd started the fight. George brought a bucket of water from the kitchen and threw it in their faces. The men came awake, sputtering and snorting as the water went up their noses.

Bo and Scratch had their guns drawn again. They showed the Colts to the men, and Bo said, "You fellas just take it easy. Sit there on the floor, and don't try to get up."

"You can't do this," one of the miners protested as he wiped water out of his eyes. "We didn't do nothin'."

"The hell you didn't," Bella said. "You caused a couple hundred dollars' worth of damage, and who knows how bad you hurt some of my regular customers."

The men glared at her.

"We're going to have to lock you boys up," Bo went on. "You're under arrest for assault and disturbing the peace, and you'll stay locked up until after the election, when Mankiller's got a real judge who can decide what to do with you."

That brought more protests and words of alarm from the miners. "We can't leave our claims alone that long!" one of them said. "Somebody'll come along and take all the gold out of 'em."

"You should'a thought of that before you agreed to do Pa Devery's dirty work," Scratch said.

From the looks of surprise that appeared on the faces of the men, Bo knew that Bella's hunch was right. Devery was behind the riot that had broken out here tonight.

The miners concealed the reaction as best they could, but it was too late. Bo said, "What did Devery do? Threaten to take even more of what you make from your claims, or promise to take less?"

"I don't know what the hell you're talkin' about," the first man replied in a surly voice. "I ain't seen Devery in weeks."

"Me, neither," another man said, and the rest of them chimed in with similar denials.

"You know," Bo said, "as long as the damage gets paid for, Deputy Morton and I might see our way clear to forgetting about the charges. That way you wouldn't have to stay locked up in a smokehouse for a week or more, and your claims wouldn't be unprotected for that long." He saw hope start to creep onto the faces of the men, then added, "But you'd have to be willing to testify why you came in here tonight and started a riot for no apparent reason."

It was like slamming a door. Several of the men shook their heads. One said, "You'll have to lock us up then, Deputy. We ain't talkin'."

Bo tried not to let his disappointment show on his face. At the same time, he wasn't really surprised. Devery had probably threatened to kill the men if they ever said anything about his involvement in tonight's trouble. They were more afraid of him than they were of being locked up and possibly losing some gold from their claims.

"All right, if that's the way you want it. George, have you got a shotgun?"

George nodded. "Yes, sir, Deputy, I sure do."

"Do you mind getting it and coming with us while we lock these fellas up?"

"I don't mind at all." George smiled. "Fact is, I reckon I'll enjoy it."

Bo and Scratch searched the prisoners, removing several knives and a couple of pistols from them. Then the Texans and George marched the disgruntled prisoners down the street at gunpoint. They attracted a lot of attention along the way.

When they reached the smokehouse that would serve as a makeshift jail, they herded the men inside the windowless, thick-walled structure. Earlier in the week, Bo had picked up a padlock from Abner Malden's store and hung it on the hasp of the smokehouse door. He snapped it into place now, and barred the door as well. As sturdy as the building was, the prisoners had no chance of getting out.

"That's a pretty small space for half a dozen men," Scratch commented quietly.

Bo nodded. "I know. I don't reckon we can really leave them in there for a week or more. But they can suffer for a day or two. Maybe then they'll be more willing to talk about why they went loco at Bella's Place tonight."

"I ain't gonna hold my breath waitin'," Scratch said with a shake of his head. "I reckon those hombres are plumb scared of Devery. Too scared to talk."

"I'm afraid you're right," Bo said.

George went back to Bella's, and the Texans returned to the sheriff's office. They both had to identify themselves before Biscuits O'Brien would unbar and unlock the door and let them in, which Bo thought was a good thing.

"Any trouble while we were gone?" he asked Biscuits as they came in.

The sheriff shook his head. "No, it was quiet." He gestured toward the desk, where three shotguns were lined up, pointing toward the door. "I was ready, though, in case anything happened."

Scratch grinned. "See, Biscuits, you're gettin' the hang of bein' a real lawman."

Biscuits wiped the back of his hand across his mouth. "Yeah, well, I about jumped out of my skin at every little sound. Some whiskey sure would've steadied my nerves. All that damn coffee I've been drinkin' has got me as jumpy as a cat."

"Whiskey might've steadied your nerves for a few minutes," Bo said, "but then they would've been shot to hell again. You're better off not drinking, Biscuits."

"I know." Biscuits heaved a dispirited sigh. "Hell of a note, ain't it?"

As the Texans took off their hats and settled down for the evening, Scratch asked, "You still think Devery's gonna try to bust out those prisoners back in the cell block, Bo?"

"I'm starting to doubt it. Judging from the visit he paid to Bella's this afternoon, he's decided to try to win the election and go at the problem that way. Now, he may resort to shady means to do it, like threatening Bella, but for now I think he wants votes more than he wants those boys out of jail."

It wasn't destined to be a peaceful evening. A short time later, someone heaved a barrel through the front window of one of the saloons. The men who did it vanished into the shadows before anybody could even get a good look at them, let alone stop them.

When Bo and Scratch talked to the saloon's owner, Bo acted on a hunch and asked the man, "Did Pa Devery pay you a visit today?"

The saloon keeper frowned in surprise. "Yeah, as a matter of fact, he did. He wanted me to tell everybody who comes in my place to vote for him in the election next week."

"But you didn't agree to that, did you?"

The man shrugged. "I said I couldn't afford to take sides in something like that. Folks want to be able to come in my place and get a beer or a shot of whiskey without being bothered, no matter who they plan to vote for."

Bo and Scratch looked at each other and nodded. That was just the start of it. More windows were busted out during the night. Someone broke into both general stores and slung manure all over the merchandise. Coffins stacked behind Sam Bradfield's business were chopped to pieces with axes. Somebody tied ropes to the corral posts at the settlement's other two livery stables and pulled the fences down. The wave of malicious sabotage continued washing over Mankiller until after midnight, and Bo and Scratch always seemed to be one jump behind the varmints who were responsible for it.

More than once during the night, Scratch said bitterly, "Damn Deverys!"

Bo agreed with him, but they had no proof. Unless they could catch somebody in the act or convince those miners in the smokehouse to talk, it appeared that things would stay that way.

Finally, in the wee hours, the town settled down. The Texans hoped it would stay that way as they returned to the sheriff's office to trade off catching a few hours' sleep.

"Why don't one of you take the cot and the other one the sofa?" Biscuits suggested. "I'm here, and since I quit drinkin', I haven't been able to sleep much anyway. It's hard to doze off when you still feel like there's ants crawlin' all over your skin."

"If you're sure . . ." Bo said.

Biscuits nodded. "I'm sure. Get some rest."

Bo stretched out on the sofa while Scratch took the cot. It was even money which place was the least uncomfortable. Saying that either one was actually comfortable would have been going too far.

Bo wasn't sure how long he had been asleep when what sounded like two sudden peals of thunder jolted him awake. As he sat up sharply on the sofa and swung his legs to the floor, two more roaring reports blasted out.

Biscuits stood behind the desk, wide-eyed in the dim light from the turned-down lamp. "Somebody's shootin' off a shotgun down the street," he said.

Bo shoved his feet in his boots and reached for his gun belt. "I know."

By the time he was on his feet and had the belt buckled, Scratch came out of the back room, also ready for trouble. "Sounds like a war breakin' out," he said.

"If it was, it was a short one." Bo had heard the four blasts, but no more.

"We'd better go see what happened," Scratch said. He glanced at the sheriff. "You still all right to stay here, Biscuits?"

"Yeah, I guess." Biscuits nodded toward the desk, where the three shotguns still lay. "I haven't even unloaded those Greeners yet."

"I wouldn't," Bo said dryly as he put on his hat.

Biscuits let them out and locked up behind them. The Texans drew their guns as they started down the street toward the area where the shotgun blasts had originated. Bo wasn't sure where the shots had come from—he'd been asleep, after all, when the first two went off—but he had been able to tell the general direction from the second pair of reports.

Most of the saloons in Mankiller never closed, but the hour was long after midnight so that they weren't very busy anymore. A few men came to the batwings to peer over them curiously. The street was empty except for Bo and Scratch and stayed that way.

Lyle Rushford stepped out on the porch of the Colorado Palace as the Texans passed. "I reckon you heard the shots," he called to them.

Bo and Scratch paused. "That's right," Bo said. "You have any idea where they came from?"

Rushford waved a hand toward the lower end of the street. "Down there somewhere. Do you want me to come with you while you check on them?"

Bo shook his head. "No thanks. This is our job, not yours."

"Yeah, but I've got a stake in what goes on in Mankiller, too," Rushford said as he came down the steps and took a pistol from inside his coat. "If there's trouble, I'm happy to lend a hand."

"Suit yourself," Scratch said. He was peering down the street. "Bo, ain't that smokehouse where we locked those fellas up down yonder about where those shots came from?"

The same thing had just occurred to Bo, and the thought brought with it a chill that pierced to his core. "That's right," he said. "Come on."

The three men hurried along the street toward the smokehouse. As they approached, Bo couldn't see anything unusual or threatening around the building. It looked just the way it had when he and Scratch and George put the prisoners in it hours earlier.

"What's got you so worried about the smokehouse?" Rushford asked. "Did you say something about locking somebody in there?"

"The men who caused that riot at Bella's this evening," Bo explained. "Yesterday evening, now, I reckon, since it's after midnight."

"Oh, yeah, I heard something about that."

They came up to the sturdy, squarish building and stopped in front of the door. Bo sniffed the air and thought he smelled the faint tang of powder smoke.

Scratch pounded a fist on the door and called, "Hey in there! You fellas all right?"

There was no answer.

Scratch tried again. "Damn it, speak up! Are you all right? Is anybody hurt?"

Silence was all that came from the smokehouse.

It might as well have been empty.

Bo checked the padlock, thinking that maybe the shotgun blasts had blown it off so that the prisoners could be freed. The lock was intact, though.

"Son of a bitch," Bo muttered, suddenly so shaken that he indulged in one of a very occasional profanity. He smelled something besides the gunsmoke, a coppery scent that set all his nerves on edge. "We need to get in there."

Scratch and Rushford grabbed the bar and lifted it from its brackets. As they set it aside, Bo took out the key and twisted it in the padlock. The lock snapped open. He took it out of the hasp and pulled the door toward him.

The mingled smell of gun smoke and blood suddenly grew stronger. Bo reached in his pocket and found a lucifer. Holding the match up in his left hand, he snapped it to life while he gripped his Colt in the other hand, ready to fire if need be.

No one in the smokehouse represented a threat, though. The prisoners were nothing now except more work for Sam Bradfield.

Rushford glanced past Bo at the grisly scene. The flickering light from the lucifer revealed blown-apart bodies scattered all over the ground inside the smokehouse. It was obvious what had happened, although the how wasn't so clear.

"Check around back," Bo told Scratch.

The silver-haired Texan came back a moment later. "There's a ladder propped against the back wall. I climbed up far enough to see that somebody chopped a hole in the roof. It ain't a very big hole, though. Not big enough for anybody to escape through."

"But big enough for the barrels of a shotgun, I'll bet," Bo said bleakly. "Whoever it was climbed up there and probably told those boys inside that he was there to get them out, so they'd stay quiet. Then he chopped out the hole, stuck the gun through, and let off both barrels. There wasn't time enough between the first pair of shots and the second for him to have reloaded, so he must've had somebody helping him. The man on the ground handed up another loaded shotgun, and the killer emptied it, too, just to make sure he didn't miss anybody with the first two barrels."

"My God," Rushford said in a voice thick with shock. "I've never seen anything like this in my life. This was the cold-blooded murder of, what, six men?"

Bo nodded. "Yeah. Six men." He started to take a deep breath, then stopped because he didn't want to drag that much blood-tinged air into his lungs. "Six men who can never testify against Jackson Devery now."

CHAPTER 27

The campaign of terror that Bo and Scratch attributed to the Deverys, even though they couldn't prove it, subsided somewhat over the next few days. It didn't end completely, though. A couple of miners who had spoken up against the Deverys were jumped in a dark alley one night and beaten and kicked until one of them died and the other would probably never be more than a shell of a man. A mysterious fire nearly burned down the assay office. Francis O'Hanrahan, who had been an outspoken critic of the Deverys for a long time, limped into town one day with a bloody bandage tied around his leg. A bushwhacker had put a bullet through his thigh.

Bo knew good and well that Jackson Devery was orchestrating the whole thing, but the old devil was cunning. He didn't leave any tracks, and since the murder of the miners who had started the fight at Bella's, he didn't enlist any outsiders in his cause, either. There wouldn't be any more witnesses who had to be disposed of.

Slowly but surely, the brutal tactics began to have

an effect. Everyone in Mankiller had been excited at first by the prospect of an election and a real town government. If the talk could be believed, Lucinda and the others were going to be elected in a landslide.

By the time the election was only a day away, though, more people were saying that it might be better to vote for the Deverys. The excuse they gave was that Jackson Devery and his family had founded the town, after all, and so shouldn't they be the ones to run it?

Bo didn't believe for a second that people really felt that way. They were just afraid of what could happen if the Deverys lost. Mankiller might become a gun-blazing battlefield. Some of the citizens declared their intention to not even vote and advised their neighbors to do the same. That way, if anything bad happened, it wouldn't be their fault.

Bo overheard so many conversations like that that he began to grow disgusted. It would serve those folks right, he thought, if the election were called off and he and Scratch just rode away and left the town gripped in the iron fist of Jackson Devery. Biscuits O'Brien would be happy if that happened. He could go back to drinking himself to death.

But Bo knew that he and Scratch wouldn't abandon the town. They had made too many friends here in Mankiller, among them Lucinda Bonner. She had been deftly fending off Scratch's romantic overtures, and Bo didn't blame her for that. She had more than enough on her plate right now as it was. He felt sort of sorry for his friend, though. Scratch was a hopeless romantic and always would be, and any time a woman didn't return his affections, he honestly couldn't understand it.

The rally was still scheduled for that night. The speakers' platform had been erected in front of the Colorado Palace Saloon, and the red-white-and-blue bunting was draped from the balcony railing. Bo was worried that the Deverys would do something to try to disrupt the speeches, but there was no way to protect against that ahead of time. They would just have to wait and see what happened and deal with it then.

Late that afternoon, the Texans dropped in at the café to see how Lucinda was doing. She was working behind the counter as usual, but she seemed nervous.

"I don't know how in the world I got talked into this," she said with a little laugh as she poured coffee for Bo and Scratch. "I never made a speech in my life, and at my age I've got no business starting now."

"What do you mean, at your age?" Scratch asked. "A beautiful woman is eternally young, Lucinda, and you certainly qualify."

"I don't need any flattery right now, Scratch Morton," she told him sternly. Then her expression softened and she added, "But I appreciate it, anyway." She looked at Bo. "What time is all this silly hoopla supposed to start?"

"Around eight o'clock, as soon as it gets dark," Bo said. "You know that, Lucinda. You helped work out the time."

"Oh, I suppose I did. I'm so flustered I just can't remember anything right now."

"You're going to do just fine," Bo told her.

"Remember, folks in this town like you and want to see you win."

"Some of them do. The girls and I have heard a lot of people say that they're voting for the Deverys."

Bo couldn't deny that, since he'd heard the same thing. So he just shrugged and said, "When it's over, we'll count up the votes and see what the outcome is. That's the way it's supposed to work."

Lucinda planned to close the café early to give her time to prepare for the rally. She shooed everybody out a short time later, including the Texans. They went back to the sheriff's office.

"You're going to have to continue keeping an eye on things, Biscuits," Bo told the sheriff. "Scratch and I will be making sure that nobody causes any trouble at the rally."

Biscuits nodded. "I know. I've gotten used to it. I reckon if I was gonna be a real lawman, I'd be best as a jailer. I seem to be able to handle that job."

"You are a real lawman," Scratch said, "and you can handle whatever it is you need to handle. Why, it's been a week since you took a drink."

"Yeah, and it's been one hell of a year."

"I said a week."

"I know what you said," Biscuits replied, "and I know what it feels like." He held out his hand, palm down. It still trembled a little, but not nearly as much as it had been a few days earlier. "Look at that. It hasn't been long since that thing would bounce around like it was full of Mexican jumpin' beans."

"Pretty impressive," Bo agreed. "We're proud of you, Biscuits."

The sheriff grunted. "Better wait until I've actually done somethin' worth it before you're proud of me."

"Reckon we'll be the judge of that," Scratch said.

A crowd began to gather in the street as twilight settled over the town. A feeling of celebration was in the air, sort of like Fourth of July. Bo hoped that no kids would start setting off firecrackers. The popping scared horses and could be mistaken for gunfire, which might prompt some trigger-happy hombre to slap leather himself.

Carrying Winchesters, Bo and Scratch walked over to the saloon and took up positions on its porch. From there they could see the townspeople in front of them in the street. Bo glanced up the hill at the Devery house. It squatted there silently, a couple of windows glowing with lamplight so that they looked like the eyes of a malevolent frog.

Lyle Rushford came out onto the porch and hooked his thumbs in his vest. "Looks like we're going to have quite a turnout," he said.

"Close to half the town's here already," Scratch said, "and quite a few of the miners have come in from the hills, even though they can't vote in the election. Can't blame 'em for bein' interested in how it all turns out, though. What happens here in town has an effect on them, too."

"Have you spoken to Mrs. Bonner lately? I know she was nervous about making a speech tonight."

"She still is," Bo said. "I'm sure she'll do fine, though."

"Of course she will. Lucinda Bonner is a very intelligent and decent woman, in addition to being undeniably lovely."

Scratch's eyes narrowed. "You sound like you're a mite sweet on her, Rushford."

The saloon keeper chuckled. "Well, can you blame me? I'm not sure she'd ever have anything to do with an old reprobate like me, but I've been thinking lately that I ought to find out for sure."

"I don't know that I'd advise that——" Scratch began, but Bo interrupted him.

"Lucinda's a grown woman. I'm sure she can make up her own mind about such things."

"That's what I thought," Rushford said. He took out a cigar, lit it, and then sauntered back through the batwings into the saloon.

In a low voice, Scratch said, "Dadgummit, you know Lucinda can do better than a saloon man, Bo."

"Yeah, like some old mossback of a fiddlefooted Texan," Bo said with a grin. "We'll be moving on one of these days. Rushford looks like he's going to be here for a while. Maybe from now on."

"Yeah, yeah, I reckon you're right about that," Scratch said grudgingly. "And you're right about it bein' up to her, too. But that don't mean I'm givin' up."

"Never thought you would," Bo said.

The candidates began to show up. Wallace Kane and Harlan Green were first, followed shortly thereafter by Sam Bradfield.

"Doc Weathers will be here in a little while," the undertaker reported with a grin. "He's got a baby he's delivering at the moment."

"That's a heap more important than speechifyin'," Scratch said.

Colonel Horace Macauley was the next one to

join them at the steps leading up to the back of the speakers' platform. The elderly lawyer was even more of a dandy than usual this evening, sporting a fancy vest and a silk cravat with a big diamond stickpin in it.

"I see that Mrs. Bonner isn't here yet," he commented. "No doubt like any woman, she wants to make an impressive entrance."

Bo pointed out. "I imagine she just had a lot to do."

Dr. Weathers showed up a few minutes later, passing around cigars bestowed on him by the proud new father of the baby he'd just delivered. "Mother and infant are doing fine," he said in response to a question. "Mankiller has a new citizen this evening, a fine, healthy baby boy."

That just left Lucinda, Bo thought as he slipped his watch out of his pocket and opened it. Almost eight o'clock, and there were at least three hundred people gathered in the street, waiting to hear what the candidates had to say.

A stirring in the crowd made him glance up. He snapped his watch closed and put it away as he saw Lucinda making her way across the street, with her daughters Callie and Tess following her. All three women wore simple gowns that they made look expensive and elegant. They looked lovely.

Someone began applauding, and a cheer suddenly went up to greet them. By the time the three women reached the back of the platform, Lucinda was blushing furiously.

"I'm not sure I can go through with this," she said.

"Sure you can," Scratch told her. "I got all the faith in the world in you, Lucinda."

"So do I," Bo added.

"We need to discuss the order in which we'll speak," Colonel Macauley said. "Why don't I go first? I'm accustomed to speaking in court, so I can make a few opening remarks, then introduce the rest of us in turn."

"That sounds good to me," Wallace Kane said. "I don't think it matters which order the rest of us go in, except that Mrs. Bonner needs to speak last, since she's running for mayor."

Bo wasn't sure that was a good idea, since it would give Lucinda even more time for her nerves to act up, but the others all quickly agreed with Kane's proposal.

Chairs had been set up on the platform, three on each side of a pulpit borrowed from the First (and only) Baptist Church. Macauley went up the stairs with a sprightly step and positioned himself behind the pulpit, raising his hands for silence as more cheers and applause came from the crowd. He let the noise go on for a minute, then motioned for quiet again. This time he got it.

"I guess we're actually going through with this," Lucinda whispered to Bo and Scratch.

"Yes, ma'am," Scratch said. "Don't you worry about a thing. Bo and me will be keepin' an eye out for trouble."

The Texans split up, going to either end of the platform as Colonel Macauley began his remarks in a booming voice that carried easily, having been trained in courtroom oratory.

"My friends and fellow citizens of Mankiller! I have unexpected but splendid news to report to you this evening! Our respected and beloved physician, Dr. Jason Weathers, has just told me that we have a newcomer among us this evening! A fine, healthy baby boy was added to our population a short time ago! Let's hear it for the lad!"

That brought on a new round of whooping, hollering, and clapping. When it died away, Macauley continued, "Yes, a new baby was born in Mankiller today, which is always a cause for rejoicing!" The colonel poked a finger in the air dramatically, "But ask yourselves this question, my friends, for it holds tremendous importance! Ask yourselves . . . *what kind of town will that child grow up in?*"

The intensity of that question made the crowd remain silent. Macauley allowed that moment to stretch out for several seconds, then thundered, "Will that child grow up in a town ruled by gun and knife and fist? Will he grow up fearing for his very life because Mankiller is ruled by bloody-handed barbarians who utilize threats and intimidation and violence . . . even murder . . . to enforce their greedy, corrupt tyranny?" The colonel's nostrils flared above his sweeping mustache as he drew in a deep breath. "Or will that child come to manhood in a community where law and order is the rule of the day, where justice is served, where people are free from the threat of wanton brutality? Think hard on each and every one of those questions, my friends, because the answers to them can be found in only one place!" Again he paused to let the tension and drama increase, before finally leaning forward and saying in an intimate tone, "The answers, my friends, can be found only in the hearts of each and every one of you."

Bo suppressed the grin of admiration he felt trying to stretch his mouth. The colonel was good at what he did. Like a hellfire-and-brimstone preacher, he had the audience right in the palm of his hand.

Macauley took off his top hat, pulled a handkerchief from the pocket of his vest, and mopped sweat from his forehead. That was a calculated move, giving the crowd time to buzz a little about what he had just said. Then he replaced the handkerchief, put the hat back on, and said, "Now, let me introduce to you the people whose mission it is to transform Mankiller into that town of law and order and justice of which I just spoke. As you know, I am a humble candidate for the office of judge, and these gentlemen want the opportunity to serve you in the positions of town councilmen. Dr. Jason Weathers! Harlan Green! Sam Bradfield! Wallace Kane!"

Each of the men climbed to the platform as Macauley called their name. They waved and smiled and looked embarrassed by the applause and cheers. As Bo looked on, he wondered why nobody had thought to have a brass band here. That was all this spectacle needed. Maybe Mankiller didn't have enough musicians to form one.

"And now, last but certainly not least, the person who will lead us as our mayor! You all know her and respect her and enjoy the food that she and her lovely daughters and her brother serve in their café . . . Mrs. Lucinda Bonner!"

Lucinda cast frantic glances at Bo and Scratch,

both of whom smiled reassuringly at her. Callie and Tess urged her toward the steps. Lucinda went up them like she was climbing the thirteen steps to a gallows.

Her face lit up with a smile, though, when she reached the top. The biggest cheers of all went up from the crowd.

It was so noisy that Bo couldn't make out the words when Scratch turned and called to him. He recognized the alarm on Scratch's face, though, so he hurried over to join his old friend.

"What is it?" Bo asked, leaning close so that he and Scratch could hear each other.

"Look up yonder!" Scratch said, pointing up the hill with the barrel of the Winchester in his hands.

Bo looked and felt his heart sink. A large group of men, at least twenty strong and led by Jackson Devery, had emerged from the old house at the top of the hill. They were marching steadily toward the rally.

And they all had guns in their hands.

CHAPTER 28

Bo and Scratch weren't the only ones who had seen the Deverys coming. Several people in the crowd had noticed them as well and started calling out in alarm. That spread quickly. Frightened, angry cries overwhelmed the cheering and clapping. A feeling of panic jolted through the gathering.

"Colonel, settle the folks down!" Bo called up to Macauley. "We'll see what the Deverys want."

He hoped they weren't coming down the hill for a showdown. If bullets started to fly, it was a certainty that innocent people would be hurt and probably killed. Not to mention the fact that the Texans were outnumbered ten to one and wouldn't stand much of a chance, either. Bo hadn't realized that Pa Devery could put together such a formidable force. Obviously, there were a lot of cousins and hangers-on that he hadn't heard about yet.

Bo and Scratch hurried along the boardwalk until they were past the crowd and then cut into the street, blocking the path of the advancing Deverys. Jackson Devery was right out front, of course, striding along arrogantly. He had a gun belt strapped around his waist and carried a Henry rifle. A black Stetson was crammed down on his shock of long white hair.

Luke and Edgar followed Devery, one to each side and a step back. The rest of the bunch spread out from there until it almost filled the street from one side to the other.

Bo and Scratch planted their feet in the dirt of Main Street. Bo raised his voice and ordered, "Hold it right there, Devery!"

Jackson Devery came to a stop and glared at the Texans. The others followed suit. Devery said, "Get the hell out of the way, Creel! This is a public street, and you can't stop us from walkin' on it!"

"We can stop you from disrupting that political rally behind us, though," Bo said. "That would be disturbing the peace, and that's against the law."

Devery sneered at him. "Nobody said nothin' about disruptin' the rally. Hell, we came to join in, didn't we, boys?"

Shouts of agreement came from the men behind him.

Bo frowned. "What do you mean, join in?"

Devery nodded toward the speakers' platform, where Colonel Macauley had succeeded in quieting down the citizens. The colonel and the other candidates stood there watching anxiously as Bo and Scratch confronted the Deverys.

"They're makin' speeches about how folks ought to vote for them, aren't they?" Devery asked.

"That's right."

"Well, don't the ones of us who're runnin' for office have a right to do the same thing?"

The question took Bo by surprise. "You want to make a speech and ask people to vote for you?"

"They'll be a lot better off if they do," Devery declared, "and I think I got a right to tell 'em that."

Bo looked over at Scratch, who shrugged. "It's a free country, I reckon," the silver-haired Texan said. "And I can't think of any law against makin' speeches. If there was, all them blasted politicians back in Washington'd be behind bars. You know, come to think of it, that ain't such a bad idea."

Bo looked at the platform and called, "Colonel, you're our legal expert."

Macauley spread his hands. "Mr. Devery is correct. He has a right to speak. However, this is a private rally. If Mr. Devery wishes to stage a rally of his own, no one can stop him."

Lucinda suddenly moved to the edge of the platform. "No," she said, her voice carrying clearly. "He can speak here if he wants to." She looked directly at Jackson Devery. "We're not frightened of you any longer, Mr. Devery. That's the biggest reason that Mankiller is about to change. The courage of these citizens is the reason." She swept her hand toward the crowd. "And once we've elected a legitimate government, you and the others from your family will face justice for the crimes you've committed! You won't be able to run roughshod over everyone in the area and extort so much money from them that they can't even make a decent living, no matter how hard they work!" Her voice shook a little from the outrage she obviously felt. "Your day is done, Mr. Devery. Done. But . . . if you wish to speak . . . come up here. Tell the people you've oppressed whatever it is you want to say."

Devery looked so mad he was ready to pop again.

But he controlled it and started to stalk past Bo.

Bo moved, getting in Devery's way and resting the barrel of his Winchester at a slant against Devery's chest. "The lady invited you to talk, that's all. If you start any trouble, you'll be the first one I ventilate."

"Get the hell out of my way," Devery growled.

Bo stepped aside. Devery headed for the platform. Scratch pointed his rifle at the rest of the bunch.

"You hombres stay back," he ordered.

Luke pointed at the platform and said, "Edgar and Granville and me got a right to be up there. We're runnin' for office, too, ain't we?"

Bo shrugged and told his old friend, "Let them pass, I guess." He lifted his voice. "The rest of you stay put. You can see and hear all right from where you are."

Luke, Edgar, and a younger Devery who had to be Granville followed Jackson Devery to the platform. They climbed up the steps. The four Deverys gathered at one end, the six other candidates at the other end.

Colonel Macauley stepped to the pulpit. "All right," he boomed to the crowd, "we'll hear from the town council candidates first."

Bo and Scratch stayed where they were, between the Deverys and the rest of the crowd, as the speeches began. The Texans had attended other political rallies, and what was said tonight in Mankiller wasn't much different from the things they had heard before. One by one, Dr. Weathers,

Wallace Kane, Sam Bradfield, and Harlan Green trooped up to the pulpit and promised that if they were elected, they would do their very best to serve the interests of everyone in Mankiller.

Then it was Luke's turn. He stood there looking uncomfortable and said, "If you folks know what's good for you, you'll vote for me and my kin. There wouldn't be no town here if not for us! We'll run it right, the same way we always have!"

Then he turned the pulpit over to his cousin Granville, who looked even more nervous about speaking in front of the crowd. "Uh, you should, uh, vote for us because . . . because there'll be trouble if you don't."

Luke gave him a sharp poke in the side and frowned at him.

Granville hurried on, "I mean, we'll take care of all the troublemakers who come into our town and think they can get away with anything." He turned his head to glower at Bo and Scratch. "There won't be no more phony lawmen killin' people right and left. Yes, sir, things'll go back to bein' just the way they were before, only, uh, better. Yeah, that's it. Things'll be better."

Luke took hold of Granville's collar and pulled him away from the pulpit. "That's enough. You said your piece. Now it's Pa's turn."

"Not yet," Macauley said as he stepped forward. "First we'll hear from the judicial candidates, starting with myself. Friends, you know my record! You know about my exemplary background as a practicing attorney in Virginia, and you know about my sterling service to the Old Dominion during the War of Northern Aggression!"

That drew a few frowns and jeers from the crowd, which included both former Confederate and Union soldiers.

"But that's all in the past!" Macauley hurried on. "What matters is right here and now in Mankiller, Colorado, the place that all of us have chosen to call home! The place that has a chance to grow into a decent community if you good people will seize the opportunity to elect me and my companions to lead you! You have my solemn oath that should you elect me as your judge, I will see to it that the law is enforced fairly, justifiably, and honorably! I know the law, and before God, I am an honest and humble man! No more can be asked of a jurist!"

Bo wasn't so sure about that humble business, but he figured Macauley was honest enough.

"Now," the colonel went on, "we'll hear from my opponent." He motioned Edgar forward without giving him any more introduction than that.

The liveryman shuffled up to the pulpit and peered out at the crowd. "You folks know me, too," he said. "I ain't loud, and I don't carry on much. But fair is fair, and I know it when I see it and I ain't afraid to say so. I reckon you can't ask for much more than that from a judge, neither." He nodded and stepped back.

Bo actually thought that was a fairly impressive speech, despite its brevity. Edgar struck him as being basically honest, but he had lived in the shadow of his brother Jackson for so long and done everything that Jackson demanded of him, that he couldn't be trusted. That was a shame, because under different circumstances, Edgar might have made a decent town councilman. Not a judge, though. He just wasn't qualified for that.

"That just leaves the two candidates for mayor," Macauley said. He turned to look at Devery, who jerked his head toward Lucinda.

"I don't care what you people think of me," Devery snapped. "I was raised to let ladies go first."

"Such chivalry," Macauley muttered. "A shame the other honorable virtues were not enculcated along with it." Before Devery could make any retort, the colonel held out his hand to Lucinda. "Mrs. Bonner?"

Lucinda had lost her nervousness during her earlier outburst, and it hadn't come back to bother her. She looked very calm and self-possessed as she stepped up.

"I've already said what I have to say. Now it's up to you citizens to make the real difference. Vote tomorrow with the courage of your convictions. Thank you."

The simple speech drew more cheers and applause than any of the others. It went on for a couple of minutes before Jackson Devery stepped forward and silenced the crowd with a glare.

"These people—" He flung a hand toward the candidates at the other end of the platform. "These people been talkin' to your hearts. I'm gonna talk to your brains and your guts. You're all smart enough to know that it ain't wise to vote against me and my kin."

"Is that a threat?" Colonel Macauley demanded.

Devery's head snapped toward him. "I didn't interrupt you, you old blowhard, so keep your trap shut while I'm talkin'! And no, it ain't a threat. It's a fact." He pointed toward the crowd. "And ever' one of those folks know it. They know it in their head, and they know it in their gut." He took a moment to sweep his gaze over the crowd, dragging it out as if he were studying the face of everyone there so that he could remember them. Then he said, "You know what you better do."

With that, he turned and walked off the platform, taking Luke, Edgar, and Granville with him. The crowd stood there quietly. The buzz of conversation didn't start up again until all the Deverys went back up the hill to the old house that had disgorged them.

"The son of a bitch put it plain enough," Scratch said to Bo. "What I can't figure out is why he's goin' to this much trouble. Why's he want to win this election instead of just grabbin' power with all the guns on his side?"

"Because in the long run, guns aren't enough," Bo said. "Santa Anna had a lot more guns than we did, but in the end that didn't stop us from booting him out. Same thing was true of King George and the American colonists a hundred years ago. Devery's trying to scare folks into supporting him, and that won't work, either. People have to believe in their leaders, like we believed in Sam Houston."

"Well, I reckon they can believe in Lucinda, after those speeches she made."

Bo nodded. "They were pretty good, all right."

He and Scratch went to the back of the platform, where Lucinda and the other candidates were coming down the steps. Callie and Tess greeted their mother with hugs. Now that it was all over, Lucinda looked nervous again.

She turned to Bo and Scratch and asked, "Did I do all right?"

"You did more'n all right," Scratch assured her.

"You said just the right things, and anybody with a lick of sense is gonna vote for you."

She shook her head doubtfully. "I'm not sure." Jackson Devery pretty much came right out and said that if he and the others aren't elected, they'll take revenge on the town."

"Let him try it," Colonel Macauley said. "Let him just try it, and he'll see what happens then!"

"What *will* happen then?" Lucinda asked. "You all saw, he had at least twenty men with him. Twenty well-armed men who are used to violence and who'll do whatever he tells them to do. What do we have in answer to that threat?"

Everyone's eyes swung to Bo and Scratch.

Scratch grinned and shrugged. "Ten-to-one odds," he said. "Nothin' to worry about."

But Bo knew from their worried expressions that no one here tonight believed that.

CHAPTER 29

The morning of June 5, election day in Mankiller, dawned beautifully. At this elevation the heat of summer hadn't taken over yet, so there was still a pleasantly cool crispness to the air. The sky over the mountains was a deep blue, dotted here and there with white clouds swept along by a good breeze. It was the sort of day that made a man feel glad to be alive.

And if he and Scratch were still alive at the end of it, Bo reflected, he would be glad about that, too. Maybe even a little surprised.

When they got to the Colorado Palace Saloon, they found the doors closed and locked. Scratch rapped on one of the doors, and after a moment Lyle Rushford looked out the window to see who was there and then came over to unlock the door.

"We closed down a short time ago," Rushford explained as the Texans came into the saloon. "Some of my regulars didn't like being kicked out, but I told them we'd be open again tonight, after the election's over."

"Appreciate you volunteering the use of your place," Bo said.

Rushford shrugged. "It's the biggest room in town. Anyway, in the long run it'll be good for business. People will hang around to find out what the results of the election are, and then they'll already be here when they want to celebrate afterward."

"Let's hope there's somethin' to celebrate," Scratch said.

"There will be," the saloon keeper replied. "I've got a good feeling about it."

Bo hoped Rushford was right. If the vote went against the Deverys, what could Jackson Devery do? He couldn't seriously think that he and his family could gun down all the winning candidates, along with the town's lawmen, and get away with it. Could he?

The problem was, Bo honestly didn't know the answer to that question. He didn't know how crazy drunk with power Jackson Devery really was.

The election was scheduled to last from nine in the morning until three in the afternoon. That would give every man in Mankiller enough time to vote. Bo and Scratch planned to be on hand the whole time, just to make certain there were no disturbances.

Rushford's bartenders were moving the tables back, creating a large open space where people could line up to vote. They would be given ballots at one table, stop at another table to mark them, and then drop the ballots in a strongbox with a hole cut in the lid that sat on a third table.

"We'll leave you to finish getting ready," Bo told

the saloonkeeper. "We'll be back before the voting starts, though."

Rushford nodded. "You don't think Devery will try to keep people from voting, do you?"

"There's no tellin' what that varmint might try," Scratch said.

The Texans walked up the street to the café. The place was very busy this morning. Lucinda might be the mayor of Mankiller before the day was over, but for now she was hustling to get breakfast cooked and served for all her customers. She barely had time to greet Bo and Scratch with a smile.

"Go on back to the kitchen and tell Charley I said to feed you," she told them.

"Yes, ma'am," Scratch said. "I ain't gonna turn down that offer."

They helped themselves to coffee in the kitchen, and Charley Ellis set plates heaped with food in front of them. He asked, "Does that sister of mine know what she's doing?"

"By feedin' us on the cuff, you mean?" Scratch shook his head. "I don't know, she's liable to go broke doin' that."

"No, I mean this loco mayor business. Devery's not gonna let her get away with it."

"He won't have any choice in the matter," Bo said. "It's up to the voters."

Charley's disgusted grunt showed just what he thought of that idea.

After the Texans had eaten, they stopped at the counter in the front room long enough for Bo to ask Lucinda, "Will you be coming down to the Colorado Palace later?"

She shook her head. "It looks like I'm going to be busy here all day. Just send someone to get me when it's all over . . . if you need me."

"We will," Scratch said confidently.

They took a quick turn around town. Most businesses were open and doing a brisk trade. The hitch rails were full, as usual, and a lot of people were on the boardwalks and in the street. An air of excitement gripped the town. Folks smiled and greeted Bo and Scratch by name.

The only Deverys they had seen so far were the trio locked up in the jail.

When they returned to the sheriff's office, they found Biscuits O'Brien eating the breakfast that Callie Bonner had delivered to him when she brought over the prisoners' meals. Bo thought something was different about the sheriff, and after studying Biscuits for a moment, he asked, "Did you shave and wash up?"

Biscuits grinned sheepishly. "Yeah, I did."

"And he even brushed his hair, looks like," Scratch said. "I'll swan, Biscuits, what's gotten into you?"

"It's election day," Biscuits said. "Maybe by the time the day's over, I'll be a real sheriff."

Bo told him, "You already are. You've done a fine job guarding those prisoners."

"Nobody's tried to take 'em away," Biscuits pointed out.

"You'd better keep a close eye on them today," Bo said. "Devery might try to take advantage of all the commotion going on and bust them out."

Biscuits patted the stock of one of the shotguns lying on the desk. "I'll be ready for him if he does."

From the cell block, Thad called, "Hey, deputies! Creel! Morton!"

Scratch stepped over to the door and swung it open. "What do you want?"

Thad gave the Texans an ugly grin. "Just wanted to take one last look at you bastards. You're about to learn that you can't mess with the Deverys."

"You're on the wrong side of the bars to be sayin' anything like that."

"For now," Thad said. "For now."

Scratch slammed the door. "I shouldn't let that ugly little varmint get under my skin," he muttered, "but he does."

"Come on," Bo said. "Let's get back over to the saloon."

Men were already lining up outside the Colorado Palace, even though the doors were still locked and it was half an hour until they would open for voting. Bo and Scratch made their way through the crowd and knocked on the doors. Rushford let them in again. By now the room was set up the way it was supposed to be. Rushford took a big gold watch from his pocket, checked the time, and said, "Now all we have to do is wait."

The half hour passed slowly, but it passed. And finally, when the hands of Rushford's watch pointed at nine and twelve, he nodded to the Texans. Bo went over to the door, twisted the key in the lock, and opened it.

"The election's on," he called to the crowd outside, which now filled the street. Cheers and whoops went up from the townspeople. Bo thought again that they really needed a brass band here in Mankiller.

As men surged toward the door, he held up a hand to slow them down. "One at a time," he said. "Line up Indian style, one at a time. That's the only way this'll work."

With Scratch standing close to the tables where Rushford's bartenders sat to run the election and Bo ushering the men into the saloon, the voting got under way. Bo cautioned the men not to talk about who they were voting for.

"That's why they call it a secret ballot," he said.

One of the men pointed to the middle table. "The fella sittin' there can see who I put down," he said. "So can the other two."

"Maybe, but they're not looking. They've sworn to be impartial."

"How do we know that?" a new voice demanded. Bo looked around to see Luke Devery in the doorway. The men who'd been lining up there a moment earlier had shrunk back away from him. "Pa says he wants me to watch the whole thing and make sure nobody cheats."

"Fine," Bo said, waving Luke into the room. "Go right ahead. Just don't say anything to anybody while they're voting. That wouldn't be proper."

"Nothin' about this whole business is proper," Luke said. "The only proper thing is the Deverys runnin' Mankiller, the way we always have."

"Nothing stays the same," Bo said, "whether we want it to or not."

Luke stomped over behind the tables and took up position there, with his arms folded across his chest and a scowl on his bearded face. Bo saw a few of the men glancing nervously at him as they voted.

That was exactly why Luke was here, to make men think twice about voting against the Deverys. Bo knew that, but there was nothing he said he could do about it. Luke was right when he said he had a right to monitor the election and make sure it was fair.

Scratch asked, "How come you ain't voted yet, Luke?"

Luke replied, "Deverys do things together,"

"Yeah, so I've heard," Scratch said dryly. "That had somethin' to do with gettin' your brothers and your cousin arrested in that whorehouse ruckus."

Luke didn't say anything to that, just glared even darker.

An election was an exciting thing . . . at first. But then it became more tedious for the folks who had to stay there the whole time. The hours dragged by, and the crowd thinned out, although there were still quite a few people in the street. The only incident occurred when a couple of men tried to sneak through the line and vote a second time, but one of Rushford's bartenders recognized them and turned them away.

Then there was a stirring in the people outside that caught Bo's attention. He stepped onto the porch and looked up the hill, the same way everyone else was looking. Then he turned his head and called to those inside, "The Deverys are coming."

Luke snorted. "Did you think the rest of us wouldn't show up, Creel? One thing you better learn while you still can . . . Deverys don't never give up. Never."

Bo came back inside. A minute later, Jackson

Devery marched in, his head held high and defiant arrogance etched on his face, as usual. He sneered at Bo, Scratch, and Rushford and said, "We're here to vote."

"I'd say you're a legal resident of the town," Bo told him. "Go right ahead."

Devery got his ballot, marked it, and tossed it contemptuously into the strongbox. Luke went next, then Edgar and Granville and one by one all the other Deverys and Devery kinfolk. When they were finished, Jackson Devery asked, "How long does this sham of an election run?"

"Until three o'clock," Rushford said. He checked his watch. "That's a little over an hour from now."

Devery's lip curled. "Enjoy the time you got left," he said in a menacing tone, then led the rest of the family out of the saloon. Luke stayed behind to continue his job as election watcher.

None of the other candidates had voted yet, but they came in a short time later as a group. After they voted, Wallace Kane asked, "Where's Mrs. Bonner? Shouldn't she be here?"

"She said she was too busy at the café to come down until the election was over," Bo explained. He thought of someone else who wasn't there and turned to Scratch. "Maybe one of us ought to go over to the jail and stay there for a while so Biscuits can cast his vote."

"I'll do it," Scratch said. "Be glad for a chance to stretch my legs. This democracy business is inspirin'," as all get-out, but it's a mite tiresome, too."

Biscuits showed up a few minutes later, having been relieved by Scratch. "Rube and Sim are startin' to get worried now," he told Bo. "They've realized that if their side doesn't win, they're in trouble and might be locked up for a while."

"What about Thad?"

Biscuits shook his head. "He's still convinced that he'd gettin' out of there today, one way or another. He says his uncle won't let us get away with takin' Mankiller away from him." Biscuits rubbed his jaw.

"I ain't sure but what he's right."

"We'll play the hand out to the end," Bo said. That end finally came. A short time after Biscuits had voted and returned to the jail, Rushford checked his watch again and then snapped it closed.

"Three o'clock!" he announced. "The election's over. Everybody out except the deputies and my men."

"I'm stayin'," Luke said. "I ain't budgin' until every damn one of them votes is counted."

Rushford looked at Bo, who nodded. "Seems fair enough, even though Luke's a candidate, too. I'd rather his family had someone else here as their representative, but I reckon we can live with this."

"Get to it, then," Luke snapped.

When everyone was gone except Bo, Scratch, Luke, Rushford, and the three bartenders, the drink juggler who was in charge of the strongbox opened it up. One of the other bartenders brought out a chalkboard on which he had written the names of all the candidates. The man at the strongbox said, "I'll take out each ballot one at a time and read the votes. You mark 'em down on the chalkboard, Gus."

"I want to see those ballots," Luke said.

Bo said, "Once they've been counted, you can have

a look at them. You'll see that nobody's cheating here, Luke. This has been an honest election, and it's going to stay that way."

The bartender at the strongbox took out the first ballot, which had been folded by the man who cast it. He unfolded it and said, "One vote each for Mrs. Bonner, Colonel Macauley, Doc Weathers, Mr. Green, Mr. Bradfield, and Mr. Kane."

The man at the board made a mark beside each candidate's name.

Luke stuck out his hand. "Lemme see that." He took the ballot, glared at it, then tossed it down disgustedly onto the table.

The bartender fished out another ballot and said, "One vote each for Mrs. Bonner, Colonel Macauley, Doc Weathers, Mr. Green, Mr. Bradfield, and Mr. Kane."

Ten ballots had been counted before one came up that contained votes for the Devery faction. That was the way it continued. Luke's face grew darker and darker with anger as it became obvious that most of the citizens of Mankiller had defied the Deverys and voted against them. Luke, his father, and the other members of his family who had run were losing in a landslide.

Luke remained there until the bitter end, though. Finally, all the ballots were counted, and Rushford announced, "The results are exactly the same in every race, gentlemen. The slate of candidates headed by Mrs. Lucinda Bonner has defeated the slate of candidates headed by Jackson Devery by a count of 364 votes to 89 votes. Effective immediately, Mrs. Bonner is the mayor of Mankiller, Colonel

Horace Macauley is the judge, and the town council consists of Dr. Jason Weathers, Wallace Kane, Sam Bradfield, and Harlan Green."

Luke couldn't contain himself anymore. "This won't stand!" he burst out. "By God, this won't stand!"

He stalked to the door, jerked it open, and stomped out of the saloon. The people waiting in the street for the results of the election could tell by his expression and demeanor who had won. Cheers erupted.

Scratch looked over at Bo. "What do you reckon the Deverys will do now?"

"I don't know," Bo replied with a shake of his head, "but I'd bet a hat it won't be anything good. We'd better get back over to the jail——"

The wild celebration going on in the street suddenly quieted, causing the Texan to look toward the saloon doors in alarm. Luke had left one of them open when he stalked out, and one of the townies appeared there, eyes wide. Bo recognized him as little Ernie Bond, who always seemed to be the bearer of bad news.

That wasn't about to change now. Ernie gulped and said, "Deputies, come quick! There's a bunch of strangers with guns ridin' into town, and they look like they're ready to start shootin' the place up!"

CHAPTER 30

Trailed by Rushford and the other men, Bo and Scratch hurried outside, drawing their guns as they did so. Bo wondered if Jackson Devery had sent for the newcomers. They might be more Devery relatives, or even hired gunfighters.

He wasn't prepared for what he saw when he and the others came out on the porch of the Colorado Palace, though.

A dozen riders were stopped in the middle of the street. They were well armed and looked plenty tough, but they didn't possess the cold-eyed menace of professional gunmen. Bo recognized several of them, including the broad-shouldered, big-gutted, craggy-faced man in the lead.

"Big John Peeler," Bo said in surprise. "What in blazes are you doing here?"

Peeler thumbed his hat back on his graying hair and grinned down from his horse. "Lookin' for you and Morton," he said.

"You trailed us all the way up here from New Mexico?" Scratch asked.

"I sure did. Left Joe in charge of the Circle JP and brought some of the boys from the crew with me. Figured I needed to track you down."

From just behind the Texans, Rushford asked quietly, "An old enemy of yours, deputies?"

"You could say that," Bo replied. He didn't take his eyes off Peeler. "You must be pretty mad, Big John, to come all the way up here just to settle a score with us."

Peeler frowned. "Settle a score? What are you talkin' about, Creel?"

"That fight we had just before Scratch and I rode out."

"You mean when you walloped me over that little trick I pulled on Case Ridley?"

"And on us," Scratch said. "You could've got us killed, Peeler."

The big cattleman sighed. "Yeah, I know. I get these ideas in my head sometimes, and they ain't always good ones. Like usin' you boys as bait for Ridley and tryin' to grab off some of the Snake Track range. Yeah, I was mad for a few days after that tussle we got into, Creel, but then I realized you were right to jump me."

"You did?" Bo asked.

"Sure. That's when I knew I had to find the two of you . . . to apologize to you and ask you to come back to work for me."

Bo and Scratch couldn't have been more surprised if Peeler had sprouted wings and started flying around right in front of them. Peeler was obviously sincere, though.

"Well, what do you say?" he prodded. "Come on back to the Circle JP with us?"

Bo tapped the badge pinned to his coat. "In case you haven't noticed, Big John, Scratch and I already have jobs. We're deputies here in Mankiller."

Peeler waved a hand. "That can't be as good as workin' for me."

"You might be surprised," Bo said dryly. "We sort of like it here, don't we, Scratch?"

"Yeah," the silver-haired Texan agreed. "And we've sort of got a full plate right now, too."

Peeler looked around at the now-silent crowd. "Yeah, I can see that somethin's goin' on. Some kind of celebration?"

"An election," Bo said. "Mankiller just elected a mayor, a judge, and a town council."

"Yeah, and the hombre who's been runnin' things around here ain't gonna like it, either," Scratch added.

Peeler's rugged face hardened. "If you fellas got gun trouble, me and the boys'd be glad to pitch in and lend a hand."

"We appreciate that——" Bo began, but a sudden outcry interrupted him. He swung around and saw a slender figure staggering down the boardwalk toward them. Even though he had seen her only a few times, he recognized Myra Devery, Edgar's daughter. But something was wrong with her.

The girl seemed to be on the verge of collapse. Scratch sprang to catch her. As Scratch steadied her, Bo saw that Myra had a bruise on her cheek, and a trickle of blood leaked from the corner of her mouth. Someone had beaten her.

"What happened, Myra?" Bo asked her.

She drew in a ragged breath. "My . . . my Uncle Jackson."

"Why would he do a sorry thing like that?" Scratch asked as he frowned in anger.

"Because I tried to . . . to stop him . . . when he was hitting and kicking my pa."

Peeler moved his horse closer to the boardwalk and said, "Is this the fella you were talkin' about causin' trouble, Creel?"

"That's right," Bo said. He turned back to Myra. "Why would Devery attack his own brother like that?"

"Because he's gone crazy! He's got all the men in the family stirred up and ready to come down here and kill everybody who's been standing up to him. He said he'd burn Mankiller to the ground before he'd let anybody else have it!"

That was exactly the sort of thing Bo had been worried about. Devery was so full of pride and hate and arrogance that he couldn't accept defeat. He would rather destroy everything, and everybody he considered an enemy, along with any innocent folks who got in the way.

"The only one who tried to talk sense to him was my father. He said they couldn't just start burning and killing. Then . . . then Uncle Jackson hit him with a rifle butt, knocked him down, started kicking him . . . I tried to get him to stop, but he backhanded me and knocked me down, too. I got out of there and thought I ought to come warn you—"

A thunderous roar suddenly shook the ground

and drowned out whatever Myra was saying. Bo and Scratch looked toward the jail in shock and saw smoke rising from behind it.

"Dynamite!" Scratch yelled. "They blasted the jail to bust the prisoners out!"

"Come on!" Bo said as he broke into a run toward the site of the blast. Behind him, Scratch pressed Myra Devery into Rushford's arms and then took off after his old friend.

Big John Peeler twisted in the saddle and shouted to his crew, "We're with Creel and Morton! Follow their lead!"

Echoes from the explosion still rolled through the town. Gunshots sounded through them. The shots came from the jail.

The dynamite blast was more than just an attempt to free the prisoners, however. It was also a signal, Bo realized as rifle-waving Deverys, led by their patriarch, burst from the house at the head of the street and started down the hill, yelling and shooting. Jackson Devery was trying to make good on his threat to destroy Mankiller for turning on him.

"Off the street!" Bo bellowed as screams and chaos broke out all around him. "Everybody get off the street!"

He thought fleetingly about Lucinda and hoped that she and her daughters and brother would lie low in the café, hopefully out of harm's way. But there was no time to check on them, not with hell on the prowl in Mankiller.

Gunfire still came from inside the sheriff's office as the Texans reached the front door. It wouldn't

budge, and Bo knew that Biscuits O'Brien must
have it locked and barred on the inside.

"Around the back!" he told Scratch. As they
started around the building, he saw that Peeler and
the cowboys from the Circle JP had dismounted and
were following, guns drawn and ready.

Smoke and dust clogged the air. Bo fought his
way through the stinging, blinding stuff. As he
reached the back of the building, he saw shadowy
figures fleeing.

"Hold it!" he shouted, but the men didn't slow
down. Instead, flame spurted from gun muzzles. Bo
heard bullets whining through the air around him.
He returned the fire, but he couldn't see where he
was shooting. The men disappeared into the clouds
of dust.

There had actually been two blasts set off at the
same time, Bo saw, blowing holes in the walls of
both cells. Those were desperate measures, because
Thad, Reuben, and Simeon could have easily been
hurt in the explosions. When Bo peered through the
ragged holes, though, he saw that both cells were
empty.

"Biscuits!" Bo shouted through the hole in what
had been Thad's cell. "Biscuits, are you in there?"

The only answer that came back was a groan.

"Sounds like he's hurt," Bo told Scratch. "He
must've tried to fight them off from the office."

"We can't get in there," Scratch said. "The front
door's locked, and so are those cells." He jerked his
head toward the street. "Besides, we got the rest of
the Deverys to deal with."

Bo knew that Scratch was right. Still, he hated to

abandon Biscuits without even checking to see how badly he was hurt. That would just have to wait.

"Come on," he said grimly. "The bunch that busted out the prisoners will probably join up with the others, so we'll have the whole blamed family to fight."

"Except for Edgar," Scratch agreed. He looked at Peeler. "You sure you want in on this ruckus, Big John?"

Peeler grinned. "Just try to stop us! Right, boys?" Mutters of agreement came from the Circle JP cowboys. Bo waved for them to follow him as he and Scratch started for Main Street again.

They came out into a hornets' nest. The townspeople had scurried for cover, as Bo had ordered, and some of them were putting up a fight. Bullets flew everywhere, shattering glass in windows, thudding into walls, chewing splinters from hitch rails and porch posts. Bo drew a bead on one of the Deverys and fired. The man dropped his rifle and spun off his feet, reaching to clutch the shoulder that Bo's bullet had just shattered.

Scratch opened fire, too, as did Peeler and the rest of the Texans' newfound allies. The Deverys had launched their attack as a fairly compact group, but now they split up and spread out, and the battle rapidly turned into a series of gunfights that sprawled up and down the street.

Bo spotted Jackson Devery shouting orders to his kinfolks and targeted the clan's patriarch. Devery moved just as Bo squeezed the trigger, though, and the shot missed. Devery disappeared behind a wagon.

Bo grabbed Scratch's shoulder and shouted over

the tumult, "Let's head for the café! I want to make sure Lucinda's all right!" He had a feeling, as well, that Jackson Devery might try to reach the newly elected mayor. Even though Lucinda was a woman, she was also a symbol of how Mankiller had slipped out of Devery's hateful grasp, and there was no telling what the crazed man might try to do.

Bo and Scratch dashed along the boardwalk. As they did so, a volley of shots came from across the street, splintering the planks right behind them. Bo glanced in that direction and saw several of the Deverys crouched behind some barrels on the porch of Abner Malden's store. He and Scratch returned the fire as they ran. A man Bo recognized as Simeon Devery flew backward as a bullet struck him in the middle of the forehead. He sprawled on the porch, blood welling from the hole.

Simeon's brother Reuben suddenly leaped onto the boardwalk in front of the Texans, blocking their path. He had a shotgun in his hands and a murderous scowl on his face. As the twin barrels swept up to blast the boardwalk clean, a couple of pistol shots cracked close by. Crimson spurted from Reuben's throat as the slugs ripped into it. He flung his arms up as he fell, the shotgun slipping from his fingers and spinning away.

Harlan Green stepped out of the hotel. Bo hadn't even noticed they were in front of the place. Smoke curled from the barrel of the pistol in Green's hand. Bo gave him a curt nod of thanks, then he and Scratch raced on toward the café.

It looked like the Deverys were regrouping, led by Luke and Thad. They surged into the street in front of the café. Behind Bo and Scratch, Big John Peeler bellowed, "Come on, boys!" When Bo glanced over his shoulder, he saw that not only were Peeler and the Circle JP cowboys backing the Texans' play, but so were a group of townspeople who had decided to stand and fight. He saw familiar faces everywhere: Doc Weathers, Lyle Rushford, Harlan Green, Sam Bradfield, Wallace Kane, the two storekeepers, even little Ernie Bond. They had learned that democracy and freedom weren't always just handed to people. Sometimes those ideals had to be fought for.

Guns blazed and men fell, but the groups were too close together. They slammed into each other, and the battle was suddenly hand to hand. Rifles became clubs instead of firearms, and fists thudded against flesh. Bo and Scratch waded into the middle of the melee, striking out to right and left as they fought their way toward the café.

Luke suddenly loomed up in front of Scratch. The silver-haired Texan saw a familiar gun belt sporting a pair of holstered, ivory-handled Remingtons strapped around Luke's waist. "I knew it!" Scratch yelled. "I knew you stole my guns, you son of a bitch!"

Luke swung the rifle in his hands at Scratch's head. Scratch ducked under the blow and stepped in to slam a right and a left into Luke's belly. Luke doubled over. Scratch grabbed the rifle and drove it up, catching Luke under the chin with the breech. That forced Luke's head back and knocked him off his feet. He rolled away and came up clawing both Remingtons from their holsters.

Scratch dropped the rifle and palmed out his Colt. Flame geysered from the muzzle as he fired. The bullet struck Luke in the chest at close range and knocked him down again. This time he didn't get up. He lay there gasping for breath as the ivory-handled revolvers slipped from nerveless fingers. His chest stilled and his eyes began to glaze over.

A few yards away, Bo found himself facing Thad Devery, who had gone as loco as a rabid wolf. Thad yanked a knife from his boot with his good hand and slashed at Bo with the blade. Bo leaped back to avoid the knife, but he stumbled and fell. Thad changed his grip and leaped after Bo, raising the knife high and then bringing it down at the Texan.

Bo caught hold of Thad's wrist with both hands and twisted sharply as Thad landed on him. Thad screamed and convulsed as the blade stabbed deep into his own belly. Bo pushed, driving the knife even deeper, all the way to the hilt. Breathing raggedly through clenched teeth, he lay there with Thad on top of him and watched as Thad's eyes, only inches from his, slowly drained of life. When Bo shoved him away, the man was dead.

Bo climbed wearily to his feet and saw Scratch buckling on his gun belt with the holstered Remingtons. "Got your guns back, I see," he said.

"Yeah, Luke had 'em." Scratch glanced around. "Appears that the fight's just about over."

That was true. The Deverys had been overcome. Some of them were dead, others were wounded, and others had been battered into unconsciousness.

Unfortunately, the same was true of Mankiller's citizens and the cowboys from New Mexico. Some of them had fallen and would never rise. Big John Peeler was still on his feet, though, bleeding from several gashes on his face as he grinned at Bo and Scratch.

"Quite a scrap," he said. "If this is the sort of ruckus you fellas usually get mixed up in, I want you to come back to the ranch with me even more!"

Bo had a good mind to tell Peeler what he could do with that invitation, but at that moment, a harsh voice shouted, "Creel! Morton!"

They swung around and saw Jackson Devery coming out of the café with one arm wrapped around Lucinda's waist while the other hand held a gun to her head.

"I want you to see what you've done, you damned Texans!" Devery shouted into the suddenly stunned silence that fell over the street. "You may have taken my town away, but this bitch will never be the mayor! You bastards stand there and watch while I blow her brains out!"

"You pull that trigger, you'll be dead two seconds later," Bo warned.

A savage grin stretched Devery's mouth. "You think I don't know that? You think I want to live in a world I can't bend to my will no more?"

"You're a sick son of a bitch, Devery," Scratch said. "A mad dog. You need to be put out of your misery, and everybody else's misery, too."

"You go right ahead and do it," Devery snarled, "but not until I pull this trigger!"

"Jackson, no!"

Edgar Devery pushed through the crowd, coming out to face his brother from a distance of about twenty feet. Jackson Devery looked surprised to see him. Edgar's face was covered with bruises and blood. One eye was swollen almost shut. Devery had probably thought that he'd left his brother for dead in the old house at the top of the hill.

Edgar was still alive, though, even though he swayed slightly on his feet.

And he clutched a shotgun in his hands.

"Let Mrs. Bonner go, Jackson," Edgar said. "This is over now."

"No, it ain't," Devery said. "It ain't over until I say it's over."

Edgar grunted. "Still got to be the big boss of everything, don't you? You was always that way. Had to get whatever it was you wanted, and you didn't give a damn about anybody else. You still don't care who gets hurt, do you?" Edgar's voice shook with grief. "My boy Thad's dead. Your sons are all dead. You tried to kill me, you could've killed Myra, and you destroyed the rest of your family. And still all you care about is more killin'!" He raised the shotgun. "Let her go, or I'll kill you."

Devery stared at him. His voice shook when he spoke, too, but with rage and insane hatred. "You'd turn on me, on your own brother?" he demanded.

A hollow laugh came from Edgar. "After all this, that'd be funny, Jackson . . . if it wasn't so sad."

"You . . . you . . ." Devery couldn't even find the words to express his lunacy. He flung Lucinda away from him, out of the line of fire, and jerked the gun in his hand toward his brother.

Edgar pulled the shotgun's triggers first.

The double load of buckshot smashed into

Devery, lifting him up off his feet and dropping him on the porch of the café. The bloody, shredded thing that landed on the planks barely resembled a human being. Even some of the hardened cowboys from New Mexico had to turn their eyes away.

Edgar slowly lowered the shotgun and turned to face Bo and Scratch. "I hated to do that," he said. "I purely did. But somebody had to stop him, and I figured it was better if it was . . . if it was . . ."

He dropped the empty shotgun and would have collapsed if Bo hadn't caught hold of his arm to steady him. "Take it easy," Bo said. "We'll find your daughter. She can look after you."

"She . . . she's alive?" Edgar asked.

"She was," Bo said as he looked at the bodies sprawled in the street.

A lot of other people had been alive, too, who weren't anymore. There would be plenty of mourning in the settlement over the next few days.

But life would go on, and for the first time in these parts for a good while, it would be filled with hope and promise instead of fear and tyranny.

Some fights were always worth fighting. Bo and Scratch, along with their fellow Texans, had learned that at the Alamo, at Goliad, at San Jacinto. And it was just as true decades later and hundreds of miles away, in a place called Mankiller, Colorado.

CHAPTER 31

"Sorry I let you down," Biscuits O'Brien said from the bed where he lay swathed in bandages, in one of the rooms in Dr. Jason Weathers's house. "I tried to stop 'em when they busted in to take the prisoners, but I didn't expect 'em to blow the blasted wall down."

"Nobody did," Bo told the sheriff with a smile. "That just shows how far Devery was prepared to go to get what he wanted."

"Loco as a hydrophobia skunk," Scratch said from the other side of the bed. "Don't you worry, Biscuits. You done fine."

"And you're going to make a good lawman for this town," Bo added. "The town council has already voted to keep you on."

"With . . . a couple of deputies . . . I hope," Biscuits said.

"Well . . . for now," Bo said. "But Scratch and I came to Mankiller to look for gold. We haven't forgotten about that."

They said so long to Biscuits for the time being.

The sheriff had been wounded in several places during the fierce gunfight at the jail, but Dr. Weathers seemed convinced that he would make a full recovery.

The Texans left the doctor's house and headed for the café. Evening had settled down over Mankiller. The bodies had all been toted away, the badly wounded were at the doctor's place, and the Deverys who weren't seriously hurt had retreated to the big old house at the upper end of Main Street. Edgar Devery, who was now the leader of the family, had assured Bo and Scratch that there would be no more trouble. Jackson Devery had browbeaten many of his relatives into going along with him, and with Jackson dead, the family might be able to take its place as part of the community. Edgar had promised to do his best to see that that came about.

Bo believed him. Edgar was badly shaken up and grieved by everything that had happened, and he didn't want it ever happening again.

Plenty of evidence of battle could still be seen in the broken windows and in the bullet holes that pocked the walls of most of the buildings. That damage could be patched up. In a few weeks, Bo thought as he and Scratch strolled through the evening, you wouldn't be able to tell that a life-and-death struggle had taken place here.

They went into the café and found it busy as usual. Lucinda was behind the counter, pouring coffee and setting plates of food in front of the customers on the stools. Callie and Tess delivered meals to the tables. Charley was whistling in the kitchen as he cooked.

Lucinda pushed cups toward the Texans and filled them with coffee. "How's Biscuits?" she asked.

"Doc Weathers says he'll be all right," Bo reported.

"You told him we want him to stay on as sheriff?"

"Yep," Scratch said. "He made us promise to keep wearin' these deputy badges until he gets back on his feet."

"You're not going back to New Mexico with Mr. Peeler?"

"Not hardly," Scratch said. "Big John ain't quite as bad as we thought he was, and we're obliged to him for his help today, but we don't hanker to work for him no more."

"Besides," Bo said, "we have jobs here for a while."

"And after that?" Lucinda asked.

Bo shrugged. "Like we told Biscuits, we came here to look for gold."

"There are other ways to find your fortune in life," Lucinda said softly.

That was true, Bo reflected, but not necessarily in the way that Lucinda meant. For him and Scratch, their real fortune was their freedom, the ability to saddle up and ride on when the notion struck them, to answer the endless call of the frontier that always drew them to see what was over the next hill.

That call could be answered another day. Bo took a sip of the fine coffee and reminded himself that he and Scratch would need to make their rounds soon.

For now, they were still the law in Mankiller.

THE FIRST MOUNTAIN MAN SERIES BY
WILLIAM W. JOHNSTONE

The First Mountain Man
0-8217-5510-2 $4.99US/$6.50CAN

Blood on the Divide
0-8217-5511-0 $4.99US/$6.50CAN

Absaroka Ambush
0-8217-5538-2 $4.99US/$6.50CAN

Forty Guns West
0-7860-1534-9 $5.99US/$7.99CAN

Cheyenne Challenge
0-8217-5607-9 $4.99US/$6.50CAN

Preacher and the Mountain Caesar
0-8217-6585-X $5.99US/$7.99CAN

Blackfoot Messiah
0-8217-6611-2 $5.99US/$7.99CAN

Preacher
0-7860-1441-5 $5.99US/$7.99CAN

Preacher's Peace
0-7860-1442-3 $5.99US/$7.99CAN

Available Wherever Books Are Sold!

Visit our website at www.kensingtonbooks.com

THE MOUNTAIN MAN SERIES BY WILLIAM W. JOHNSTONE

Available Wherever Books Are Sold!

Visit our website at www.kensingtonbooks.com

THE LAST GUNFIGHTER SERIES BY
WILLIAM W. JOHNSTONE

The Drifter
0-8217-6476-4 $4.99US/$6.99CAN

Reprisal
0-7860-1295-1 $5.99US/$7.99CAN

Ghost Valley
0-7860-1324-9 $5.99US/$7.99CAN

The Forbidden
0-7860-1325-7 $5.99US/$7.99CAN

Showdown
0-7860-1326-5 $5.99US/$7.99CAN

Imposter
0-7860-1443-1 $5.99US/$7.99CAN

Rescue
0-7860-1444-X $5.99US/$7.99CAN

The Burning
0-7860-1445-8 $5.99US/$7.99CAN

Available Wherever Books Are Sold!

Visit our website at www.kensingtonbooks.com

THE EAGLES SERIES BY
WILLIAM W. JOHNSTONE

___ **Eyes of Eagles**
0-7860-1364-8 $5.99US/$7.99CAN

___ **Dreams of Eagles**
0-7860-6086-6 $5.99US/$7.99CAN

___ **Talons of Eagles**
0-7860-0249-2 $5.99US/$6.99CAN

___ **Scream of Eagles**
0-7860-0447-9 $5.99US/$7.50CAN

___ **Rage of Eagles**
0-7860-0507-6 $5.99US/$7.99CAN

___ **Song of Eagles**
0-7860-1012-6 $5.99US/$7.99CAN

___ **Cry of Eagles**
0-7860-1024-X $5.99US/$7.99CAN

___ **Blood of Eagles**
0-7860-1106-8 $5.99US/$7.99CAN

Available Wherever Books Are Sold!

Visit our website at www.kensingtonbooks.com